CASINO KING

CARFANO CRIME FAMILY
BOOK 1

REBECCA GANNON

newsletter, blog, shop, and links to all social media:
www.rebeccagannon.com

Content Warning

This book is intended for those 18 and over and contains graphic violence that may make some readers uncomfortable.

More by Rebecca Gannon

Pine Cove
Her Maine Attraction
Her Maine Reaction
Her Maine Risk
Her Maine Distraction

Carfano Crime Family
Casino King
The Boss
Vengeance
Executioner
Wild Ace

Standalone Novels
Whiskey & Wine
Redeeming His Reputation

To all of those who feel like they don't really come alive until the night, a black rose blooming in the shadows, only needing that one person to see them hiding there amongst the other lost souls and bring them out into the moonlight to see that the dark isn't a place to ever shy away from, but where kings and queens rule, this is for you.

THE CARFANO FAMILY

Leo (d)
(m) Katarina (d)

Michael (d)	Salvatore (d)	Anthony	Richard	Maria
(m) Anita	(m) Teresa	(m) Francesca	(m) Christina	(m) Carmine
Leo, Alec,	Nico, Vincenzo,	Stefano, Marco,	Saverio,	Matteo, Elena
Luca, Katarina	Mia	Gabriel	Gia, Aria	

(m) – married / (d) – deceased

"born from fire, she danced with flames
with a power that shook the devil's domain"
- r.h. Sin

DANCE SONGS FROM CASINO KING:

1. "High" by Dua Lipa – solo in the beginning
2. "King" by Niykee Heaton – private dance in Alec's penthouse
3. "Sweet Emotion" by Aerosmith – partner dance with Jeremy
4. "Deeper" by Valerie Broussard – solo at the end

SONGS THAT INSPIRED ME WHILE WRITING:

1. "Like That" by Bea Miller
2. "Dreams" by Wet
3. "Sorry" by Shaylen
4. "Concentrate" by Demi Lovato
5. "Holy" by Justin Bieber ft. Chance The Rapper
6. "SexBeat" by Usher
7. "Comeback" by JoJo ft. Tory Lanez and 30 Rock
8. "Lonely Hearts" by JoJo
9. "So Bad" by JoJo
10. "Devil" by Niykee Heaton
11. "So Good" by Dove Cameron
12. "We Belong" by Dove Cameron
13. "Bruises" by Lewis Capaldi
14. "Waste Away" by Jaira Burns
15. "Electric" by Alina Baraz ft. Khalid
16. "A Little Wicked" by Valerie Broussard

CHAPTER 1
Tessa

The music flows through me like a warm breeze, touching me with heated possession as it takes me over entirely. I pull the audience into my orbit, entrancing them with every movement and look.

The bass drives my heartbeat.

The rhythm moves my body.

The tempo thrums my senses.

The lyrics sway my emotions.

Here on stage, I'm the me I need to be. Everything I hold onto all week comes out, and I feel free. I feel lighter. Everything I do and don't have doesn't matter when I'm up here. It's just me.

The lights swirl and flash, and in between the beams, I look out to the first row, seeing him.

I knew he'd be there.

Every Friday night for the past month, he's sat at the same table against the wall, half in the shadows, watching, his eyes always on me.

I can feel them caress my body like he's undressing me, possessing me, and covering every inch of me in all of the thoughts running through his mind of what he wants to do to me.

From the glimpses I've gathered over these four weeks, I still haven't seen him fully. His face remains either partially or fully in the shadows, only his square jaw making an appearance when he leans forward to reach for his drink.

His dark suit is tailored perfectly to his built frame that I know holds great power beneath the expensive material. Even from up here on stage, I'm drawn to him. To the air of authority, strength, and confidence he exudes.

My eyes slide over him as I spin, bend, lift my arms in the air, and sweep my leg up and around. They're like magnets being pulled towards the force that wants them the most.

After the second show with him in the audience, I came back to my dressing station to find a bouquet of black roses, and I knew right away they were from him.

The next week, the same thing, this time accompanied by a little black velvet box containing diamond stud earrings and a note with a simple A as a signature.

Then last week, another bouquet of black roses and a velvet box. Only this time, it was a diamond tennis necklace, and the note had more than just a single letter.

I want to see how this looks on stage next week.

-A

I have both the earrings and necklace on now, and I know the diamonds are catching the lights in blinding glimmers.

My back arches as I lift my leg in the air and spin, my red sequin fringed skirt fanning out from my body, my eyes sweeping over him again, giving him a small smile there in the shadows.

I feel weightless – my limbs moving through the air like they're a part of it.

His hand tightens on the whiskey glass in front of him as I glide across the stage, the song almost coming to an end. With one final fan of my leg, I hold it near my ear as I lift up on my toes and spin, then end in a split with my back arching to touch my thigh behind me.

The clapping of the audience fills my head as the lights fade and the curtain falls.

I only started dancing here at The Aces six weeks ago, and I already have a solo. The show's manager saw something in me right away, and while the other girls who have been here longer might have a slight issue with that, I couldn't care less when I'm up here.

Tonight is the first time I'm performing my solo, and for these three and a half minutes, I can let myself break free and become one with the inner me that fights to find her way out every other minute of the day.

Every time I practiced this week, I thought of *him* sitting there watching me, knowing the feel of his eyes on me would make me better and would drive me deeper into a trance.

And I was right.

The Friday night show at The Aces is something unlike anything I've ever known or been a part of. The casino has a number of other shows they put on the other days of the week – burlesque, comedy, dance companies, unbelievable talents. But the Friday night show is a combination of show girl and modern and contemporary dance and ballet, with a touch of burlesque in how we dress and perform. It's an overall sexy show, and I have to admit the costumes were a big draw for me.

I also teach dance at a studio in town, and I had come to see a Friday show a couple of months ago after the mom of one of the kids I teach gave me her tickets when she found out she couldn't go last minute. I was entranced from beginning to end, and right away, I knew I had to find a way to be up there with those dancers. I wanted to feel as free as they all looked.

And two weeks later, I was.

If I had to give a classification to my solo, it would be something along the lines of a contemporary ballet piece. It's not rigid like classical ballet, which is what I grew up trained in. Here on this stage, my body is loose and free to move how it desires – how my emotions desire.

Changing my costume for the finale, I wait for the other routines to finish and then get in line with the other girls. We're dressed in classic show girl costumes with big red feather headpieces, a red sequined bra and panty set, red rhinestone thigh-high wrap-up heels, and a matching rhinestone choker necklace that has long strands of red crystals hanging down our torsos like chandeliers.

After the final curtain falls, I make my way back to my

station, and once again find a bouquet of black roses and a jewelry box waiting for me. They always magically appear while I'm on stage for the finale.

Brushing my fingers over the soft, velvety black rose petals, a small smile pulls at my lips. It's such a fitting color for him. I have a feeling most of what he owns is black.

Opening the jewelry box, I suck in a quick breath at the sight of a diamond bracelet that matches the necklace I got last week.

This is too much. It's all too much.

Nobodies like me don't get gifts like this from anonymous sexy strangers for no reason.

Pulling the note from the envelope resting against the flowers, I run my fingers over the script. He has beautiful handwriting. So much so, I know he could seduce a woman with that alone if he wanted to.

Congratulations on your solo. You were mesmerizing.

-A

I need to know his name. I need to know *something* about him other than either his first or last name begins with an A and he likes to gift black roses and expensive diamonds to a woman he doesn't know beyond watching her dance.

I go through the routine of changing out of my costume, taking off my show makeup, and throwing my hair up into a bun. With the armor gone, it's back to reality, and it's back to the fact that no mystery man would find the real me as fascinating as the one I embody on stage.

Carefully, I place the bouquet of flowers and jewelry in my bag and head out, smiling politely at the dancers still left backstage.

I make my way through the back halls of the casino and out the side door that leads to the parking lot.

Most of the other girls change into party clothes and either head out into the casino to gamble and cozy up to the high rollers at the tables, or go to the casino's club, Royals, to try and pick up wealthy men who can show them a good time for a night or two.

Never me, though. I don't even own any going-out clothes. At least not like what the other girls wear.

That's why I was drawn to this show and why the version of me on stage is never going to be the real me, no matter how much I wish it was. I can't afford a single costume that I wear, and I work three jobs just to keep a roof over my head and food on the table. But I'd never complain. I teach three dance classes twice a week, I work at a fifties style diner in town two shifts a week, and then I dance the special Friday night show here at The Aces which also has rehearsals for it twice a week. To be in the show, I had to cut back on a couple diner shifts, but it's more than worth it for how it makes me feel.

I'm always busy, I'm always tired, and I don't have any time for a life outside of work, but I love what I do. It's all I have.

Checking the parking lot to make sure no one's around, I make my way over to my well-loved little Nissan. I'm always cautious when it's late and I'm alone, and even more so knowing I have a bag with *very* expensive jewelry in it.

Getting back to my apartment, I drag my feet to the bathroom for a hot shower before I pass out for the night. My legs are more tired than usual from the extra practicing I had to do this week for my solo, and as I drift off, the only thoughts in my mind are ones of a mysterious man in the shadows who makes me feel like the most beautiful thing in the world when I never have before.

CHAPTER 2
Tessa

Swiping primer across my lips, I dip my finger into the red glitter pot and press it on top, matching my eyes.

Pursing my lips, I turn my head back and forth to watch the light catch on the glitter before applying my fake lashes and mascara.

My solo is next, so I make sure to put on my diamonds for him to see. My mystery man hasn't been here for the other numbers, but for some reason, I feel like he'll miraculously show up for my solo, unable to stay away.

Every night this week, I've taken the jewelry out and held them, wishing I knew the man behind them.

Touching the necklace, I give myself a small smile and

put on my red sequin tassel skirt and red bikini styled top.

Red always makes me feel sexy, and as I tie my red satin pointe shoes around my ankles, I do a little spin in front of the mirror to make sure they're tight enough.

Walking over to the stage area, I get a smile and nod from the show's manager, Dan, and return it with my own, getting in the zone for the seduction I'm about to perform. That's what my solo is – a seduction. And I love every second of it because it's so opposite of who I am normally.

When the music changes and the curtain rises, I spin out onto stage, the crowd's applause filling my ears. But when my eyes float over to the table against the wall, it's still empty, and my smile slips momentarily.

I've gotten used to having him there, and without feeling his eyes on me, it feels like my performance isn't as powerful. I know I'm good, but he makes me better.

After the show, I walk back to my station with the other girls, and my eyes are immediately drawn to the bouquet of black roses waiting for me.

What? How?

I reach for the card and eagerly pull out the thick cardstock from the envelope, needing to see his beautiful script.

I'm sorry I couldn't be there tonight, I had business to attend to. But I know you were beautiful as always.

-A

Opening the jewelry box, I'm once again struck speechless. Nestled in the velvet is a pair of dark red ruby stud earrings with little diamonds surrounding the stone.

They're absolutely stunning, and I know they'll look beautiful with my solo costume. Which I have a suspicion was the drive behind him choosing these.

The pad of my finger circles the tiny diamonds around the ruby and my mind wanders to the image of who he is and why of all people he's chosen *me* to shower with extravagant gifts and attention.

Maybe one of these days I'll finally find out.

Changing into my post-show clothes, I wipe my makeup off as best as I can before I can get home to take a shower, and start making my way down the small back hallway. My thoughts drift to the beautiful earrings in my bag and I bite my bottom lip to keep from smiling like a fool.

I have no reason to think anything other than he's a man who likes to give the woman he enjoys seeing dance gifts, but I can't help thinking of what it would be like to be with a man like that. A man with expensive taste who probably has a big important job, an expensive car, a fancy house, and gets whatever he wants.

Men like that are usually already taken, though, which is probably why he's stayed anonymous these past five weeks. He's probably married with a girlfriend on the side, and I'm just something pretty he likes to look at when he's bored.

It doesn't feel like that, but I don't know...

Pushing those thoughts away, I drift back to thinking about what it would be like to feel his eyes on me when he's standing directly in front of me. Those are more pleasant thoughts.

Taking my keys out of my bag, I unlock my car, and as I reach for the door handle, I see a shadow loom over me right before a hand grips my upper arm and spins me around with a roughness that has me squealing out a strangled cry.

The face of a complete stranger fills my vision, and I manage to let out a scream before his hand covers my mouth, filling my senses with the scent of cheap beer and cigarettes.

"Don't scream," the man growls. My wide eyes stare up at the imposing figure, knowing straight away he's most definitely not my mystery man. He drinks expensive whiskey, wears expensive Italian suits, and would never lie in wait for me in the parking lot just biding his time until he can make his move. "I saw you dance earlier. You're so sexy."

"Get off of me," I try and say behind his hand, but it comes out as a muffled string of inaudible words.

Bucking my body forward, I try to break free from his grip, but his hand on my arm just tightens as he pushes me against my car.

Panic starts to set in when I can't make him budge, and my wide eyes look around for anything and anyone who can help me, but I come up with nothing.

"Stop fighting me," he snarls. Pulling his hand away from my mouth, I suck in a ragged breath like I hadn't had oxygen for minutes when it's only been a few seconds.

"Get off of me!" I yell in his face, trying to push him off of me.

A sharp sting flashes across my cheek and my head is jerked to the side, pain automatically spreading from where he hit me.

"I said don't scream!" His harsh voice drips with malice, and I know he's not going to stop at just cornering me to talk.

No. I refuse.

Struggling with every ounce of strength I can manage in

the pinned down position I'm in, I fight him. I grunt and huff and manage another scream before he backhands me again and clamps his hand over my mouth. A putrid taste fills my mouth knowing I can't fight off a man twice my size who's determined to have me however he wants me.

I don't know how long I struggle to break free, but just when I've all but given up hope that I'll come away from this without having his filthy hands all over me, he's suddenly yanked away from me.

A man dressed impeccably in a dark suit throws him against the nearest car by the neck, punching him in the face. "Who the fuck do you think you are hitting a woman?" His deep, angry voice is sharp and pointed. He punches him again in the face – hard. "She said no." Punching him in the gut, the bastard folds over with a pained grunt.

Relief floods my tightly wound muscles now that I'm free from the clammy grip of my attacker, but when I try to say something, no words will form from my constricted throat.

My savior gives him another hard punch to the gut that crumples him to the pavement, and then he straightens and turns to me. He's quite handsome, with tanned skin, dark hair, and eyes that look like they hold a million secrets.

"You okay?" he asks in a much gentler tone than he was using a second ago. "I'm sorry I didn't get over to you quick enough."

"I'm…I'm okay. Thank you," I manage to say through my short intakes of air. Forcing a few deep breaths into my lungs, I tell him in a much stronger voice, "Thank you."

He gives me a curt nod and turns back to the balled-up man on the ground. He's a lot less intimidating like this, and

I'm tempted to get in a couple kicks of my own, but hold back.

Lifting my hand to my cheek, I wince, and my suit-clad rescuer looks me over, his eyes surveying my face in the dim parking lot light.

"I have to make a call." Pulling out his phone, he dials quickly, not having to wait long before someone on the other end answers. "There's been an incident," is all he says as an opening. "She was attacked at her car." He looks at me and then toes the man on the ground.

I only have his one-sided conversation to listen to, but he's speaking as if he and the person on the other end of the line know me, when I have no idea how that's possible. I don't know him. I would remember meeting someone like him.

"He hit her," he says low, rubbing his forehead as he pulls the phone a few inches from his ear like the person on the other end is yelling. "What should I do? ... Got it. See you then." Slipping his phone back into the inside breast pocket of his suit jacket, he looks at me with guarded eyes.

"Who was that?" I whisper. "Who are you?"

"You're coming with me to have the doctor look you over."

"What? No. I'm not going anywhere with you. Thank you for helping me, but I'm okay to go home on my own."

"I can't let you do that. I have orders, and he's going to expect you to be there when he gets back from the city."

"That still doesn't make me miraculously know who you are, or who *he* is."

"The diamonds and flowers in your bag say otherwise."

"What?" I breathe, the air vanishing from my lungs in a

single breath.

"He's had me watching you, but after tonight, I'll be lucky if I see another day for letting this fucker touch you." He toes the guy on the ground again, and he groans.

"You've been watching me?" I ask in a small voice, completely caught off guard by that. "For how long?"

"About a month."

"Why?"

"You can ask him that yourself later. I have to make another call before we head up."

Head up? Head up where? I'm so thrown by what's happening that I just lean back against my car and tighten my grip on my gym bag, my mind trying to play catch up.

"Come to the employee lot, I have a package that needs to be delivered to the basement," my rescuer says into the phone and then hangs up, turning back to me. "Grab whatever you need from your car."

"Why?"

"Because you're coming with me."

"I never agreed to that. I don't even know your name."

"Lorenzo. But you can call me Enzo."

"And the man you first called?" I want to know the name of my mysterious A.

He just smirks and gives me a small shake of his head. "You can ask him that later, too."

"Wow, you're just full of information," I say sarcastically, my resolve starting to come back.

Another impeccably dressed man emerges from between the cars and my grip on my gym bag tightens as I take a small step to the side. He's much scarier than Enzo, who I can tell has a lighter side beneath his tough exterior. But not this man. He's all muscle beneath his suit, with a hollow look to his eyes that chills me to the bone when he gives me a once over.

He doesn't say a word as he hoists the man who attacked me off the ground and pushes him towards the back door I came out of just minutes ago.

"Where's he taking him?" I whisper.

"The basement."

"What's in the basement?"

"Nothing for you to worry about. Grab what you need and let's go, the doctor should be here soon."

"I don't need a doctor, and I'm not going anywhere with you."

"Not your call. Boss says he wants you safe and in his place."

"I don't know your boss," I reiterate, feeling like a broken record. "I'm not just going to let you take me up to his place."

Yes, I want to know the man in the shadows who's been on my mind day and night for over a month, but I also have enough self-preservation to not just go with this stranger because he saved me.

"One second," is all he says, pulling his phone out again and dialing a number. "She's refusing to come with me because she doesn't know either of us." He pauses, listening to the man on the other end and then nods, handing me the phone. "Here."

"What?" My voice is barely above a whisper.

"He wants to talk to you."

With a trembling hand, I reach for the phone and take a deep breath to ensure I'll be able to speak.

"Tessa." His smooth, deep voice floats through the phone and into me, my hand curling around the phone a little tighter. My name sounds like a caress coming from him and I feel it coat my insides like warm, raw honey – sugary sweet with a touch of roughness.

My breath leaves my lungs and I angle away from Enzo so he can't see my reaction.

"Go with Enzo and let the doctor check you out."

Again, his voice does something to me that I'm not used to. My stomach knots and my heart starts beating a little faster.

"I'm fine," I tell him softly, but wince internally at the lie. The truth is, my face is starting to throb, and my arm is sore from where he grabbed me.

"You're not," he says firmly, his voice dropping an octave. "*He hit you.* I'm leaving the city now and I'll deal with him when I get back in a couple of hours, but I want you safe."

"I'll be safe at my apartment."

A low growl comes through the phone at my response. I have a feeling he must be used to getting what he wants from everyone around him when he commands they do something. But I'm not like that. I've been on my own for a long time now and only know how to rely on myself. No one else.

"I need you to go with him, Tessa. We'll talk when I get there."

I think about the prospect of going back to my dark, empty apartment, knowing I'll be up all night thinking about him anyway, and decide that finally being able to meet him, and see him, is a much more desirable option.

"Okay."

"See you soon," he says, his voice holding a little less edge, and hangs up.

Sighing, I hand Enzo back his phone and he doesn't say anything as I fall in step beside him, heading back inside. You need a pass card to re-enter, but Enzo has one.

Walking through the cement hallways, I start to feel the fatigue of the day catch up with me, and my face throbs even more where that asshole hit me. Reaching up, I press the pads of my fingers to my cheek bone and area around my eye, and suck in a sharp breath.

Luckily, Enzo doesn't say anything since I was so adamant about being fine, but he looks down at me with concern in his eyes. He guides me around what has to be the entire perimeter of the building to an elevator that requires his handprint and retinal scan to open.

"Pretty tight security I see," I comment casually as I step into the sleek grey elevator car.

"This elevator goes to the penthouse. Very few people have direct access."

Leaning against the cold metal wall, I lower my bag to my feet but keep ahold of the strap.

So, we're going to the penthouse. My mystery man must be a very important man if he has the penthouse at The Aces – the best hotel and casino in Atlantic City. And Enzo must be pretty trustworthy if he's one of the few allowed access to his home.

The ride to the top is long, but when the doors slide open, I muster the strength to lift my bag back onto my shoulder and step out into a small hallway with only one door ahead of us. With this door, in addition to a handprint and retinal scan, it requires a keypad entry code.

Enzo holds the door open for me, and the second I step through, my eyes widen. This place is huge. He must have the entire top floor to himself.

The living room in front of me has floor-to-ceiling windows spanning the entire length of the room, giving me an uninterrupted view of the city, boardwalk, and ocean. The bright lights from the other casinos and hotels reflect off the dark water crashing against the shore. It's beautiful.

I was right in that my mystery man loves black. Everywhere I look, it's the predominant color, with splashes of grey, white, and red.

A massive chandelier hangs in the middle of the living room that's dripping with crystals, the light dancing off of it casting beautiful shadows across the ceiling. A big leather couch and two chairs face a fireplace half-wall that divides the left and right side of the room, with a large flatscreen TV hanging above the mantle.

The other side of the fireplace wall is a smaller living room library area, with a wall of floor-to-ceiling mahogany bookshelves and two leather chairs facing the fireplace.

To my left is a massive kitchen and dining room that has me dreaming of cooking something just so I could use the beautiful equipment.

I've never seen a place like this. It screams money, power, and status, and I feel out of place in my plain clothes and modest upbringing. I don't know this kind of wealth.

"Take a seat," Enzo instructs. "The doctor is on his way up."

Nodding, I don't bother commenting that all I need is an icepack and an aspirin because I know he'll just say it's not my call and I'll have wasted my breath. So, I take a seat at the end of the plush leather couch and place my bag tightly by my side – a small comfort to keep me grounded.

I'm staring out the large windows next to me when the door opens a few minutes later, and I turn to see another man in a suit walk in. He's older, maybe in his mid to late forties, with salt and pepper hair around his temples, and carrying a leather doctor's bag.

"Tessa, I presume?" he asks me, walking right over to take a seat in the chair next to me.

"Yes." I nod.

"I'm Joe. Can you tell me what happened?"

Swallowing, I look down at my hands in my lap and play with the ring on my right middle finger. "I was about to get in my car after work when a man came out of nowhere and grabbed my arm." I lift my right arm to show him, and frown when I see a large handprint has started to form. "He spun me around and pinned me to my car with his hand over my mouth." My stomach rolls at the memory of his taste. "I tried to break free, but he was much stronger than me. And when he removed his hand, I yelled, which is when he backhanded me across my face. Twice." I turn my head so he can see. "And then Enzo came and tore the guy off of me."

"It's a good thing he was there."

"Yeah, it was." I don't like the fact that I had a man following me for a month and I had no idea, but I'm also glad he was there tonight. I know things would have gone completely different if he wasn't.

"Do you mind if I look at your injuries?"

"No, it's fine." I don't really have a choice anyhow, I add silently.

Joe lifts my arm and gently runs his hands over the finger bruises, making me wince slightly – a movement he doesn't miss. I've always bruised easily.

"I'm sorry. Can you turn your head?" With the same gentle touch, he presses down on the area around my eye and along my cheek bone, all of which makes me cringe and bite my lower lip to hold back from whimpering.

It hurts, but not enough so that I think anything is actually fractured. He was stronger than he looked, and I think he had a ring on too, making it worse.

"You're a strong woman. If he had hit you any closer to your eye, then you'd have a lot more bruising that would take a lot longer to heal than what you have here."

"How do you know?" I ask out of pure curiosity, and he gives me a small smile.

"I've been doing this a long time. I've seen every injury you could possibly imagine. You just need to ice it and take a few aspirin."

Just as I suspected. "Thank you."

"Here." Enzo hands me an icepack wrapped in a towel, a few white pills, and a glass of water. Wow, he's quick.

"Thank you."

Nodding, he goes back over to the door where he's been standing guard. I don't see the need when the only people who could even get in here have to pass a three-tier security system, but I'm guessing he just does as he's told.

Swallowing the pills, I press the icepack to my cheek and lean back into the couch as the doctor gathers his bag and stands.

"It was nice meeting you, Tessa."

"You too, Joe. I'm sorry you were called here for this."

"It's my job. Goodnight." He nods, and Enzo opens the door for him.

Once again, I'm struck with how tired I am, and this time, I let my eyes fall closed.

CHAPTER 3
Alec

My older brother, Leo, leans back in his leather chair and interlocks his fingers across his stomach. "Business good, Alec?"

"Better than good." I nod, taking my seat at the table next to my younger brother, Luca.

Once a month, we have our family meeting in Manhattan, and all of the family branches come together, including myself and our cousins from Miami.

Leo made these meetings more frequent since he took over from our father in order to keep a tighter hold on all of our business dealings and make sure we're all always on the same page.

Today is Friday though, so that means I'm missing Tessa dance.

Tessa Lyons. My obsession.

I've had one of my men following her since the first night I saw her in order to gain all the information I could find out while also keeping her safe.

She makes me crazy, and I can't afford to be crazy when I need a level head to be who I am.

I want her, but I can't have her. She's too good. Too pure. That hasn't stopped me from wanting her with every fiber of my being, though. I've held back from going to her, but I don't know how much longer that will last when I can't seem to keep away from watching her dance every week.

She's a fucking goddess on stage.

"Alec?" Leo calls my name, and I snap out of my visions of Tessa in one of her little dancer outfits and heels walking towards me before I grab her and throw her down on my bed, spreading her out for me to see and feast on before she wraps those sexy long legs of hers around my hips.

"Alec," Leo says again, his voice harsher. "What the fuck is going on? Are you listening?"

"Yes, I am." The table has filled up with every high member of our family now, with Leo sitting at the head, his relaxed posture I know to be a false bravado he wears. He's wound tighter than a coil wrapped around a spring, always on the verge of exploding.

"You sure?"

"Yes." The word comes out harsher than I meant it to, and he levels me with a stare that would make most men piss themselves, and has.

Sitting up straighter, I push Tessa out of my head so I

can focus on the rest of the meeting. The Albanians are trying to encroach on our territory, but that shit is not going to happen.

When my phone starts buzzing inside of my suit jacket pocket, I'm struck with a bad feeling. My men know of tonight's meeting, and they know that Vinny is taking care of business while I'm here. I'm not to be interrupted unless it's serious.

Discretely, I check who's calling, and when I see Enzo's name, my blood turns to ice. He wouldn't be calling me unless something happened with Tessa.

Standing in a rush, I disregard the glare from Leo burning into my back and hold the phone to my ear.

"What happened?" I ask straight away, fisting my hand in my pocket so no one sees how tense I am. Every muscle in me is tight and ready to attack.

"There's been an incident. She was attacked at her car."

"WHAT?! What did he do to her?"

"He hit her," Enzo says, and I explode, feeling my anger rolling off of me in waves as my blood goes from ice to boiling.

"*Where the fuck were you?*" I growl out. "YOU WERE SUPPOSED TO BE WATCHING HER!" I explode, pacing the small space by the window.

"What should I do?"

"Take her to up to my place and call Doc. I'll be there as soon I can to deal with him. And you," I make sure to add.

"Got it. See you then."

Hanging up, I clench my phone so tight I think it might break, but hold back from throwing it across the room so I can call for an update on Tessa.

"Alec!" Leo barks. "What the fuck is going on?"

My eyes scan the room and I see everyone looking at me with questions in their eyes.

"I have to go."

"Who is she?"

"She's mine," I tell him, and his eyes widen, then narrow. "And she was attacked after work today."

"Who did you have on her?"

"Enzo," I say through a clenched jaw.

"Go. I'll discuss this with you later." Nodding, I leave the conference room in an angered haze. I need to make sure Tessa is okay.

Taking the streets of Manhattan as fast as I can, it takes every ounce of control I have to not fucking punch everything surrounding me.

My grip on the steering wheel is so tight, my knuckles are turning white from loss of blood flow. But it's the only thing I have to focus on without snapping the wheel in my hands.

Enzo is one of my most trusted soldiers, and I gave him the task of watching over Tessa this past month. He'll have to pay for letting anyone touch her.

I rarely, if ever, go to the shows in my casino, but last month I needed a break from the shit I have going on with the Triads, and I found myself using the table I always have reserved for me or my associates. I wanted to get lost in beautiful women dressed in outfits that leave little to the imagination, and what I found was Tessa.

Every Friday night since, I've sat at that same table and watched her, my mind coming up with a thousand different ways I want to take her.

She's beautiful beyond belief, and when she's dancing, I'm mesmerized. My mind is on nothing but her. She's an angel dressed like the devil, tempting me with the way she moves.

The moment I saw her, all I thought was *mine.*

I've kept my distance, though. I've sent her flowers and jewelry after every show, but I've remained anonymous. When she wore the earrings and necklace for me last week…it made me so fucking hard, I could barely walk out of the show without going to her. It was like she was wearing me, and I wanted to finally claim what I've known is mine for weeks.

From what I've learned about her, I know she's alone. She doesn't know the world I live in, and I don't want to drag her into it. But while I've tried to be a good man, something I've never been known or described as, all I want is her in my bed. Her in my kitchen. Her in my living room. Her in my car. Her with me, any way I can have her.

Clenching my hands even tighter around the steering wheel, I hit it with my right palm and rub my jaw, trying not to think about how tight my pants have gotten. Just the thought of her gets me harder than I've ever been, and I don't like that all the men in the audience tonight were watching her and wishing they could have her when I'm not there.

I'm fucking crazy.

She makes me fucking crazy.

But I have a right to be when some piece of scum thinks he can put his hands on her. I'm going to fuck him up before killing him so he knows what it feels like to have the unwanted hands of someone stronger than him slowly stealing the life from his piece of shit body.

Leo is going to tear into me at some point later, but I don't give a shit. I've dealt with my older brother my entire life and he doesn't scare me. No one does.

Leo may be the head of the family and rule over our entire empire from his tower in New York, but I'm the ruler of Atlantic City. I could have been his underboss, but I never wanted that. Our father knew that, too, so he trained Leo to take his spot and my younger brother, Luca, to be his underboss.

I always wanted AC as my own. When I turned eighteen, I came to live at The Aces with my uncle Sal. He showed me how to run the business, and when he and my father were both murdered outside of one of our restaurants in Brooklyn, Leo and I stepped into our roles even though we hadn't foreseen doing so until we were much older.

In the five years we've ruled together, we've doubled our family's profits. With that, though, comes enemies and targets on our backs, which is why I've tried to stay away from Tessa. But she's not a woman I could ever stay away from for long.

My phone starts buzzing in my pocket, and I see the screen on my car's dashboard show that Enzo is calling me again. Hitting accept, I bark out, "What?" I'm already pissed at him.

"She's refusing to come with me because she doesn't know either of us."

"Put her on," I tell him. There's no fucking way I'm letting her escape me now.

I hear the phone exchange hands, and I know she's there, but she doesn't say anything.

"Tessa," I say low, not wanting to scare her. "Go with Enzo and let the doctor check you out."

"I'm fine," she says softly, but I hear the hitch in her voice that tells me she's not.

"You're not," I say hard, keeping my voice under control. I don't want her to hear my anger. Not at her, but at the situation. "*He hit you.* I'm leaving the city now and I'll deal with him when I get back in a couple of hours, but I want you safe."

"I'll be safe at my apartment."

Growling, I wring my hands on the steering wheel. "I need you to go with him, Tessa. We'll talk when I get there."

I need her to not be difficult on this.

"Okay," she finally agrees, and I breathe a sigh of relief.

"See you soon." Ending the call, I press my foot down on the gas. Her voice…it does something to me. Delicate, yet strong. It makes me wish I was there with her to see her eyes. To see for myself if she's okay.

The night I'm not there is the night she needs me.

Once I hit Jersey, I fly down the highways, no law enforcement agency daring to pull me over. I own their asses, and they know I can get them fired with a single phone call.

Hitting 100mph, I weave through the cars on the Parkway with only one thing on my mind. Tessa.

When I get to The Aces, I pull right into my private level of the garage and nod at one of my men standing guard at the elevator. Placing my hand on the pad, the laser scans my eye, and the doors open for me.

I'm big on security, and when I took over, I made sure the entirety of The Aces was updated so I always have control and can monitor who accesses what and when.

Going through the process of giving my handprint, retinal scan, and number sequence in the keypad at my penthouse door, I walk inside my home, my eyes landing on Tessa straight away. She's leaning back against the couch with an icepack held firmly to her left eye, and my anger flares again, burning deep inside of me.

Her long legs are stretched out in front of her and she looks small and fragile. I know she's not, though. A woman who is, could never handle being with a man like me. Tessa's strong. She knows loss. She knows pain. She knows independence. She knows how to survive.

Facing Enzo, I give him a look that makes his eyes immediately fall to the floor. He knows he'll pay for letting my woman get hurt on his watch.

In a few long strides, I'm beside Tessa. Looking at her, my anger wanes slightly at seeing that she's asleep. She was comfortable enough in my home to let herself fall asleep. I don't know why that fact means something to me, but it does.

I sit in the leather chair beside her and place my hand on her leg. Her eyes flash open in an instant, darting all around before settling on me.

Her hazel eyes are like rare jewels — a swirl of green and brown that comes together to form a unique color all her own. Mesmerizing. They hold my gaze for a long moment before they wander over my face and body. I stay silent, letting her take me in. When her eyes meet mine again, they have something in them that I can't read.

"What's your name?" Those are the first words she says, and her voice cuts me deep, shooting straight to my dick.

Jesus fucking Christ. It's even better in person.

Her hand holding the icepack against her face falls to her side and my hands clench in fists.

Reaching out, I grip her chin lightly, and turn her face so I can get a better look at the swollen area around her eye and the bruise that's forming.

My jaw clenches as I try to keep my anger at bay while my eyes sweep over her face before locking with hers. It's a straight shot to my dick once again. Her eyes hold so much strength and power, mixed with a little fear that I know is because of me.

Brushing my fingers over her bruise, Tessa closes her eyes briefly, a little sigh leaving her lips as she leans the slightest bit into me. That little separation of her pouty lips is giving me visions of how they'd look stretched wide around my cock. I know I'm an asshole for thinking that while she's hurt, but she's reacting to my touch. To me.

She's fucking amazing.

"I'll be back, *bella*." Standing, I stalk towards the door, but stop when I see Enzo still standing and looking down. Grabbing him by the throat, I slam him against the wall. "You were supposed to be watching her," I growl out in a low voice so Tessa can't hear me. "You let him touch her." I squeeze his throat a little tighter. "I trusted you with her. And the only reason I'm not going to put a bullet in your brain right now is because she's here and I don't need her seeing that side of me yet. This is your one chance, Enzo."

Releasing him, I walk out and straight into the waiting elevator. Punching the B button, it reads my fingerprint, and the doors close. The basement isn't accessible to anyone but myself and my men. It's deep below my casino and isn't in the building's blue prints, so no one knows it exists. The only entrance is through this private elevator, making it the perfect place to do my business.

Turning the next corner, I give my finger print and punch in the passcode to the door that grants me access to all of the rooms down here. There's a conference room, security room, fully stocked artillery, and soundproof rooms for interrogations.

Tessa may not know it yet, but she's mine, and what I'm about to do is my first act of my promise to protect her. To protect the strength I see in her eyes that I never want to see snuffed out by the evils of this world. I may have stayed away, but that was before she needed protecting, and before I touched her and saw the look in her eyes that made me never want to look away.

I pass a few of my men as I walk through the conference room and out into another hallway that leads me to one of the holding rooms. Nodding at Gino, who's standing outside the door I need, he opens it for me, and I wait for the click of the door closing before I take a step towards the man handcuffed to a metal chair in the middle of this cement box.

I'm usually the one giving the orders to do the dirty work these days so it never traces back to me, but this time I'm making an exception. This is personal.

"Look at me," I command, and the sorry excuse of a man lifts his head, his eyes going wide. "What's your name?"

"T-Trent," he stutters, his fear showing.

"Do you know who I am Trent?"

"Y-Y-Yes."

"Do you know why you're here?" My voice never wavers from its low, indifferent tone, and the little prick starts shaking like he's freezing, while also sweating bullets.

He gives up on talking and just nods his head.

"You touched my woman tonight." I take a step closer. "You put your dirty hands on her." Another step. "You hit her." Another step, and I'm towering over him. He shrinks down, somehow thinking that'll save him from what I'm about to do to him. "Look at me," I growl, the animal I keep caged wanting to come out, needing to see the fear in his eyes.

Lifting his head slowly, his eyes meet mine, and I give him a predatory grin as I shrug out of my suit jacket. I drape it over the empty chair in the corner and remove my ace playing cards cufflinks, rolling my sleeves up to my elbows.

Sliding my hands into a pair of leather gloves left on the chair for me, I unlock the handcuffs holding him to the chair and toss them to the ground. "Get up."

"W-What?"

"Get up."

"I c-can go?"

"Sure, why not?" I say with controlled casualty.

Standing back, I make it seem like he'll be able to pass by me, but the second he takes a step, my fist slams into his face, taking pleasure in the sound of his bones crunching beneath my fist.

A scream is torn from him that sounds like music to my ears. His pain is my pleasure, and the blood trickling down his cheek is a beautiful sight.

Picking him up by his shirt, I throw him against the cement wall, gripping his throat tightly. The sound of Trent gasping for air fills my ears, and I smile sadistically as I squeeze his throat just a little more.

His hands try to scratch at mine, but it's without much

effort when all he gets is leather, and he slowly starts to fade before me, his eyes losing the will to live. But just when he's about to pass out, I release him, letting him fall to the floor in a heap. He coughs violently, sucking in ragged breath after breath.

My foot rears back and kicks him in the ribs, and another scream is torn from him as the air he so preciously needs leaves his lungs in a rush.

Toeing him on the ground, I grip him by his shirt and haul him up onto his knees, punching him in the face again.

"Let's see what hand you hit her with. Lifting his hands, I see the right one has a ring on it, and I know instantly that that's the one he used. "I don't think you'll need this hand anymore, do you?" I taunt, and he whimpers like a fucking scared little girl.

I pull out a switchblade from my pocket, and Trent's eyes widen. Placing his hand on his thigh, I stab the knife through the back of his hand and straight into his leg, pinning it down. His garbled scream echoes around my head and I grip his throat.

"You won't be leaving here alive, Trent." Pushing him to the floor, I grab him by the hair and hoist him up so his back is to me, not wanting to get his blood all over me.

Yanking the knife out of his leg, he screams again, a little weaker this time due to the blood seeping out of him, and I hold the knife to his exposed throat.

Jesus fucking Christ, he's crying.

"No one touches my woman without dying," I tell him, slicing the knife clean across his throat. Blood spurts out from the cut and I push him to floor as his tries to cover the open wound, but it's useless.

I wipe the knife off on his pants and wrap it in my handkerchief, putting it back in my pocket to clean thoroughly later. Removing the leather gloves, I leave them on the chair for Gino to use when he takes care of the mess, and grab my jacket.

I step around the blood pool forming and leave the room, turning to Gino by the door. "Clean it up."

"Yes, sir." He nods, and I walk back out the way I came, feeling better than I did when Enzo first called me.

The way everyone was looking at me in the meeting after he called... Leo especially, gave me a look that said it all – be careful.

He had someone once, years ago. He never told anyone, and he never brought her around, but we all knew. He'd disappear most nights and he'd never pick up women when we went out. But when he took our father's place, that was the end of whatever they had together. He stopped disappearing for chunks of time and became the hardened, ruthless man that I know today.

He doesn't talk about it, and I would never ask. Feelings aren't something we ever share in my family. Feelings make you vulnerable. Feelings get you killed.

All the men in our family know the consequences of having a woman in their lives. Especially a woman not from our world who doesn't know the score of what they'd be getting into when they're with one of us.

My mother was never in love with my father. I don't know if my aunts and uncles were ever in love either. Marriage to us is a convenience, a business transaction, a means to an end. I'm sure they were fond of each other in some way or another, even friends. But a real relationship?

Not even close.

The only two people I ever saw in my world who truly cared about one another were my grandparents. They were an anomaly, though. Where my grandfather was hard, my nonna was soft. Where he was tough, she was forgiving. And where he was ruthless, she was caring. They were opposites from both ends of the spectrum, but they worked. The only time I ever saw that man smile was with her, and that was when he thought no one else was around.

My nonna taught all of her children and grandchildren how to respect the attributes of a woman. She taught us what one can offer a hardened man with no redeeming qualities other than his loyalty and devotion to his family name. A man like me. She showed us there is a possibility for truth and love, which is why I always preferred being at my grandparent's house over mine.

But that was quickly taken from them when my nonna got cancer and my grandfather had to watch her die right in front of his eyes each day, with no power to change the outcome.

That was when we all saw what love can do to a man. He was destroyed. Without her, he was nothing more than a shell of himself, and it drove him to an early grave right along with her with a heart attack.

I never wanted that for myself.

CHAPTER 4

Tessa

"Are you hungry?" Enzo asks from somewhere behind me. I haven't moved from my spot on the couch since I arrived almost four hours ago, and I've just been staring at the unlit fireplace in front of me for the past hour.

My mystery man is sexier than I could have ever imagined. And now that I've seen him up close, and looked into his dark eyes, I realize nothing I could have come up with in my head would have done him justice.

He's dark. He's dangerous. I saw it in his eyes, his walk, his posture, and his entire aura and demeanor. But there's something else there. Something I can't help but be drawn to while still remaining just the slightest bit afraid of him.

I need to know his secrets, what makes him tick, why he comes to watch me every week, why he leaves me lavish gifts without ever having met me, and why he's had someone following me.

"Tessa?"

Blinking out of my thoughts, I look up at a concerned Enzo, and remember that he asked me a question.

"Yes?"

"I asked if you were hungry."

"I don't know," I say honestly. I know I was when I left The Aces after the show, but my stomach turned to lead the moment I thought my life was going to be left in the hands of that asshole.

"I can make you something. Toast? Soup? Or do you need a strong drink?" he offers, and I give him a small smile.

"A drink, I think."

Nodding, he walks over to the dry bar in the corner of the room against the wall of windows and pours me a hefty glass of amber liquid from a crystal decanter.

"Whiskey?" I ask when he hands it to me, and he gives me a curt nod. "Thanks."

Taking a sip, it goes down smooth, spreading through me with a warmth that pools in my stomach. I've never had expensive whiskey before, and so I take another sip, savoring the sweet burn on my tongue before swallowing.

When the front door opens, I know who it is immediately by how the frayed nerve endings in me spark alive and I jump where I sit, the liquid in my glass almost spilling over before I steady my hand again.

My God, he's beautiful. Beautiful in the way lightning is when it cracks across the sky during a summer thunder storm

— powerful, dangerous, electric, uncontrollable, a force of nature. You want to get closer, you want to dance in the warm rain, but you know if you do, then you risk getting struck. You risk getting burned. You risk everything. Including your life.

But if you survive, you cheat death, and that's a euphoric rush straight to the soul, making you feel more alive than ever before.

He's a force of nature with a direct line straight to my core, heightening everything I'm feeling.

He's probably somewhere around thirty, but every trace of youth has been wiped from him. Every inch of him is all man.

I can't help the slight shaking in my hand as I bring the crystal tumbler to my lips again and take a larger sip than before, needing the whiskey to calm my nerves.

He watches my every movement, his eyes darkening when my tongue peeks out to lick the drop of liquid left behind on my upper lip.

"How are you feeling?" His voice is as smooth as the whiskey sliding down my throat, and pools just as warmly in my stomach, loosening the knot that formed the moment he walked out the door earlier. I knew he was going to pay the man who attacked me a visit. I felt his anger rolling off of him when he saw my bruised face. And while taking comfort in knowing he hurt him right back for me should make me feel like a bad person, it doesn't.

If he's not taught a lesson now, what's to stop him from going after another girl the next night he's drunk? And that woman most definitely won't have a secret bodyguard like I did to rescue her from the fate I narrowly escaped from.

"What's your name?" I ask him for the second time, needing to know that more than anything right now. I want to call him something other than my mystery man. I need something to grab onto right now when everything about him is so carefully veiled.

Draping his suit jacket over the chair beside me, he walks over to the bar and pours himself his own glass of whiskey before taking the seat beside me. The sleeves of his crisp white dress shirt are rolled up to his elbows, exposing his tanned muscular forearms that I'm having visions of seeing flexing on either side of my head as he thrusts into me.

Looking away, I clear my throat and shift where I sit. He's a lot to take in. He has too much of a presence for me to relax.

"Alec Carfano," he says, and I repeat the name in my head, letting it roll around in there, and loving the way it feels. It's sexy. It's strong.

I look back up at him, his dark eyes pulling mine to his. "Alec Carfano. It suits you," I tell him, and immediately wonder why I said that. But his lip twitches, almost like he wants to smile but doesn't remember how.

"You think so?" Leaning back in his chair, he eyes me speculatively over the rim of his glass as he takes a long drink, my eyes drawn to his throat as he swallows.

"Yes," I whisper, my eyes meeting his again. "Why am I here?"

"Because I want you to be."

"Why did you have me followed?"

"Because you needed protection."

"From what?"

"I think tonight speaks for itself."

"And I'm grateful, but it still doesn't answer my question."

He stares at me for a long, silent moment. Using it, I'm sure, to contemplate whether or not to answer me honestly.

"I wanted to make sure you were safe."

"Why? From what?"

"Just accept the answer, Tessa. That's all you're getting tonight."

Well, then. Placing my half-full glass on the coffee table, I stand. "Fine, then I want to go home. Enzo?" I look over to him by the door, but he just looks at Alec.

"You're not leaving," Alec says in a matter-of-fact tone, his voice dropping just a little lower. Enough to send a shiver down my spine and make my legs give out so I'm sitting again.

"Why not? I'm fine, and I want to go back to my apartment."

"You can stay in one of my guest rooms tonight. I want you safe."

"I'm plenty safe at my apartment. I'm not anticipating another incident as I'm sure you took care of him in the basement when you left before." Alec's eyes momentarily dart over to Enzo, giving him a sharp glare at the mention of the basement like I was never supposed to know about it.

"What did you do to him?" I ask softly.

"Don't ask a question you're not ready to hear the answer to, *bella*," he says, and a chill runs through me. I think he did more than just rough him up.

Darting my eyes away, I try to decide how I feel about that. But Alec doesn't give me time to, because he places a finger under my chin and lifts my gaze back to his, all thoughts leaving my brain. "Stay tonight. I don't want you alone."

"I have work tomorrow."

"That has nothing to do with tonight."

His eyes are dark, pulling me in like two black holes until I feel like I'm free-falling into them, not knowing where I'll end up.

"Okay." The word is spoken as if he reached inside of me and pulled it out himself.

"Good. Are you hungry?" He leans back in his chair and breaks eye contact, allowing me to blink out of my hypnotized state.

"No. I'm just tired."

"I'll show you where you can sleep." Standing, he takes a sip of his whiskey and then holds his hand out for me. I stare at it for a second too long, contemplating how touching him would feel, before I tentatively place my smaller one in his.

His warmth immediately envelopes me and I feel a current travel up my arm, straight to my chest.

I don't know this feeling. I'm both scared and excited. Calm and wound up. I'm unsure of everything aside from my desire to stay the night.

Walking down the hallway, we pass a few closed doors before he opens one on the right.

Silently, I step inside before him and look around, clenching my jaw to keep it from dropping to the floor.

It's amazing.

Floor to ceiling windows line the exterior wall, giving me a view of the opposite side of the city and ocean from the living room's windows. I have the urge to go over to them to take it all in, but his hand surrounding mine anchors me to where I stand.

"The sun is bright in the morning, so you might want to close the curtains," he says as I look at the large, king-sized bed that looks like heaven waiting for me.

"Okay," I say softly, the quiet of the room loud to my ears.

"My sister stays with me when she's in town, so you should have whatever you need in the closet and bathroom, which is right through there." He lifts his chin to the door off to the right. "Use whatever you need. Wear whatever you want. She'll never know it's gone."

"Okay," I repeat. I don't know what else to say. I'm feeling overwhelmed at being out of my element in a place like this, and my exhaustion isn't helping either.

"I'm in the next room over, so if you need anything, just knock." His eyes turn a shade darker, and I have to look away with all the images I'm starting to have of us in this big bed after telling him exactly what I need.

"Okay," I whisper, feeling like an idiot that that's all I can come up with to say for the third time.

Releasing my hand, I feel the loss immediately as his eyes slowly roam over me before silently leaving the room. The click of the door closing makes me physically relax now that I'm alone.

Why am I here?

Why did I agree to stay?

Not that I had much say in the matter, but still. I could have had more of a backbone and insisted that I leave. Although I wouldn't have been able to use the elevator without either him or Enzo anyhow, so I'm essentially imprisoned here until Alec says I can go. Well, imprisoned is a strong word considering I caved rather quickly to his demand that I stay the night by simply looking into his eyes.

I liked the idea of him wanting me to be safe too much to put up much of a fight. I haven't had that in a very long time – someone looking out for my safety. Not since my brother.

A pang in my chest at the thought of James has me rubbing the spot over my heart absentmindedly. It's been six years, and I still see that day play out in my head as if it were yesterday.

Shoving it back down, not willing to go there tonight, I walk through to the bathroom and my eyes widen. It's huge, with marble everywhere I look. The floors, tub, shower, countertops. Everything in here screams money and elegance, and I'm way out of my element. But even so, I fully intend on allowing myself to enjoy every minute of tonight because I don't know when I'll ever get the chance to take a bath in a marble tub again.

Filling the tub with hot water, I look under the sink and find an assortment of bubble bath powders, soaps, shampoos, and conditioners. I can definitely tell this is a woman's bathroom, and one with expensive taste.

I find that surprisingly sweet that he lets his sister stay with him when she visits. I wonder where she normally lives and if he has any other siblings.

Sprinkling in lavender powder, I sink into the hot water and sigh, my sore muscles from all the extra practicing I've been doing feeling relief on contact.

I may be out of my element with all of this lavishness, but I know I could get used it pretty quickly. Leaning my head back against the edge of the tub, I close my eyes, letting all my worries and unanswered questions dissolve into the hot water.

I don't know how much time passes, but when the water cools, I reluctantly move to the shower to wash my hair with products that smell like honeysuckle and amber, and I relax all over again.

Wrapping myself in a fluffy robe that's folded neatly on a shelf by the sink, I look at myself in the mirror for the first time since being hit, and tears immediately pool in my eyes.

Turning the light off in a rush, I quickly walk out of the bathroom and pad across the bedroom carpet to the walk-in closet.

"Oh, wow," I breathe.

I'm surprised Alec's sister doesn't live here full-time with how packed it is of everything – clothes, shoes, coats, bags, accessories.

It feels weird to pick out pajamas from someone else's closet, but that soon passes when my fingers brush over a pretty pink silk pajama set, loving the way it feels against my skin. Pulling it out, I notice it still has the tags on it, and catching a peek of the price, my eyes bug out. Who spends that much on pajamas?

I hesitate on whether or not I should put them back and choose something else, but the material is unlike anything else I've ever worn and so I give in, telling myself that it's okay for tonight. It's not like I'll keep them.

Crawling into bed, I turn and look out the windows. It's comforting knowing the world continues to move down below.

At this time of night, whoever is still in the casinos are either trying to win back their losses or cash out their day's winnings. Those who have drank too much are stumbling back to their rooms with whoever they chose to keep their bed warm for the night. Or, if a woman is lucky, she has a steady man by her side, holding her up as she tries to walk in a straight line in her heels without falling on her face.

I love living in a city that never sleeps. Like a mini Las Vegas. Not that I would feel safe walking around at night. Clearly, by what happened tonight. But I like knowing I could, and knowing the other lost souls are awake with me.

We're alone together.

I wonder if Alec feels the same about living here. And with the thought of him, and the reminder of where I am, my mind starts racing, no longer tired. He said he's in the next room over, which brings along with it images of him sleeping naked with the sheets tangled around his hips, and suddenly I feel too hot for the covers. Throwing them off, I start pacing the room.

I want to know everything about him. But most of all, I want to know, why me?

Walking into the closet, I put on the matching silk robe I find and then peek my head out the door, needing a glass of water or something to calm my nerves. I don't see or hear anything, so I tiptoe down the hall towards the kitchen, but practically jump out of my skin when I see Alec sitting in one of the chairs on the library side of the fireplace.

He's still dressed in his suit pants and white button-down, with a drink in one hand and a stack of papers in the other.

"Oh, um, I'm sorry. I didn't think you'd be out here. I'll just go back–"

"No," he says, cutting me off. Looking me up and down,

his eyes rake over my body like a slow caress, making me feel as if I were naked by the way his gaze feels against my skin. My body immediately reacts with a heated flush and a pounding pulse that settles between my thighs.

"Do you need something?" His eyes finally meet mine, and I wrap my arms around my waist to keep from melting on the spot.

"I was just going to get some water. I couldn't sleep."

"Have a seat." He nods at the chair beside him. "I'll get it for you."

Doing as he says, my thighs come in contact with the cold leather of the chair and a shiver runs through me. Returning, he hands me a cold bottle of water and places a plate of cheese and grapes between us.

"If you're hungry. I know you didn't eat."

"Thank you." I twist off the cap on the bottle and let the water slide down my throat, cooling my suddenly hot body from being so close to him.

"You couldn't sleep. Is the bed not comfortable? Would you rather I—"

"No," I say, cutting him off. "No, it's the most comfortable bed I've ever laid in. I even had a relaxing bath and shower. My mind just won't turn off."

"I know the feeling. What's keeping your mind awake?"

"Just…things." I pop a grape in my mouth, avoiding his gaze. It's too penetrating. I'm afraid he'll see every dirty thought I've had about him that's kept me from sleeping.

"Care to elaborate?"

"Care to tell me why I'm here?"

"My place is the safest in the city."

"That's not really an answer," I counter, sipping my

water. He doesn't say anything, and his stretched silence makes me rethink my response. "Never mind. I'll let you get back to your work." I go to stand, but he reaches out, placing a large hand on my forearm to stop me.

"Stay. I've worked enough for tonight."

My eyes swing to his, and I lean back in the chair again when I see the sincerity in them, tucking one of my feet up under me while he places his stack of papers to the side.

"What kind of work do you do?"

He flashes me a little smirk and rubs his jaw. "I own The Aces."

My eyes widen. "You own this hotel/casino?" No wonder he has the penthouse.

"Yes. The Carfano name owns many businesses. This one is mine." He swirls the glass in his hand and keeps his eyes on me as if he's watching to see how I'll react to what he just told me.

"What other businesses do you own?"

"This and that."

"Okay. You're just adding more questions to the pile." I eat a little slice of cheddar cheese and a couple of grapes and lean my head back, closing my eyes briefly.

"I can answer a few of them for you. Maybe not all right now."

Rolling my head to the side, I give him a small smile. "Which would you like to answer first?"

Alec takes a sip of his whiskey. "I never go to shows in my casino," he starts, "but I needed something to distract myself for a while where no one would bother me. That's when I saw you." His dark eyes hold mine captive, and a chill runs down my spine. "So beautiful. I've never seen anyone like you. The way you move..." He rubs his bottom lip with his thumb. "I couldn't go near you, though. I still know I should stay away. But after tonight, I don't think I can anymore."

"Why would you stay away?" I whisper, my throat tight.

Swirling his whiskey, he takes another sip. "For many reasons." Pausing, he captures my gaze once again and my breathing quickens. No matter how much I want to look away, I can't. "You want to know why I bought you those gifts?"

I give him a slight nod, knowing my voice would give away my nerves at having his full attention.

"Because I wanted to see you in them. I knew you'd look even more beautiful. And when you wore them for me with that sexy little smile"–he smirks–"I knew right then and there I'd buy you every fucking diamond in the world if you'd wear them for me like that."

Leaning forward with his elbows on his knees, his dark eyes hold mine with unwavering attentiveness, making my stomach twist in knots and my core clench with need. "I chose black roses because I see the darkness in you that you try and hide from the world. It's what drives you to dance. It's what keeps you at a distance from everyone around you. You're a black rose blooming on stage, but you close up again once that final curtain falls."

"How?" I breathe, unable to finish the question. How does he know all of that about me?

"Reading people is what I do. I'd be dead by now if I couldn't."

"Why was Enzo following me?"

"For reasons such as tonight. He'll have to deal with

what's coming for letting anyone touch you."

"Please don't," I say quickly, my pulse quickening. "He saved me. He was keeping his distance like I'm sure you told him to so I'd never know he was there. That's why he didn't get to me right away."

"Enzo has to be punished. I can't have my men thinking I'm any less than the man I am."

"What does that mean?"

Staying quiet, Alec just takes another sip of his drink as his eyes move to take in the darkening bruise around my eye. I lift my hand to it and turn away.

"You don't have to hide it from me, Tessa," he says, his voice strained from concealed anger. "You're fucking beautiful, bruise or not."

A blush spreads up my neck and I keep my eyes on my lap.

"Look at me, *mia bella rosa*." The term of endearment rolls off his tongue in perfect Italian, making my heart beat a little faster and my body flood with heat.

I risk a look back over at him and see his eyes have softened, making him look a little less like he's ready to kill at any given moment.

"You don't ever have to hide from me."

Biting my lower lip, I give him a small nod and keep my head raised, not letting myself shy away from him. I want to be the blooming black rose he sees on stage right now, not the closed off Tessa I am every other minute of the day.

He rewards me with the slightest of smiles. Just the lift of the corner of his lips, but it's the sexiest thing I've ever seen. Mix that with the way his eyes seem to see into the deepest parts of me I don't let anyone into, and my chest tightens. I feel my nipples harden, the thin satin fabric doing nothing to hide my reaction to him.

His eyes dart down, and the little smirk on his sexy lips grows by a fraction while his dark eyes swim with desire.

I've never had a man look at me like this, like I'm every fantasy come to life and he wants to devour me whole. The longer he stares, the heavier my chest feels, and the more the silk starts to feel like it's too tight. Too suffocating. He could rip it from my body right now and I wouldn't protest. I should, but I wouldn't.

Tearing my eyes away, I look at the unlit fireplace in front of me and sip my water, needing to calm down.

"Don't worry, Tessa," he murmurs, low and hypnotic. "I won't touch you until you're ready."

My head spins. My vision blurs.

Clearing my throat, I stand on shaky legs, realizing though, that the pajamas and silk robe leave the entirety of my legs on display, and I can feel his eyes burning my skin with their heat.

"I...I think I'll try going back to sleep now."

"You sure?" he taunts. "I thought we were just getting started."

"With what?" I ask, my slight fear evident in my voice.

"With me answering your questions."

"You answered enough."

"If you say so," Alec says smoothly, his hypnotic voice making me look back at him. He appears so relaxed in the way he's sitting and watching me – leaned back, legs apart, elbows resting casually on the arms of the leather chair. But I can see the underlying current of his prowess. He's ready to strike at his prey at any moment. And right now, that's me.

"You look scared, *bella*."

"Should I be?" I ask, sounding braver than I feel.

"I'd never hurt you," he says, and I hear the sincerity of his words. "But everyone else..." He lifts one shoulder slightly. "They don't get the same assurance. Especially if they hurt you."

I shouldn't find that so flattering, and yet I do. I know he'd never physically hurt me. I can feel that. But hurt me in every other way...that's what I'm afraid of.

"I don't need protection. I've been on my own for a long time and I've done just fine."

"Just fine isn't good enough for someone like you."

Turning the water bottle in my hands, I look past him and out the windows, forcing a deep breath. "You don't really know me," I say softly.

"Goodnight, Tessa," he says as a reply, with a gleam in his eye that says he might know more about me than I think.

"Goodnight," I whisper, walking back down the hall to my room for the night. I crawl right under the covers and curl into a ball on my side, pinching my eyes closed.

I didn't expect any of this.

This is why I was afraid to ever meet my mystery man. Over this past month, I've formed an illusion of him in my mind of who he could be, what he'd look like, and what he'd be like. And now that I've met him, all of those expectations have been thrown out the window.

He's better than all of my imaginary versions.

He's so much...*more.*

CHAPTER 5
Tessa

Waking up to the morning light, I blink my eyes open, remembering where I am the moment I see the ocean through the floor-to-ceiling windows.

I can't believe how beautiful it is. I've never stayed on the top floor of a hotel or apartment building before, so I never knew views could be so nice. I see why people pay for them now.

Climbing out of bed, I pad across the plush cream-colored carpet. In the dark last night, I hadn't noticed that there's a balcony off of the room, and as I slide the glass door open, the thick, warm morning air hits me like a heavy dose of reality.

It's the dead of summer, and while I love laying out on the beach, I hate the constant muggy stuffiness that hangs heavy in the air most days.

Taking a deep breath, I lean on the railing and scan the city before me.

The beach is already peppered with colorful umbrellas, and the boardwalk has a few joggers and families walking together, ready for a day of rides, games, and food.

The waves crash on the shore in a hypnotic rhythm, and after a few more minutes out here, I start to feel the heat getting to me, so I duck back inside to the cool air conditioning.

Heading into the bathroom, I comb my hair out, saying a silent thank you that it dried straight last night despite sleeping on it while slightly damp. I brush my teeth with a new toothbrush I find in one of the vanity drawers and wash my face, wincing when I touch the area around my eye.

I toss the pajamas I borrowed into the hamper in the corner of the bathroom and dress in my yoga pants and tank top from last night so I don't have to borrow any more clothes. It wouldn't feel right to leave here with something that isn't mine.

Looking at myself in the mirror, I cringe, and dig around in the bathroom drawers until I find concealer. But after applying an ample amount, it doesn't help in the least. It actually makes it look slightly worse, so I wash it off, deciding to make peace with how I look for now. Alec's already seen me, so there's no reason to hide behind makeup.

In the light of day, staying the night doesn't seem like the best choice on my part. Last night, my emotions were running on high after being attacked and then rescued, and then meeting Alec. But now, I don't know. I feel awkward and out of place.

I know I can't hide in here forever, so I take a deep breath and open the door. I make my way down the hall and see Alec straight ahead, sitting at the dining table off of the kitchen reading the newspaper and drinking coffee.

He looks up when I approach, and his eyes immediately scan down my body and back up. His expression doesn't change, just his eyes. They turn a shade darker as if I were standing before him in lingerie and not fully clothed, and I have to grip the back of the chair in front of me to steady myself.

"Would you like coffee?" Alec asks, his smooth voice both revving me up and calming me down simultaneously.

"Yes, thank you."

"Take a seat." He nods, pouring me a cup from a French press. Sliding the cup and saucer towards me, I add a little cream from the white porcelain creamer between us and take a sip, letting the liquid gold slide down my throat, waking me up further.

Mmm, it's delicious. It's probably some high end, quality coffee that's better than anything I could ever find on the local grocery store shelf.

"Breakfast is on its way up."

"Oh, okay. Thank you."

"Why are you nervous, Tessa?" he asks, studying me as he takes a drink of coffee. "I thought we would be past that after last night."

I divert my eyes, studying the coffee in my cup. How could I *not* be nervous around him? His presence is formidable. And he can't be serious that I would be less nervous around him after last night. He said he wasn't going to touch me until I was ready...

What does that even mean? I don't think I'll ever be ready for his touch. It'll ruin me for every other man. I already know that. A man like him doesn't touch without fire.

"Don't worry, we'll have plenty of time for you to get used to me."

I look back up at him and see that same almost-smile as last night that makes my insides churn and take flight. "I will?"

"Yes," is all he says, going back to reading the paper.

A minute later, Enzo strolls through the door with a small food cart. He brings over covered plates to me and Alec and then takes the third for himself over to the kitchen island where he takes a seat on a stool to eat.

"Thank you, Enzo. Why are you over there?"

"Because I told him not to bother us."

"You're not still mad at him for last night, are you? I told you he helped me."

Alec's eyes dart to mine and holds them with a hardness that sends a chill through me. "He was too late. Did you not see yourself in the mirror?"

"I did." I look away, biting into a slice of crispy bacon, deciding to let it drop. I know he'll never see it my way.

We eat in silence, and I don't realize how hungry I am until my plate of eggs, bacon, and toast is clean.

"I have to get home and get ready for work. Will Enzo be taking me down to my car? I can't access the elevator myself."

"You don't have work today."

"What? Yes, I do," I answer, confused. "I work the

lunch shift at Lucy's Diner Saturday afternoons."

"Not today." Alec folds the newspaper neatly and places it on the table, pouring himself a fresh cup of coffee.

"And why not?"

"Because I already had your boss informed that you're unwell and will be out for the next week. At least."

"You did what?" I ask incredulously, my eyes widening. "You had no right to do that. I need to work, Alec. I have bills. Rent."

"That's taken care of. You just have to worry about healing."

"I'm fine." I sigh. "And what do you mean about it being taken care of?"

"I took care of everything," he tells me casually, continuing to drink his coffee like he isn't telling me something absurd.

"No."

"No?" His eyebrows raise and a little smirk graces his lips.

"I don't need you to take care of anything for me. I manage just fine," I say proudly, squaring my shoulders.

"I never said you didn't, or couldn't. I'm telling you that from here on out, I'm here to take care of everything."

"Alec," I say through a laugh. "You can't be serious."

"Why can't I be?"

"Because that's crazy. You're crazy."

He shrugs. "I've been called worse, *bella*. And there's no debate to be had here. You don't have work at the diner or the dance studio this week."

My anger flares. "How dare you. You called the studio too? Those kids need me. They really look forward to class."

"There's a substitute lined up."

I place my palms flat on the table and take a deep breath. "Alec," I say calmly. "You can't just swoop in and start controlling things. I already thanked you for everything you did in helping me last night, but my life is my own. I like my job at the diner and I love teaching dance to those kids."

"But you love your Friday nights more," he counters. I open my mouth to deny it, but he cuts me off. "Don't try to tell me otherwise, Tessa. I've seen you up there."

He's right. But what he doesn't get is that I can't be her full-time. I can't be that Tessa more than just Friday nights. She's my escape from reality, and I worry that if I play her too often, she won't be effective anymore, and I never want *that* Tessa to become mundane or a chore to be.

"I'd like to go now." I look over to Enzo who I know is trying not to listen to our conversation, but I know has heard everything. "Will you take me down, please?" I ask him kindly.

He looks to Alec and then back to me. "Sure."

"I'll just grab my bag." Standing, I go and get it from the room I was in and then meet Enzo at the front door. I was only gone a minute, but Alec isn't at the table anymore, and he's not in the kitchen or living rooms either.

"He had business to attend to," Enzo tells me, seeing me looking around.

"Okay." I nod. "Let's go."

CHAPTER 6
Alec

Tessa is going to be the death of me. Punching in the code for the elevator, I ride it down to the basement, shoving my hands in my pockets to keep from hitting the fucking walls.

I've never felt so out of control and in need of controlling someone else so much before.

But one of the reasons Tessa is so fucking insanely beautiful is her air of freedom. On stage, she's wild and free, and I wouldn't dare tame her. Although when she was sitting in front of me last night, vulnerable and hurt, all I wanted was to hold her. I would do anything to help her and keep her safe – a concept as foreign to me as letting someone out of a gambling debt. Never happens.

I've never cared. That's how I've been able to run this city and keep it mine.

Reaching the basement, I walk into our offices to call Leo on my secure line. I would normally do business like this in my penthouse office but I had to leave before I dragged Tessa into my bedroom and never let her leave.

She's too distracting and I have shit to do that requires my full attention. Also, Tessa fired up and directing it at me... I was close to laying her out on the table and giving her a better use for her passion.

I want to hear her scream.

I want to hear her moan my name as I sink deep inside of her.

Fuck.

Pounding my fist on the table, I punch in Leo's number. While I was in New York last night, my men broke up another underground gambling ring by the Triads. They've been steadily trying to gain a foothold in Atlantic City over the past six months, and this is the third time I've had to break up one of their underground games.

I snuff them out every time, and they just come back up like weeds in the darkest corners of my city.

I got the intel Thursday night from one of my private gambling room waitresses. She was asked by a higher-up Triad to come work his underground game, and the fucking bastard didn't think she'd tell her boss, who then told me.

Loyalty runs deep in my casino. I don't tolerate anything less.

Sitting back in my chair, I close my eyes briefly while the phone rings, and see Tessa's hazel eyes staring back at me, begging me to challenge her. Jesus, she's fucking sexy when she's riled up. The automatic tightening of my pants is evidence that a woman with fight turns me on more than I thought it would.

I usually need a woman completely under my command, but now the thought of Tessa giving me the same fight and fire in the bedroom as she did this morning has my dick harder than it's ever been.

"Alec," Leo answers, his voice clipped. He's always wound so tight. I don't even think getting laid would relax him. "What's this shit with the Triads? I thought we dealt with them." I can always count on him for getting down to business straight away.

"I have. This is the third fucking time they've crept back up thinking they're going to outsmart me like I don't have eyes and ears everywhere."

"Well, clearly they weren't put off by your other talks with them," he says harshly, implying I'm not doing my job.

"I did everything but wipe them all out. Is that what you're suggesting I do, Leo? Because I think we'd have a bigger shit storm on our hands if I did that."

"Don't think it hasn't crossed my mind once or twice. I'm going to schedule a sit down for us with their leader. They need to be shut the fuck down. They can run their shit underground games from here in the city. But that's it."

"Agreed."

"And with that business done for now, I'm going to need you to tell me why the fuck you think it was a good idea to walk out of the meeting yesterday for some pussy?"

My blood boils. "Don't ever refer to her like that again," I tell him low, my implications clear.

"You know who you're talking to, right?"

"Yes, my older brother, not my boss."

Leo let's out a sigh that's barely audible through the phone and I know he's rubbing the bridge of his nose like he always did when we were younger and Luca and I did something he didn't approve of.

"Alec, you know getting involved with a woman in any serious capacity isn't going to end well, right?"

"Who said anything about it being serious?" I counter, not wanting him to know how serious I already am about her.

"Because you walked out of our meeting last night. If I didn't hear you say something about her being hurt, then I never would have let you leave."

Let me leave?

My fist clenches on top of the conference table and I force myself to not say something I'll regret later. Leo is the head of the family but he's also my brother, and that fact seems to slip his mind more and more lately. He's started detaching himself from the rest of us these past couple of years, and I don't know how to reel him back towards us before we lose him.

"I had to." I don't want to explain myself further.

"Is she okay?"

"Yeah, I dealt with it."

"Is there something I should know?"

"No. The guy who hit her has been taken care of."

"Jesus," Leo breathes, but I don't want to talk about this over the phone. Our lines are clean, but I still don't like it.

"Did I miss anything after I left?"

"We discussed some shit going on in Miami and the club being challenged by the Cubans. Saverio and Matteo have it covered though, and a meeting is in place with them down there to clear up a few misunderstandings."

"Good. Why anyone thinks they can try and come in and push us out of our cities just shows how little they value their lives."

"Exactly. And Alec, we need to talk about Katarina."

"What's wrong?" I ask quickly, my blood running like ice at the thought of something being wrong with our little sister.

"She's fine. She's just driving me up a fucking wall with her talk about needing her freedom."

"She's just being dramatic. It'll pass."

"No, it won't. She tells me every chance she gets that she needs more from life than what we allow her to have."

"Leo, brother, I know the thought of loosening the reigns on her will result in something bad happening, but–"

"No fucking buts, she needs protection. This city is full of men ready to take advantage of her, and I won't let that happen."

"You think any of us want that?" I fire back. Katarina is only 21, and she's too beautiful and naive to know the world will chew her up and spit her out before she even realizes what hit her. "Look, her birthday is coming up, so why don't we throw her a party at The Aces? She can have a little fun and feel like she has the illusion of freedom for the night."

Leo is quiet for a moment, thinking it over. "Fine. I think that'll keep her at bay for a while, then."

"You know she's getting older, right? And what that means for you?" It's Leo's job now since our father is gone to make sure she's married off to a man who will be a good match, but also benefit our family.

"Yes," he hisses. "It means I'll be sharpening my

knives."

"Sounds about right," I say, taking the slightest pleasure in his discomfort.

"I have to go. Luca just walked in and we have to talk some things over."

"I have to go, too. Talk soon."

Hanging up, I lean back in my chair and scrub my hands up and down my face.

Sometimes my family name weighs so heavy on my shoulders that I wonder how my back hasn't crumbled under the pressure. But then, like right now, I remember what that name represents, and the weight just strengthens rather than destroys me.

My mind wanders back to Tessa and how she doesn't know what the Carfano name means yet. I could tell in the way she didn't react when I told her who I was.

She may not know now, but she'll soon find out what it means to be with a Carfano man.

CHAPTER 7
Tessa

I was so mad at Alec for telling my bosses at the diner and studio that I couldn't work for a week. I even tried to call them and tell them I was okay to come in, but they insisted they were fine and I needed to rest and get better. I know they don't know for what reason, but their concern was evident, and I thought that was so sweet. I hadn't realized they cared about me like that.

I'm also reluctant to admit that I enjoyed this past week. I went to the beach a few times, my first time this summer, and I made myself my favorite dinners and watched endless movies and shows that have been piling up on my DVR.

It's sad to admit, but it was the first time I had a week

off in…well…ever. I've never taken a vacation. I don't know the last time I requested off, or if I ever even have. I've only called out sick a couple of times in the past six years I've worked at Lucy's Diner and the dance studio.

It's Friday again though, and there's no way I'm not dancing in the show. The bruises on my face and arm have faded drastically, and it's nothing my show makeup can't cover.

Alec has kept his distance this week, which has been making me go a little crazy. I spent the night at his place, he's all demanding and protective of my safety, and then silence. Nothing. I still have my bodyguard though.

Every night I went to sleep with him on my mind, his dark eyes lulling me under, and every morning I woke up wishing that when I opened them, I was looking out floor-to-ceiling windows that showed me the bright sun, ocean, and the city I've grown to call home over almost a decade now.

Grabbing my gym bag, I open my front door to find Enzo leaning against the wall of my apartment.

"Hi, Enzo," I greet. "How are you?"

"I'm alright. How are you?"

"Good, thank you. I'm sorry you were given the task of following me. That can't be what you want to be doing."

"It's not so bad. You don't go anywhere that would be awkward for me."

"And where would that be?" I laugh.

"Male strip show, lady stores, lady doctor—"

"Okay, please stop." I laugh again, holding up my hand. "And what's a lady store?"

"I don't know." He shrugs. "Bras, panties, lingerie. Boss would kill me if I had to see you trying shit on like that."

"Okay, okay, okay. Enzo, first you'd have to be in the dressing room with me to see that, and that wouldn't happen. And second, I don't buy lingerie. You can feel free to report that back to Alec."

Smiling, he shakes his head. "Ready to go? I'm driving you tonight."

"Why? Sick of tailing me?"

"It would be easier if I just drove you, yes, but tonight you won't need your car."

"Why?"

"Because Alec says so."

"And I'm supposed to do what he says?"

Enzo steps away from the wall and holds his arm out, directing me to walk down the stairs first, giving me my answer.

Closing and locking my door, we head down, and Enzo opens the back door to a black Range Rover for me. "I'm not allowed up front?" I ask, tossing my bag in the back.

"It's safer in the back."

"What's with you guys and safety?"

"It's a high priority in our business, and your safety especially matters to Alec."

"Why?"

"You're still wondering why?" He tilts his head to the side, studying me.

"Maybe. I don't know. Yes."

"Get in. You're going to be late."

Realizing he's right, I climb in the back without another word, and Enzo and I ride to The Aces in a comfortable silence.

"Thanks for the ride," I say, hopping out when we

arrive.

"Wait. I'll walk you in."

"Enzo," I challenge, giving him a look. "I'm fine. I promise. Thank you for the ride, and tell Alec I'll see him at his table in a little while."

"I will." He nods, accepting my request like an order.

"Hey," I say, turning back after taking a step, curious. "Are you the one who sneaks in to leave me my gifts?"

"Yes."

"Do you watch my shows?" I like knowing Alec is there for me to dance to, but I think I'd feel weird if Enzo was there too.

"No," he says quickly.

"Alec?" I taunt, smiling, and he nods yes. "Alright, I'll see you later, I guess. Thanks for the ride, E."

"E?"

"Yeah. If you're going to be my new shadow, then I think I should be able to give you a nickname."

"Just get inside," he urges, shaking his head. But I see the little smile he's trying to hide.

Seeing Alec at his table again makes me dance better than I ever have. Every move I make is for him. I let my emotions rule my body, taking over me like I was someone else entirely. Which I feel like I am.

He doesn't keep to the shadows tonight. Alec has his chair angled in the castoff stage lighting so I can see, as well as feel, his dark eyes following me across the stage.

He didn't get to see the slight changes I made to my solo last week, and with every bend, twist, and spin of my body, I feel his intensity for me growing. If his desire was a tangible thing to see, it'd be a hazy black cloud surrounding me – filling me, changing me. My heart beats faster, my mind goes foggy, and my blood rushes like a raging river after a huge storm.

My senses are overloaded and all I can see, hear, feel, and think about is Alec. His black smoke of desire and need for me gets thicker and thicker as I dance, as if he thinks he can shield me from everyone else in the audience but him.

With my final leg lift and spin, my skirt fans out, and the crystals that make up the fringe of it glint off the bright lights. I throw Alec a sly smile when I land in a split with a backbend towards him.

The curtain falls, and it takes an extra second for me to get up and walk off stage. I feel like I was just in a trance for the past three and a half minutes, and am only now coming back into my own body and mind.

After the show, I walk back to my dressing area to find a bigger than usual black bouquet of roses with a note.

Enzo will take you up to my place. I'll be waiting.
-A

Smiling, I bite my lower lip and open the jewelry box, only to have my smile vanish as I take in the necklace. A dark, blood red ruby hangs from a gold chain, matching my earrings perfectly. It's stunning. Closing the box, I hurry to change and wipe off my makeup.

Alec scares me in the best of ways. I know I shouldn't accept his gifts. I know I shouldn't go and meet him again. I know I should stay away from him. But I also know I like the way I feel when I'm around him. I like the way I feel about myself when I'm around him.

He makes me feel seen, beautiful, important, worthy.

I haven't felt those things about myself in a very long time. The fact that he also screams danger doesn't even register as a deterrent for me. Because along with that danger comes the promise of life, and I want to feel alive again.

I want to dance in the summer storm, fully knowing I might get struck by lightning.

I almost welcome it.

"Hey, E." I smile, finding him waiting for me out in the back hallway.

"Hey, T," he replies with a small smile.

When we reach the penthouse, Enzo unlocks the door and I step through, my eyes immediately meeting Alec's, who's sitting in the chair facing me.

Standing, he buttons his crisp black suit jacket and walks towards me, his eyes holding mine the entire time.

Lord have mercy, he knows how to wear a suit unlike any man I've ever seen. As if he walked straight off Milan's runway and onto the cover of GQ, and then kept walking towards me.

Each step closer stirs the air around me. That force I felt last week at being near him, and have been craving every day since, magnifies to the point of feeling as if I'm physically being pulled into his orbit when he's right in front of me.

Reaching out, Alec lightly grips my chin between his thumb and forefinger, and I feel the touch straight to my stomach, knotting it up in anticipation and delight.

He turns my head to the side to look over my face. "How are you?" he asks, his low, velvety voice instinctively making my eyes close for a moment and a little sigh to leave my lips.

Everything he does, I react to. I can only imagine how I'll react when his touch is on more than just my face and his voice is commanding me to do whatever he wants.

Holding back a moan at just the thought of being with him, I sway where I stand, and Alec places his other hand on my hip to steady me. I feel his heat burning me through my thin cotton top, and when my eyes clash with his again, they're penetrating mine – searching for answers to questions I'm not sure I would even know how to answer.

"I'm taking you out tonight," he says low, so close to my lips that I can feel his warm breath against mine.

"You are?"

"Yes. Choose anything you'd like from my sister's closet. Something nice."

"Okay," I whisper, the knots in my stomach turning to butterflies.

Stepping back, he releases me, and I take a moment to regain myself before heading off down the hall in a blind haze to the room I stayed in last week.

After a shower, I dry my hair straight and reapply my makeup. I had hoped I wouldn't be going back to my apartment tonight, so I made sure to bring my makeup and toiletries in anticipation. A bit presumptuous, but I don't care. I thought about him nonstop this week, and I knew if he was going to be at the show tonight, then maybe I wouldn't be going home.

I play up my hazel eyes with a nude palette smokey eye and a few extra layers of mascara.

Padding across the room, I walk into the closet and run

my hand over the rows and rows of clothes. He said something nice, so I stop in front of the dresses section, one in particular catching my eye straight away.

Smiling, I know it'll catch Alec's eye too, so I pull it out and find matching heels and a small purse to go with it.

When I slip it on, I turn in the mirror and smile.

The red cocktail dress fits me like it was made for me. The red satin material is overlain with red lace flowers that seem to grow across my body like vines, inviting the eye to follow the lines.

It hits me mid-thigh so it's not too short, and the rounded neckline doesn't show too much cleavage, but the back is what's the showstopper. Thin straps hold the dress up and then crisscross in three large x's down the length of my back, tying at the base of my spine.

Reaching back, I tie the satin strings together and then slip my feet into matching red satin heels that tie around my ankles.

I just so happened to have brought my red lipstick with me as a last-minute decision, and when I swipe it across my lips, I can't help but give myself a sly smile.

If I'm going to be on Alec's arm, then I need to look like I belong there.

CHAPTER 8
Alec

Fuck. Me.

Tessa emerges from the hallway and I already regret telling her I was taking her out.

She looks so fucking good. A walking wet dream. I'm going to have to kill every man who looks at her because I know exactly what they'll be thinking when they are.

Just like on stage, she's an angel dressed like the devil, tempting me to sin. Begging me to sin.

I have enough of those to my name to buy me a one-way ticket to hell when I die, but tarnishing Tessa will be the bullet train to those fiery gates.

The blood red dress against her flawless tan skin is an all

too inviting image for me, and her caramel and honey brown hair is a silken curtain that I can't wait to grip in my fist as I drive into her.

I want those hazel eyes on me while she has those matching blood red lips wrapped around my cock, taking me so deep inside her hot mouth that I hit the back of her throat.

I don't do anything to hide how hard I am for her, and when her sexy eyes drop to my lap, I see a blush creep into her cheeks that I can't wait to feel against my own as I whisper in her ear what I want to do to her.

But I told her I wouldn't touch her until she's ready. I want her to beg for me to touch her.

This is on her.

I need to know she needs this just as badly.

Standing, I button my jacket and hold my arm out for her. Looping hers through mine, I pull her close and breathe in her flowery scent, planting a kiss right below her ear. She's wearing the ruby and diamond earrings I got her.

"You're stunning, *bella*." I feel her shiver at my words and I smile against her skin, stepping even closer so she can feel how hard I am, which sends another shiver through her. Good.

Pulling back, I take in her flushed skin and parted lips. She's a temptation I've never resisted before, but I force away every instinct I have to rip this dress off of her and haul her to my bed so I can keep to the plan I made.

"Let's go before I decide against letting everyone see you like this."

"And what about me letting everyone see you?" she asks, her voice soft and breathless, making my blood rush with how come-and-fuck-me she sounds.

She wants to keep me away from other women? Well, fuck me, I'll welcome her possession just as I know she'll welcome mine.

Not being able to hold back any longer, I give in to the man I've only ever known to be. I take what I want, when I want it. My lips crash down on hers and my arms circle her waist as she falls into me, her body mine to hold. Mine to have. And mine to take care of.

Jesus fucking Christ, her whole back is on display. Spreading my hands out, I feel the little strings holding her dress together, and I think about how easy it would be to rip them apart and free her of the dress. I want to see her.

A soft moan escapes her lips and I tighten my arms around her. My tongue slides against the seam of her lips, the taste of her like the sweet purity of a white rose I fully intend on turning as blood red as her lips.

Her surrender to my touch and my kiss without pause or question is the best gift she could ever give me.

My restraint is teetering on the edge of a fine razor blade, sharpened to kill. If I don't stop now, I'll keep going until I've carved a place for myself permanently in her so she'll never be able to forget me.

I'm a selfish bastard who wants this woman so badly, I'm willing to use every ounce of power I have, and everything I know about pleasing a woman to keep her as mine.

With one last sweep of my tongue across her lips, I tease her with what's to come as I run a single finger down the length of her spine, pulling on the little strings so she knows what I want – her out of this dress.

"Time to go, *bella*."

Her eyes flutter open, and they're so fucking glazed over simply from kissing me, that I hesitate before stepping back.

Wrapping my arm around her waist, I walk us toward the door, and I slowly start to feel her regain her composure and walk confidently beside me like she knows she belongs there.

Tessa is either going to be my salvation or my full demise. Either way, I know I'm going to love every fucking minute of it.

CHAPTER 9
Tessa

As the elevator doors close, the air between Alec and me electrifies with the kiss we just shared.

My brain is a pile of mush, my heart has a rapid beat like the wings of a hummingbird, and my core is throbbing like the steady beat of a bass drum needing the song Alec started to hurry to the crescendo and epic finale.

But that will all have to wait.

With his arm around my waist, he rubs his thumb against my hip, burning his touch through this dress and into my skin.

The doors slide open to the casino floor and I'm struck with the ringing of machines, the low lighting, and smokey air filled with both promise and sorrow.

Walking with Alec is something I've never experienced before. Where I usually try and blend in in my everyday life, Alec is the complete opposite. He commands the attention of everyone in any room he's in, and it's of no exception here.

I know he owns The Aces, but it also seems like something a little more. I see fear in the eyes of grown men while others avoid looking at him entirely, as if they're hoping he doesn't see them.

After their eyes skirt over Alec, they land on me, and I feel both the hatred and jealousy from the women and the creepy gazes of men as they take me in. All probably wondering what I did to land the attention of a man like Alec.

As if sensing my discomfort, he squeezes my waist, but we keep walking. People move from our path, giving us a wide lane to pass by, and I feel like I'm on the arm of royalty.

Who is Alec Carfano?

We clear the main casino floor and move through to the corridor that circles this half of the building. It's where the entrances are to various restaurants, intermittent with high-end jewelry and designer stores where those who hit it big can go and spend their winnings before the liquor wears off and they realize what they just wasted their money on.

The other side of the casino has a similar corridor that leads to the theater where my show is, the concert venue, and the conference center.

Alec guides me towards Carfano's, an Italian restaurant, and I look up at him, surprised.

"You have a restaurant?"

"Yes. Only the best ingredients made the authentic way. Everything from scratch."

"Oh, that sounds amazing."

"Good." He nods, opening the door for me.

"Hello, Mr. Carfano," the hostess greets with a smile as her eyes practically eat him alive. "Your usual table?"

"Yes. Thank you, Mia."

I know I shouldn't be jealous, but I can't help the flash of white-hot jealousy that races through me at him being on a first name basis with her.

She's very attractive, with shoulder length wavy chestnut hair and blue eyes that remind me of the sky on a cloudy day.

Walking us through the restaurant, little Miss Mia sways her hips in her tight pencil skirt, just inviting Alec to look. But when my eyes dart up to his face, I see he's looking around the dining room rather than her round ass on display, and I can't help but smile to myself.

"Your server will be right with you," she tells us.

"Thank you." I throw her a sweet smile, and the one she's wearing turns forced as she gives Alec one last long look before going back to her hostess stand.

Alec holds my chair out for me and my smile widens. So, he has a little gentleman in him after all.

A server comes over and hands us each a menu, his hands shaking slightly. Alec orders a bottle of wine, and when the server comes back to open it, I see him take a deep breath before proceeding, forcing himself to relax. Is everyone afraid of Alec?

"She'll have the eggplant parmigiana, and I'll have the tonnarelli cacio e pepe," Alec orders after the wine is poured, and just the sound of his voice makes the guy flinch.

"I think he's afraid of you," I say with a nervous laugh when he walks away.

"I ordered you a menu favorite, I hope that's okay."

"It is. Thank you." Truth be told, eggplant parm is my favorite.

Alec hands me my wine glass and raises his to clink against mine. With a single sip, I sigh. Oh, that's good. Smooth and full-bodied. Just like the whiskey I had in his penthouse, I've never had expensive wine, and I can taste the difference. It's delicious.

"Why is everyone afraid to look you in the eye?"

"Because they know better."

All the thoughts I've had of who he is spin around in my head, and as my eyes sweep the room, I see everyone purposefully avoiding our table. He owns The Aces, but he said his family has many businesses...which includes this restaurant.

Who are the Carfanos?

Taking a long sip of wine, I divert my eyes from him, suddenly wondering why I'm here. Why am I with a man who everyone is so clearly scared of?

"Don't do that, Tessa."

"Do what?" I adjust the silverware on the tablecloth.

"Avoiding looking at me like everyone else." Meeting his gaze, my heart does a little stutter beat. "Are you afraid of me?"

"No," I tell him honestly. When I look in his eyes, I don't see someone I should be afraid of. I see a man who is looking for something to grasp onto before he realizes the entire world is on one side of the glass with just him on the other. "Should I be?"

"Probably. If you knew all the things I've done, then you would be."

He's challenging me. He's seeing if I'll buckle under the weight of whatever he's done. But I want to know everything. I want to know and not be afraid. I want to be what no one else is to him.

Squaring my shoulders, I keep my eyes on him. "Try me."

Alec flashes me a blinding grin that makes my core clench and my breath catch. It's more predatory than a show of happiness, and holy sweet lord, this man is going to kill me with how unrealistically sexy he is.

"You're brave, *mia bella rosa.* No one's ever challenged me before."

"There's a first time for everything. And besides," I say, tossing my hair over my shoulder and leaning forward to place my chin on my knuckles, "I think you need someone to challenge you."

His eyes darken before me, turning to molten pools of dark promises that I want to swim in all night long. "*Bella,*" he practically purrs, the word rolling off his tongue like a dark angel's promise. "I want you to challenge me. I want you to be the blooming rose I see on stage whenever you're with me. I want you to give me that dark beauty that fights to be free from you but you keep locked away."

My chest rises and falls with my short little breaths. He doesn't know what he's asking for. I don't know if I can...

My fingers play with the cloth napkin in my lap, twisting and knotting it while my mind and heart are at war.

"You don't know what you're asking me for," I whisper.

"I know full well what I'm asking for." His voice drops to an octave that floats over me, blanketing me in a warmth that sends a chill through me. "I want you, Tessa. I want the you no one else gets."

"Will I get the *you* no one else gets?" I counter, needing to know if this is even real. It all feels like a dream I'm going to wake from if someone snaps their fingers.

Since he first sat at that table to watch me dance, I've felt like I've been in a dream. Men like him don't just show up and choose a woman like me to give their entire focus to.

Leaning towards me, Alec reaches under the table and takes my nervous hands in his larger one. "Yes, *bella*." I let his words soak into me, and I want to know everything about him. I want to know his secrets. I want to know *him*. "Tell me about your family," he says.

"I don't have a family," I confess, and he strokes my knuckles with his thumb. "My parents died when I was fifteen."

"What happened?"

"They were on their way to my dance showcase when they were t-boned by a tractor trailer who ran a red light. It was pouring out and he couldn't stop in time. He slid right out into the intersection." I blink away the stinging in the backs of my eyes and clear my suddenly tight throat. "My brother took care of me then. He never made me feel like a burden, and he worked three jobs to make sure I could keep dancing. But when I was eighteen, he was…" I wipe away a stray tear that escaped, and take a long drink of wine.

"When I was eighteen," I start again, "we were walking home when he was…" Swallowing hard, the words won't form, and I can't stop the flood of built up emotions bubbling to the surface. I've kept James's memory, and everything that happened that day buried so deep, that I've yet to deal with them. I can't.

"I'll be right back," I say in rush, grabbing my purse and standing. But with no idea where the bathroom is, I just walk straight out of the restaurant and into the crowd of people walking around.

I get bumped around as I blindly walk in a trance with no idea where I'm going.

"Tessa," Alec's angry voice growls from behind me as his hand grips my upper arm to stop me. "Where the fuck are you going?" Spinning me around to face him, Alec walks me over to the wall and pins me against it, shielding me from everyone around us.

"I needed air. I needed..." I try and focus on Alec's face, but it starts to blur with the tears gathering in my eyes. "I don't know," I whisper.

"You can't just walk away like that."

"I...I'm sorry," is all I can say. He places his hand under my chin and I blink away the tears, taking a deep breath to try and gather myself again. "I don't talk about James."

"Let's get out of here." Tucking me against his side, Alec walks us back to his private elevator. If he weren't there to hold me up, I don't think I'd be standing right now.

"Look at me, Tessa," he demands when the elevator doors close, sealing us in the quiet for the long ride up. "Focus on me."

I do as he says, my eyes taking in every inch of his handsome face. I memorize every feature. The strong set of his jaw that's covered in the light shadow of a beard. His cheekbones that sit just high enough to make them look like they were carved from the clay of God. My eyes move up the length of his straight nose that leads to dark eyebrows that frame his dark eyes that are rimmed in impossibly thick, black lashes that shouldn't be so masculine on a man, but are. And when I take in his eyes, I'm struck with the immediate feeling of safety.

This close to him, I see his eyes are actually a deep brown like dark chocolate and not black like I thought. Around his pupils is a thin ring of honey brown like a halo that once was, but has slowly been strangled out, with the dark always winning.

We breathe together. In and out. Until I finally feel like I have control over myself again.

"Better?"

"Yes." I nod. "Thank you. I'm sorry for—"

"I don't want your apology, *bella*. I want you to be real with me. Always."

"I've never...I mean I don't..." I trail off, not wanting to admit that I haven't had anyone in a long time to share my life with. And never on an intimate level like he wants from me.

I don't know how to be with a man. I don't know how to share my thoughts. I don't know how to express how I feel so easily like other women.

I've never done it before. Any of this.

I don't let people in because that means they'll just leave, or be forced to leave. Taken away.

I'm also scared of who I'll become if I give any part of myself to Alec, let alone the deepest parts of me that have never seen the light of day.

"You've never what?" he asks, brushing my hair over my shoulder and running his fingertips down the column of my neck and shoulder.

"What?" I breathe, my mind only focused on his touch

on my bare skin.

"Tell me everything, *mia bella rosa*. Tell me what you've never done. Tell me everything you want done to you. I can give you it all, Tessa," he rasps in my ear, his lips brushing my skin, sending a shiver down my spine. "I want to give you everything. I want you to only need me. Rely on me. Think of me. Crave me. Be consumed with me."

"Alec," I moan, leaning into him further, my legs no longer able to hold me up.

"You feel what you do to me?" he asks, pressing his body against mine so I can feel the hard length of him against my stomach. "Just the thought of you. The sound of your voice. You make me harder than I've ever been, and I'm going fucking crazy with needing you."

"Alec," I moan again.

"But I told you I won't touch you until you ask. Until you're ready. Until you beg."

I would do that, too. I know I would, or rather will. It's already a foregone conclusion. I'm already begging him in my head.

But tonight, I feel too vulnerable. Too raw.

"I know you will, too," he continues, planting a kiss below my ear, heat flaring where his lips touch me. A fire ignites in my blood, spreading wildly, and settling in a steady throbbing between my thighs.

The elevator opens at his penthouse, and Alec wraps his arm around my waist and then lifts me up into his arms, cradling me to his chest as if I weighed nothing at all.

My eyes roam over his neck, jaw, and face. Every plane and angle is sharp, defined, and sexy. I follow the bob of his Adam's apple when he swallows, and I have the urge to place my lips there to feel the motion.

I want to know everything about him, too. I want to give him everything he needs. I want to please him. I want to be good for him.

Alec's eyes dart down to mine as he walks me into the spare bedroom and places me on the bed.

Without another word, he leaves the room, closing the door behind him.

Sitting up, I take my heels off and stretch my feet, staring at the closed door like I have the power to manifest him into coming back.

When the minutes tick by with only silence as my companion, I stand up and take my dress off before sliding between the cool sheets.

I know he's leaving me here alone because I need the time to gather myself again, but I wanted him to stay.

A few more stray tears slide down my cheeks as I push the memory of my brother back down to the place I've kept him in for all these years. I'm not ready. Maybe one day.

CHAPTER 10

Alec

Fixing my tie in the mirror, I add my ace cards cuff links and don my suit jacket.

I've always felt more comfortable in a suit than anything else. It's a sign of power. Respect. My grandfather wore one every day, and my father the same. And both men were the most respected and powerful men I've ever known.

When I stayed at my grandfather's as a child, I would follow him around to see how he did everything because I wanted to be just like him. He taught me how to put on cufflinks. Hell, he taught me what a cufflink even was.

My nonna would pick his tie out every morning and help him put it on. He told me once that he let her choose his tie every day because then whenever he looked down at it, he would think of her. It was their little moment before they headed off to do whatever the day brought them.

Looking down at the deep maroon tie I chose today, I have the image of Tessa walking into my closet in nothing more than a satisfied little smile because I spent the whole night fucking her into oblivion, and she chooses this tie for me. Lifting up her toes as graceful as if she were on stage, she places it around my neck and uses it to pull me down for a kiss that makes me want to fuck her all over again.

"Jesus," I breathe, my cock straining at my zipper. I need to calm the fuck down with this woman. She's going to be the death of me if she's all I can think about. I can't have her as a distraction.

After leaving Tessa alone last night, I didn't sleep. Not one minute. All I could think about was her alone in the room next door, in bed, beautiful, and vulnerable.

I know I could have had her. I know she wouldn't have denied me if I went to her. I see it in her eyes every time she looks at me. She can try and fight it for as long as she likes, but I know it won't be long now before she's begging me to touch her. To fill her.

Heading out into the kitchen, I find Vinny, my cousin, at the counter drinking coffee and flipping through some papers.

"Hey, Vin."

Looking up, he gives me a cocky grin. "Who was that fine piece of ass leaving your place this morning? Where did you find her? I could use a woman like her in my life for a little while."

"What the fuck are you talking about?" I demand, my

words slicing the air between us like knives.

"Whoa, Alec, relax. I was just kidding if she's yours."

Turning on my heel, I stalk back down the hall and all but rip the door handle off as I slam it open, seeing the room empty.

Where the fuck did she go? How did she leave?

A primal, animalistic growl leaves my throat as I take out my phone. "When did you see her?" I ask Vinny sharply, back in the kitchen.

"When I was coming off the elevator an hour ago. I held the door for her. Why?"

"Fuck!" I yell, dialing Enzo. He has to be on her. I can't let her get away. "Enzo, where are you? Tessa's gone. Vinny let her leave." I give him a murderous look and he backs away, pouring himself another cup of coffee.

"I drove her home," Enzo tells me, and I almost crush my phone in my hand.

"Why?" I ask in a chilling, calm tone.

"She texted me, desperately asking me to come and get her to take her home."

"I didn't say she could leave."

"She said she needed to."

"And that means you should do so without asking me? Why are you so defensive of her? Do you need to tell me something?" If he tells me he wants her, I really will kill him the next time I see him.

"What do you mean?"

"You're lucky you're not here or I would fucking strangle you, and Tessa wouldn't be able to talk me out of it this time."

"You've had me following her for over a month. I've

gotten to know her. You've entrusted her with me."

"Apparently I chose the wrong person for the job if you think I wanted you in any way to get to know her. And I do trust you, Enzo. Don't fucking test that or think I'll let you get away with shit." Hanging up, I throw my phone on the counter and rub my hands up and down my face.

"What's going on, Alec?" Vinny asks, leaning back against the counter with that same cocky little smirk he always wears when he's learning something about someone that he can use against them.

"Nothing," I snap, walking over to the bar to pour myself a finger of whiskey that I shoot back in one take.

"Yeah, because nothing says whiskey at eight thirty in the morning like a woman. I heard you walked out of the meeting last week because of one. That her?"

Turning back to him slowly, I narrow my eyes. "Where did you hear that? That shouldn't have left that room." What? Are my brothers fucking running their mouths about me?

"I'm second to you here, Alec. I need to know if something in your life is going to affect me too."

"Is that so?" I challenge. "And how would my personal business affect you?"

"See? She's already changing you. Alec, man, you can't let a beautiful woman fuck with your head. I've been there, and she turned out to be a manipulative, conniving, gold digging bitch who didn't give a damn about anything but my dick and my bank account."

"Tessa's not like that," I growl like a fucking animal.

"That's what they want you to think at first." He shrugs.

"Drop. It. Now. She's not up for discussion."

"Fine." Vinny holds his hands up in defeat. "Let's talk

about why I'm here. We need to discuss this shit with the Triads."

Getting down to business, the subject of Tessa is dropped. For now, at least. I know he'll come back for answers when I'm calmer.

When I took over AC from my uncle, who was also Vinny's dad, I knew I needed Vinny with me. My brothers were staying in New York, and Vin is the cousin who always had my back growing up. He has a good business sense and knows how to get shit done. Always. No matter what I need, or what needs doing, Vinny is my guy.

The fact that he's questioning my sanity and my judgment pisses me off, and that in itself goes to show that Tessa is a problem I need to deal with.

She's making me crazy. She's making me look weak to my family, and I can't have that. I can't be pussy whipped.

I haven't even had her pussy yet and I'm already being driven crazy by it. By *her*.

Vinny leaves my house and I pour myself a drink. The entire time we were talking, my mind still went right back to Tessa.

She left before I woke up and called Enzo for help. She needs to learn that that's not *ever* happening again. If she needs help, she calls me. If she wants to leave, she can fucking tell me herself. If I let her go is my decision.

Leaning against the glass windows of my living room, I look down at the city below. *My city.*

If Tessa knew who I really was, I doubt she would've

Casino King

tried this shit with me. I can have her tracked, followed, and found with the snap of my fingers. She can't hide. There's no where she can go that I won't know or be able to find her.

Downing the rest of the whiskey in my glass, I slam it on the drink cart and take long, sure strides out of my house, needing to tell her that right now.

Folding myself into my matte black Audi R8, I peel out of the garage with only one destination on my mind.

Weaving in and out of the cars on Atlantic Ave, I arrive at Lucy's Diner in a matter of minutes. My car stands out like a diamond in a pile of rocks, and when I step through the door, every pair of eyes land on me.

I spot Tessa with her back to me at a table. She places the plates she's holding down in front of the two men sitting there, each's eyes roaming over her like she's theirs to leer at.

My blood pounds loud in my ears when I see how short her uniform skirt is and how much of her long, tanned, smooth legs are on display for every man in the place to fantasize about having wrapped around their hips.

Her long hair is pulled back in a ponytail, and when she turns towards me, it fans out around her shoulder like a silken rope I want to wrap around my fist. I'd pull her head back so I could look into her eyes and see the desire she wears so fucking beautifully for me.

Seeing me standing here, Tessa's eyes widen, and she almost drops the tray in her hands.

My eyes roam over the front of her uniform, and all I see is red. Her tits are pushed up and on display with the low cut of the dress and skin-tight fit to her hips, showing off every sexy curve of her body that is mine to explore. Not the little pencil dick pricks in this place who look at her like they'll be the ones to give her everything she needs.

Looking back at the men who she just delivered food to, they shrink at my attention, and I take in their faces, memorizing them for when the time comes that I'll see them again and teach them what happens when they look at Tessa the way they were.

Tessa places the tray on the counter and wipes her hands down the front of her apron, her chest heaving with a heavy breath that does nothing to calm me.

My jaw hurts with how tightly I'm keeping it clenched so I don't say every thought in my head. I've spent my entire life learning when to hold my tongue and when not saying anything is more powerful than words ever could be.

With small, tentative steps, she closes the distance between us. "What're you doing here?" she whispers.

I'm trying to control myself, but the longer I stare down at her, the more riled up I get. How could Enzo not tell me this is what she fucking wears to work?

Grabbing Tessa by the arm, I practically push her out the front door. She doesn't protest until we make it outside and away from the door and windows where anyone could hear or see us.

"What're you doing, Alec?" she pulls her arm free and crosses them over her chest, pushing her tits up even more.

"What kind of fucking uniform is that? Do you not see how those men were looking at you?"

"I wear less on stage and you don't seem to mind that."

"That's not the same," I growl, taking a step closer while she takes one back.

"Is that why you're here? To complain about my uniform?"

"No," I say sharply. "I'm here because you snuck out of my house this morning without a word. Without a note. You called Enzo and begged him to come and get you."

"So? Why would you care?" I take another step closer and she takes another back, this time her back hitting the cement wall of the building, not giving her any more space from me. "You left me alone last night."

"And you think that means I don't care?" I counter, and she gives me a small nod. "I left you alone because otherwise I was going to rip that little red dress from your body and spend the night fucking you until you couldn't walk straight." Her breath catches, and a flush spreads up her neck. "And I knew you would've let me even when you shouldn't."

"Why not?"

Flashing her a smile that's all teeth, I close the distance between us. "Because you needed someone who was going to be gentle with you when you were upset, and that man isn't me."

Tessa's pouty lips are separated in that sexy way I love, making me wish they were wrapped around my cock.

A low groan rumbles from me and I slam my mouth down on hers, needing to taste her. Needing to feed the beast inside of me that rattles at its chains whenever I'm near her.

Framing her face with my hands, I angle her how I want and take this kiss from her. My tongue sweeps into her mouth – tasting, exploring, claiming.

She gives into me without hesitation, her moan a straight shot to my dick as I press my hips into her, knowing that I'm the only thing keeping her upright.

Tessa's hands grip the lapels of my suit jacket, begging me to stay where I am. But the fact that we're out in broad daylight and vulnerable trickles into my mind, and I pull away. She gives me a little grunt of protest and I let my hands drift from her face to down her neck. Gripping her ponytail, she arches her back into me.

"Later, *bella*," I rasp. "We're too open here. Get in the car."

Blinking, her hazel eyes become a little clearer, and she whispers, "No."

"No?"

"I'm working."

"You're not fucking going back to work in there. Not now. Not ever."

"What?"

"You don't work here anymore, Tessa. Go grab your things. I'll wait."

"No."

"Don't test me on this. There's no fucking way you're working here dressed like that, with yourself on display for everyone to see what's mine."

"I'm not on display," she says softly, her eyes darting away from mine.

"You are. Those men in there are only thinking about one thing when you're in front of them. Go get your bag. Now. I'm not feeling very patient."

"When are you ever?" she mumbles.

"Never. It's best you learn that now."

She doesn't protest again. She just walks back inside the diner and straight through to the kitchen. Emerging less than a minute later, I open the passenger side door for her and she slides right in, the skirt of her dress riding up to show me even more of her thighs.

I slam the door closed and look over my shoulder to see Enzo leaning against his Range Rover in the parking lot across the street. He lifts his chin, but I don't respond. He and I need to talk about the arrangement between him and Tessa and decide if I need to assign someone else to her.

I don't want either of them getting attached.

Behind the wheel, I rev the engine, and Tessa lets out a little gasp when I pull out of the lot at a speed she's not used to.

"My car," she says, looking over her shoulder.

"I'll have someone drive it to your place."

Pulling back into the garage of The Aces, I open her door for her and give her my hand to help her out, and she doesn't think twice about taking it. Good.

CHAPTER 11
Tessa

I don't know what just happened, or why I didn't fight him harder on it.

Alec can't possibly think he can just show up, order me to do something, and then I'll go along with it without putting up too much of a fight.

I never saw men leering at me like he suggested, and I never thought my uniform was showing too much. He's definitely overexaggerating this entire situation.

It's like my life suddenly isn't my own anymore because Alec decided he wanted me, and I need to take some of it back.

I fought for years to build the life I have for myself. One

where I'm surviving. One where I'm breathing. One where I'm able to take care of myself.

And when someone comes along and tries to tell me any aspect of that life I made for myself is lesser than...

"Go change," is all he says when we get inside his place.

"I don't have any clothes."

He gives me a sharp look that tells me what I already know.

Sighing, I head down the hall to the guest room and right into his sister's closet. I feel like I need to meet his sister to tell her how sorry I am her overbearing and demanding brother keeps having me wear her clothes.

As I'm walking around the closet, an idea strikes me. I'm going to give him exactly what he wants.

Replacing my uniform with layers of clothes that ends with a winter parka jacket I find on one of the racks, I head out to meet him. And when he sees me, his face shuts down.

"Are you serious, Tessa?"

"You wanted me covered up," I challenge, holding my arms out to the sides.

"Take it off."

Tilting my head to the side, I give him a little smirk that has his seemingly all-knowing eyes narrowing.

I unzip the jacket slowly while Alec stands so stock still, I wouldn't think he was here with me if it weren't for the feel of his eyes following my fingers as I pull the zipper down.

Letting the jacket fall to the floor, I stand before him in another zip-up jacket, and his eyes follow my fingers again as I pull the zipper down and shrug it off.

Under that, I have on a black and white snakeskin patterned blouse that has a zipper closure down the entire front of it, and when I start to pull it down, Alec moves in a blur towards me – a panther coming out of hiding to go in for the kill.

Grabbing the front of the top with one hand, and my ponytail with the other, he yanks my head back so I'm looking up at him.

His eyes are two pools of an emotion I don't know. A mix of rage and desire, with the latter trying to fight off the first.

"What're you doing?" His voice is holding barely contained restraint, and the rough edges skirt over my skin like a welcome scratch to an itch I've had since he first started watching me dance.

I want to feel what it's like to have that restraint snap, and to be the one he releases it all on.

I need him wild. I need him unhinged. I need him so far past being able to control himself that he gives me everything.

I need everything.

"I'm giving you what you want. Me covered, but uncovered for you."

His hand tightens over mine that's holding the blouse, and his other pulls my head back even more, the bite of pain making the breath leave my lungs.

"I told you not to challenge me, *bella*. I'll always win."

"We'll see," I whisper, and he takes my mouth with a sureness I've never known, his tongue meeting mine in a fiery dance I never could have choreographed.

Pulling my ponytail, he rips my lips from his and yanks my head to the side, dragging his mouth up the column of my neck and biting me hard before whispering in my ear,

"You're testing my patience. You're lucky my response isn't to kill you like it would be anyone else." The brush of his lips against my ear has me panting for more of his mouth on me. "I'd rather fuck you into submission. Until you're so far gone, you'd do anything I tell you to."

I can't stop the moan that leaves me at his words, and I sway into his solid body. My mind is swirling with too many images of what he's telling me, unable to think straight anymore.

"You want me to? You want me to give you everything your eyes tell me you want but are too afraid to ask for?" Looking down at me, he stares so deeply into my eyes that I start to feel like he's inside of my head, demanding entrance to every place I've created to hide in.

He has the power to do this to me.

He has the power to sweep my mind – making my thoughts his, making my desires his, and leaving me with nowhere to go but directly into his path of destruction.

"Are you going to beg, *mia bella rosa*?" The phrase rolls from his tongue like a litany. A call to prayer all my own, delivered by a fallen angel.

"I need to hear you say it." His words flow through me like water, lulling me under the current until I'm drowning and have no choice but to beg him for air. Beg him to breathe.

That's what he's asking of me.

He's asking to be the air I breathe. To not be able to survive my next breath without him.

And I'm all too willing to give him that. To let him be that. I don't have the will to fight him on it.

Alec's offering to take me down to the dark depths

where he lives, and I don't know a sweeter place to find bliss.

How could I possibly deny myself the chance to be free?

I've lived in my own darkness for so long, and I don't want to walk that path alone anymore. I want to give in to the girl I am on stage. Alec can give me her. And maybe he'll find a way to help me keep her without letting myself get destroyed along the way.

"I..." I whisper, my voice not my own.

Alec's hand slides up my chest to around the side of my neck. His entire hand is large enough to cover half the circumference.

"I need you," I rasp. "Give me everything. Free me. Please," I beg, leaning into him.

"Ti darò tutto e di più. Ti lascerò sbocciare, mia bella rosa."

Slamming his mouth down on mine, I give in to him. I give in to his beautiful words that I can only assume were an agreement, with his lips now sealing the deal.

Fire races down my spine when his tongue plunges into my mouth. There's nothing sweet in this kiss.

It's all-consuming.

It's primal.

It's instinctive.

It's wild in a way that can never be duplicated.

Alec groans into me and I feel it travel through my body like an electric current, sparking alive every nerve ending.

Everywhere he touches me feels like flames licking at my skin.

His hands travel down my back to grip my ass, pulling me closer to him, letting me feel his hard body against mine.

He lifts me up swiftly and I wrap my legs around his hips as he stalks down the hall to his room.

Throwing us both onto the bed, my back hits the soft bedding, and it feels like too harsh a contrast to him.

He's the farthest thing from soft, but I welcome every hard plane he has for me to explore before I go completely insane.

I feel him between my thighs, his hard length pressing against my center a welcome relief. Moaning, he swallows it like it's his next meal, taking it from me like it's his to keep. His to consume.

His hands are all over me. So much so, that I don't even know how they can be. Sliding the zipper of the blouse down, he tears his lips away to watch as he pulls the top open, exposing my torso to him.

As if by miracle, I chose to wear my favorite bra today. It's a nude pushup with black lace overlay and leather trim, with a little leather bow between my breasts.

Alec takes a moment to let his eyes roam over me, his hand sliding down the middle of my chest. I arch up into his touch, loving the feel of his hands on me. Against my bare skin like this, it feels like making a deal with the devil – the deepest pleasure I'll ever know in exchange for my soul. And I'm all too willing to make the deal.

I'll sign in blood if I have to.

If I spend eternity in hell with Alec for it, then at least I'll know the fire racing through me is real. At least I'll always have this.

I haven't felt anything in what seems like an eternity. The only time I do, is when I'm on stage or when I'm with Alec.

He makes me feel.

He makes me want something more from life than just surviving each day.

"*Così fottutamente bella. Anche meglio di quanto avrei potuto immaginare.*" His hot tongue tastes my skin, traveling over the mounds of my breasts, following the cups of my bra.

I've never been with a man before.

I've been kissed by boys. I've been on dates with boys who only knew how to feel the shape of my body through my clothes as we frantically groped in the back of his car.

But I've never been with a man.

I've never let a man into my body.

I've never let one close enough to feel what I want them to. I keep it all to myself. Every day. My entire life. All I've done is live an existence that did just that – exist.

After my parents, it was just me and James, and he sure as hell wasn't letting any boys near me. Then after he died, I was just an eighteen-year-old all alone in the world who had to figure out how I was going to survive on my own. I didn't have time for the drama and all the uncertainties that come with a man. I couldn't afford to be flighty and jeopardize my focus on getting through each day.

But now…

Now I want it all.

I've never been wanted like this. I've never been pursued like this. I've never so badly wanted someone who I knew would break me. Break me in every possible definition of the word, and then build me up to be the woman I want to be.

Tearing the cups of my bra down, his hot mouth latches onto my nipple, sucking it deep into his mouth.

A strangled groan is torn from my lips as my back arches against him, needing to be closer to him.

Alec slides his hands under me and unclasps my bra, desperately needing to free me of the offensive fabric.

He palms my breasts – kneading, squeezing, and pinching my nipples between his fingers.

I feel every stroke like a shot straight to my center, my clit throbbing, needing his touch there more than I've ever needed anything in my entire life.

My mouth stays open as my neck arches back, his eyes capturing mine in a look that says he promises to give me everything. He promises to give me what no one else can.

His hands and mouth are everywhere, marking me and carving into my skin so everyone else will know I'm his.

Alec kisses me deep into the mattress. Detaching my legs from around his waist, he grips the waistband of my yoga pants and peels them down the length of my legs, his eyes consuming the flesh he exposes as he goes.

He's looking at me as if he's never seen a woman before. As if this is his first time too.

But I know it isn't. That's an impossibility.

Alec is all man, and I'm just a girl who hasn't felt the need to give herself to anyone before him. Before now.

This is what I've been waiting for. This all-consuming feeling.

I don't know where we'll end up when we're done, but I want to go down in flames with him. I want the heat to be the last thing I feel before I'm fully engulfed in the flames that burn me alive.

Skimming his hands back up my bare legs, they fall open at his touch, his palms pressing me open into the bed.

His eyes take me in, never missing a single beat. He's memorizing me. He's learning how I react to him.

My hands fist in the blanket beside my hips as his mouth descends, capturing my nipple in a sharp bite before dragging his mouth down my torso – a trail of fire and ice left in his wake.

The cool air hits my skin after his mouth, and a shiver racks my body, needing more of him.

Swirling his tongue around my navel, Alec keeps moving south, the apex of my thighs his destination.

"*Ho bisogno di assaggiarti. Ho bisogno di assaggiarti ovunque.*"

Ripping my thong from my body in a single snap, he licks my folds open. His tongue brands me, searing me with a sensation I never knew possible.

Alec swirls my clit with the tip of his tongue, my hips flying off the bed and into his mouth further. He sucks my tight bundle of nerves as hard as he can before flattening his tongue to soothe the ache.

With one more pass from my clit to my entrance, he circles me, teasing me.

"Alec," I pant, my mind so far past the point of coherent thought.

"*Lascia che ti adori, mia bella rosa. Voglio assaporarti sulle mie labbra per sempre.*"

Gripping my hips, he moves me up the bed. His mouth staying attached to any part of my body he can find.

Sighing, I slide my fingers through his thick mass of black hair, never having felt anything so soft.

Alec is a slew of contradictions that I want to spend every minute of every day exploring.

Still fully clothed, he stands at the foot of the bed, towering over me as he strips each article of clothing from his body.

I don't think I've ever seen a man remove his cufflinks before, but I find the act simply sexy.

Everything Alec does is sexy.

When he shrugs his dress shirt from his body, my eyes rake over his torso, trying to memorize every dip of muscle and every inch of flesh so I can pull this moment from my memory when I'm alone.

Unbuckling his belt, he pops the button of his pants open and slides his zipper down, the sound an erotic intro of what's to come.

Pushing his pants and boxers down, Alec steps out of them and stands before me completely naked.

He's perfect.

He was built for the pleasure of women.

Gripping his cock, Alec strokes himself, and I bite my lip, wanting to know what he tastes like. Wanting to know what he'd feel like in my mouth – choking me, stretching me, filling me.

"I've wanted to fill your mouth with my cock since I first saw you, needing to see those pretty lips stretched so wide you don't know if you can take any more. But you do. You always do." Alec's voice sounds like it's spoken under water. My senses drowning in him and flooding me with a need I don't think will ever be quenched.

"Are you on the pill? I want to feel you, *bella*. I don't want anything between us."

I nod, and breathe out, "Yes." Yes, to all of it. I've been on the pill since I was sixteen to regulate my cycle as a dancer. I never wanted to be surprised in the middle of class or a competition.

And I've waited my entire life for this. I want to feel him.

There's no one who I deemed worthy of having me until

Alec came and made that decision for me.

Crawling on top of me, he settles between my hips, the tip of his broad head aligning at my entrance.

His hands smooth up my body, gripping my breasts and rolling my nipples between his fingers as he pushes into me.

A strangled cry is ripped from my throat, both out of pleasure and pain while Alec utters a string of Italian words I can't even begin to decipher or understand. As if I'm being ripped in two, Alec fills me so fully, my body has to rearrange my insides to accommodate him.

Pausing when he's fully seated inside of me, he frames my face with is large hands.

"*Mia bella rosa*," he says, his voice strained – pained. "Am I the first man to be inside of you? Am I the first man to feel this tight, hot pussy strangle my cock like a fucking silken tunnel?"

I'm tempted to lie, but I can't. Not to him. "Yes," I hiss, my senses on complete overdrive.

"*Perché? Perché? Perché? Così perfetta.*"

"Please," I beg, the pain I felt gone, and in its place a growing pressure and desire unlike anything I've ever felt. "More."

Growling, he captures my lips in a hard, bruising kiss that leaves me breathless when he pulls back. "I won't be gentle, *bella*. Knowing I'm the only one to feel you like this makes me need to fuck you even harder."

"Please," I beg again, breathless, pushing my chest against his.

Without any further incentive, Alec pulls out and thrusts into me, my body squeezing him like it wants to keep him there.

Sounds unlike I've ever heard are ripped from me as Alec takes me like he owns me.

Alternating between my breasts, he sucks my nipples so deep into his mouth, I know I'll have bruises.

I'll have bruises everywhere.

I'll have Alec everywhere.

And that's the way I want it. The way I need it.

My body adjusts to him, welcoming him into it like it's been waiting for him all along.

Fire races up my spine as he takes me without thought, without consideration, and without cause.

Every drag out of me has me begging him not to leave, and every thrust back inside has me grateful he's chosen me to give this gift to. Him.

My nails rake down his back, needing to get closer to him. He's inside of me – filling me, feeling me, claiming me. I need a way inside of him. If he can leave his mark on me, then I can do the same to him. I want him to know I was here. I want him to remember how much I was in this with him.

We burn together.

Gripping my hips, Alec lifts them up and starts taking me with a force I know will leave me raw and sore. But it's so good that I'd take whatever I'm left with in the end.

"Not enough," he growls deep, the last of his control hanging by a thread.

"More," I pant, the whisper of my voice making his eyes flash with approval. And with another deep growl, he pulls out and flips me over. Thrusting my hips back up in the air, he enters me again in one swift movement, my strangled scream muffled by the pillows in my face.

It's deeper like this. He's touching a place inside of me that I didn't even know existed. That I didn't even know could be reached.

I feel my heartbeat in my blood, my ragged breaths scratching at my throat, and my tight, taut nipples rubbing against the soft sheets — all of it creating a storm building inside of me that's about to peak.

Alec's grip on my hips is past the point of pain and into a numb possession I know I'll crave when it's gone.

Harder. Faster.

With the leverage of this position, I feel the last of his control snap, and Alec releases his demons on me. I feel them at my back, demanding me to join him in the freedom of letting go.

With a scream torn from deep within me, I'm set free.

Alec sets me free.

My skin breaks out in a fine sheen of sweat and Alec's loud roar behind me sends a fresh wave through me. I've finally snapped his control, and I have the proof marked all over me. Inside of me. With me.

My body seizes around him, my inner muscles spasming out of control as white spots dot my eyes behind my lids and my head spins.

My eyes roll back at the intensity of it all, my mind and body at odds with how to process it all.

CHAPTER 12

Alec

I can't get enough of her.

Sliding my hands up the length of her back, I palm her perfect tits in my hands and she groans, pushing back against me.

I just fucked her like a beast and she's already asking me for more.

She's perfect. My perfect little rose.

I've never lost control like I just did with her, and she took it all. She wanted it all. And that's why my dick is still hard as fucking granite inside of her. Because fucking Tessa is a fucking revelation. It's pure heaven and hell – bliss and fire.

Wrapping my hand around her ponytail, she braces

herself on shaky elbows as I pull her head back, my other hand traveling down her stomach and between her legs.

Still inside of her, her muscles squeeze me as I rub two fingers around her clit. No longer muffled by her face in the pillows, Tessa's little mewls and whimpers of pleasure are music to my ears.

She continues to rock back into me, so I pull my hand away and yank on her hair to turn her face to the side, eliciting a strangled cry from her.

"I didn't hear you ask for more," I taunt.

I want her to beg me to fuck her again. I want to see those pouty lips ask me to fuck her again and again. I don't think I'll ever hear sweeter words than this woman begging me to give her something no one else can. Only me.

I'm glad no other man has ever had her. I'd have tracked each and every one of them down and put a bullet between their eyes for ever having touched what's mine. No man will live if they touch her.

"Please," she moans. "Alec." My name leaves her lips in a sigh that has my cock swelling even more inside of her. "I need you again. Please."

My chest puffs out like a fucking king, and I pull her up by her hair to bite her shoulder. The animalistic pride in me taking over as I flip her on her back.

Her wide eyes look up at me with a wild lust that has me about ready to fucking blow. She already made me lose control once, something I never do, and I want to see if she can do it again. I liked the feeling way too much.

"Grab the headboard," I order, and she does so without hesitation.

"Do you trust me?" I don't know why I had to ask her

that, but now that I have, it seems like the most important question in the world. I want her trust more than anything.

"Yes," she breathes, the tip of her tongue peeking out to lick her bottom lip. I see the clarity in her glazed over eyes and my cock twitches between us.

Kissing her deep into the pillows, I run my hands up her arms to cover hers that are gripping the wooden posts of my headboard.

She opens for me immediately, and I sweep into her mouth, tasting the passion on her tongue.

When I pull away, her mouth tries to follow mine, but she falls back to the pillows and bites her bottom lip when I press the swollen head of my cock at her entrance.

She's so fucking unbelievably sexy.

Pushing inside of her slowly, I take my time watching her face change the deeper I go. Her eyes flash with too many emotions, her skin flushes with heat, her lips part as she sucks in ragged breaths, and when I'm fully inside of her, she sighs with relief while her eyes turn hungry. My little black rose is blooming before my eyes.

That's who I need here in this bed with me. I bring it out in her, and it's a beautiful sight to see.

Pulling almost all the way out, I slam back in, and Tessa cries out as her tits bounce beneath me, her grip on the headboard tightening.

I bend to capture one of her nipples between my lips. Swirling my tongue around the taut peak, I bite down, her cry this time mixed with both pleasure and pain. My specialty.

I lick, suck, and bite my way to her other nipple, and give that one the same treatment. Tessa's hips buck against mine and I groan against her.

Sliding my hands down her hips and the outside of her thighs on either side of me, I grip her behind the knees and pull her legs up in front of me so her shins are pressed to my chest.

Fuck. She's strangling me in this position.

Pushing her legs down towards her, her body grips me like a fucking vice as I pull out and thrust back into her.

She tries to arch her back, but only her chest rises. She has nowhere to go but where I have her, and no choice but to take what I give her.

The bed shakes and bangs against the wall with the force of my thrusts. I don't know how to be gentle, and I don't want to be.

I want to be brutal.

I want to possess her.

I want to own her.

I want every step she takes in the morning to hurt and know it's because of how much I fucking needed her.

I know she doesn't want me gentle, either. I recognize the dark desires in her eyes because they reflect mine, and despite the innocence she wears, she's all sin.

The sound of my thighs slapping against her ass, mixed with her resound moans and pleas, is a heady combination that drives me even wilder, and I start to feel myself unravel.

Looking down at her, her eyes open and lock with mine. They're filled with pure fire and challenge me to take more of her, and the last bit of my control snaps again. Grunting, I shove her legs open to her sides and grip her shins to keep her exactly where she is, pounding into her with reckless abandon.

Tessa releases the beast inside of me that I've learned to

keep caged and locked down. When I'm not in control, I'm brutal, destructive, and wild, and it's hard to reel me back in once I've been released. But the smile Tessa's wearing as she cries out is one of victory.

So, she likes when he comes out to play…

My little rose wants the beast. She likes the beast.

Lightening shoots down my spine and I know I'm close. But I don't want this to end. I need to wreck her and push her past the point of no return so she'll always be mine.

I feel her close to the edge, and with one more push, she's detonating around me, her tight little pussy clamping down on me harder than before.

Fuck.

She's coaxing me into my own release, but I hold back.

Not yet.

I pump through her orgasm, and the beautiful sounds of defeat coming from her drive me harder still. A tear leaks out of the corner of her eye as she pinches her eyes closed. Her neck arches back, exposing all that creamy skin I want to mark with my mouth so everyone knows who she belongs to.

Me.

Tessa starts to flutter around me again, and right as she comes a second time, I growl, pulling out of her and releasing her legs to grip my cock as I come all over her stomach and breasts. The streams of white against her sun-tanned skin is a beautiful contrast that makes my chest tighten with a possession I've never known.

With a tentative hand, she swirls her fingers in my seed, and I groan at the image. She's so fucking innocent, yet she doesn't act like it or let it make her shy. She's more innocent than I thought, but that doesn't faze me in the least, or make me want to go easy on her.

It has the opposite effect.

Tessa looks up at me with a little smile that makes my blood rush as she lifts her fingers to her lips to taste me, and her little moan has me hard all over again.

"Do I taste good, *bella*?" I cajole.

"Yes. So good," she says with a little moan, her eyes flashing with a thought I can already read.

"You want to taste all of me, don't you?" I grip myself, my cock still needing more of this woman. I don't think I'll ever have my fill of her.

She gives me a little nod and licks her bottom lip before taking it between her teeth.

Standing, I lift her into my arms and carry her through to my bathroom, placing her on the edge of the marble tub. I turn the shower on, but when I go to lift her up to carry her inside, she stops me.

"Wait," she says softly, her hand reaching out to touch my thigh. I look down at her and she raises her chin. "I don't want to wash you off of me yet. I want to taste you first."

Dropping to her knees on the cold, hard, marble floor, Tessa takes my cock in her small hands. I look down at her through hooded eyes, and with her mouth an inch away, she looks up at me, her hazel eyes full of determination and desire to give me this. She wants to please me.

I smooth the backs of my fingers down her cheek, and it's the only encouragement she needs.

Swirling her tongue around the head of my cock, a low groan rumbles from my chest. Tessa runs her tongue up the entire length of me, from base to tip, and then sucks just the head into her hot little mouth.

The sight of her on her knees in front of me and those pouty lips wrapped tightly around my cock, is one I'll have engrained in my head forever.

Pulling her ponytail out, I dig my hand into her mass of silky hair and she moans around me, the vibrations sending shockwaves through me.

Tessa takes me deeper into her mouth, letting herself adjust to my girth as she goes. But there's only so much I can take before I tighten my hand in her hair and she moans again, my hips pushing myself into her mouth.

I hit the back of her throat and my head falls back, my groans echoing off the marble all around us.

I feel her choke, but she quickly recovers, swallowing around me. Grunting, I hold her to me for a second longer, her hot mouth as good as her hot pussy.

Easing up a fraction, I let her slide back up my length, her nose flaring with a much needed breath.

"Suck. Hard," I command, and her lips tighten, doing as I say automatically. "Fuck," I groan, and her eyes shoot up to mine, her pleasure at my approval shining back at me.

She lets me guide her how I want her. She lets me fuck her mouth.

Pumping my hips into her, my balls tighten as I get close, and Tessa scrapes her nails down my hips and thighs before digging them into my ass, holding me to her like she wants to keep me there.

"Look at me," I growl, and her eyes flash up to mine, giving me what I need. Fire travels down my spine and I grip her hair to where I know she must be in agony, but I can't help it. I can't stop.

The steam from the shower fills the air around us, and

with one final thrust, I hold her to me, her mouth taking as much of me as she can before her airway is completely blocked and she frantically swallows around me as I shoot my release down her throat.

Her eyes stay locked on mine and something in me shifts.

She's fucking incredible.

Releasing me with a wet pop, Tessa falls back on her heels, her chest rising in quick little breaths that make her perfect tits bounce for me, her nipples hard. Licking her lips, she rubs her thighs together, letting me know she's just as turned on sucking my cock as she is when I have my hands all over her.

Lifting her up from under her arms, I walk her into the shower and press her against the glass wall, my fingers stroking her folds.

Jesus fucking Christ. She's soaked.

"You liked sucking me off, *mia bella rosa*?" I ask, my lips brushing hers as I do.

"Yes," she moans, and I take her bottom lip between mine, sucking on it while swirling the pad of my finger around her clit.

Her immediate groan has me kissing her fully and thrusting two fingers inside of her. She whimpers, and I know she's already swollen and sore from taking me so hard and multiple times.

Good. That's exactly what I wanted.

After only a few strokes, I press my thumb against her clit and she moans into our kiss, coating my hand in her sweet cream.

The water beats down on us and I pull my hand away,

licking it clean.

"Mmm," I hum, making her eyes darken. "So good." I use the words she used to describe me, and a little smile ghosts her lips, too spent to give me anything more.

I see her losing the battle to stay upright, so I let her lean against the glass as I wash her lithe body. Dancing has given her such a sinfully sculpted body that has me wanting to worship her for the goddess that she is.

When I've washed us both, I turn the water off and pat us dry before carrying her back to my bed. Her eyes have been fighting to stay open, and the moment I place her in the middle of my bed, she curls on her side and closes her eyes.

I brush the hair away from her face, and she sighs. Reluctantly, I cover her with my comforter and then go to my closet to put on a fresh suit.

I still have work to do tonight, no matter how tempting it is to stay here with Tessa.

Dressed, I close the door behind me and meet Enzo in the kitchen. The son of a bitch is just casually leaning against the counter drinking a cup of coffee.

"I can't believe you didn't fucking tell me that Tessa worked in an outfit that has her tits and ass out for every man to see." My anger flares again at thinking about her dressed in that fifties styled waitress uniform every time she went to work there. "And you let her leave here without telling me. You're on thin ice, Enzo."

"I know." He nods.

"That's all you have to say?" I ask angrily, but keep my voice low so I don't wake Tessa. He doesn't answer me, so I close the distance between us in three long strides, gripping him by the throat before continuing. "She can't protect you,

Enzo. I don't care if she likes you. I won't hesitate to kill you if anything happens to her because you think being her friend is more important than following orders."

I release him and push away, running my hands through my hair to try and calm myself.

"I have to meet Vinny downstairs," is all I say before storming out the door.

CHAPTER 13
Tessa

Rolling over, my hand splays out in the spot next to me, but all I come up with is cool sheets where I thought I'd find Alec's warm body.

I reluctantly open one of my eyes and look around the room. The light of pre-dawn illuminates the horizon of the sky and I wonder if Alec ever even came to bed. I was so spent, I fell into a deep, dreamless sleep for the rest of the day and into the night, that still has my brain a little hazy.

Wrapping the sheet around my body, I use the bathroom and then peek my head out the door. I hear low murmuring voices down the hall and realize there's someone other than Alec here. At this time of night? Or, morning?

I wouldn't want to intrude on anything, but my stomach is growling. I hadn't eaten much of anything today since I left my shift early, and my mouth is as dry as a desert.

I search Alec's closet for something to put on, but I only find suits.

Sighing, I wrap the top sheet from his bed tightly around me and sneak out into the hall, dashing into the room next door without making a sound or being seen.

I throw on yoga pants, a bra, and a loose t-shirt that falls off my shoulder. I braid my hair so it wraps around my shoulder, and then I take a few deep breaths to ready myself. I don't know who's out there with Alec, but I guess I'm about to find out. I don't know if the other person knows I'm here, and I have the sudden rush of fear that maybe Alec wouldn't want me to be seen. But I shake the thought from my mind and pad quietly down the hall. I'm not a secret.

I see the back of Alec's head first, as he's seated in the leather chair facing the wall of windows. His guest, however, is on the couch where I sat last week with the doctor, and he looks up to see me standing there.

He's the man from this morning when I ran out of here in a panic, needing some space. He looks like Alec, but not really. A relative, maybe. He's handsome, of course, but he lacks that aura of raw power and darkness that Alec has.

He raises his chin to me and Alec turns his head, his dark eyes meeting mine and then raking down my body, sending a chill through me.

"Come here," he says, and I take small steps until I reach him. He pulls me onto his lap. "You smell good," he whispers in my ear. "What are you doing up?"

"I woke up and couldn't go back to sleep. I'm hungry," I

admit regretfully.

"Well, we can't have that," he says against my neck, kissing me there and then biting gently. I close my eyes and force myself to swallow the moan that threatens to escape me.

Gripping my hips, he stands with me and turns to the other man who's been watching our exchange with speculative eyes.

"Tessa, this is my cousin Vincenzo."

"Vinny," the man says, holding his hand out for me to shake. When I do, though, Alec makes a little grunt of disapproval and I smile.

"Nice to meet you, Vinny."

"You, too. I don't count this morning as a meeting," he says playfully, and I feel Alec giving him a look of disapproval before walking me into the kitchen.

"What're you hungry for?" he asks, handing me a bottle of water from the fridge like he knew I was thirsty. "I can order you anything you want. Breakfast? Dinner?"

"Breakfast. French toast?" I suggest, and he nods, pulling out his phone and sending a quick text.

"It'll be here shortly."

"Thank you."

Pulling me against him, he kisses the spot right below my ear that makes my core clench, and I sigh when he licks the shell of my ear. "I just have some more business to discuss with Vin in my office," he tells me.

"Okay," I reply, breathless.

Leaving me, he nods at Vinny to follow him in the opposite direction, past the dining room to the hallway on the other side.

I wait on the couch, and maybe ten or fifteen minutes later, Alec comes back to answer the door and hand me my plate of food.

"The remote is there," he points at the coffee table. "If you want to watch something."

"I'm fine. I promise." I give him a reassuring smile and take the lid off of the plate, the heavenly scent of French toast and bacon wafting up to my nose. "This is perfect. Thank you."

"I have to keep you sustained so we can go another few rounds." His deep voice fills my every sense, and rounding the couch, he brushes my bare shoulder and whispers in my ear, "Are you sore, *bella*? Do you still feel me inside of you?" His warm breath blows against my sensitive flesh, goosebumps breaking out where it does.

Oh…

Pressing my thighs together, I bite my lip, nodding yes. And yet despite the intense soreness I feel, I know I wouldn't be able to deny him if he were to say he needed me right this moment. My body comes alive around him without any prompt. It's just him.

"Enjoy your food," he rasps, scraping his teeth across my neck and then disappearing.

Releasing the breath I didn't know I was holding, I toss my braid over my shoulder and take a deep breath to calm myself down.

Alec is going to destroy me. I already know it.

My body, my heart, my soul…all of it.

I feel like I'm going to have a heart attack every time he's near because my heart starts beating wildly to a rhythm all its own. My body feels like it's on fire whenever he touches me and is inside of me. And my soul, my very spirit and essence, is starting to tie itself to his with every look, touch, and kiss we share. He wrecks me in the most delicious of ways.

He's too much.

With a shaky hand, I reach for the silverware and unroll it from the napkin. I need the TV to distract myself, so I put on the first movie I find and sit back on the couch.

I don't know how long I sit here after finishing my food, but when I lay down to finish watching the movie, my eyes close on their own.

When I wake again to the bright sun streaming through the windows, my head is resting on Alec's lap, and he's mindlessly combing his fingers through my hair.

I turn to look up at him. "What time is it?"

"After ten."

"Did you get any sleep?"

"No," he says, running his fingers through my hair and then skirting them down my back to swirl them in the sliver of exposed skin before the waistband of my pants.

"My sister is coming today."

"What?" I ask in a panic, sitting up in a flash. "When? Should I go?"

"No," he says firmly, his brows clashing together. "She's coming to make sure her birthday party has everything she wants. Plus, she wants to meet you. Apparently, Vinny likes to run his mouth to my siblings." Alec shakes his head, rubbing his jaw.

"Oh...um..."

"Don't worry about a thing, *bella*. She'll be nice. Just go get ready and I'll have coffee and food sent up."

Nodding, I go off to take a shower and dry my hair

straight before applying a light layer of makeup. Deciding what to wear is more of a challenge considering my choices are all his sister's.

I go with a pair of dark rinse skinny jeans that have the lowest price tag hanging from it, and a pretty, semi-sheer mint green blouse. Tucking it into the jeans, I add a brown belt with a gold H buckle to tie it all together before slipping into a pair of strappy flat brown leather sandals.

With one final look in the mirror, I decide I look as good as I'll ever be in someone else's clothes. I've never had to worry about making a good impression on someone's family before, and I have to wipe my clammy palms down the sides of my thighs as I head back into the living room.

Alec turns around when he hears me approaching, and his eyes eat me alive from head toe, letting me know he approves.

"Do I look okay? These are her clothes. I don't want her to think I'm some thief stealing her things. You brought me here yesterday right from work."

"*Bella*," he starts, the Italian sentiment rolling off his tongue in such a way that lulls me into a relaxed state. "Never doubt your beauty," he says fiercely. "And my sister won't say a thing. Don't worry about her."

Checking his phone, Alec grabs my waist and gives me a hard kiss that has me gripping the back of the couch to steady myself when he leaves me to open the door.

"Hey, Alec," a young woman's voice greets warmly, wrapping her arms around him. He returns it, and I'm genuinely shocked for some reason. I know she's his sister, but he didn't strike me as a man who hugs many people, so I'm assuming he saves it just for her. "Where is she?" I hear her ask, and I stand with my back ramrod straight, wringing my hands in front of me.

Alec steps aside, and I'm greeted by the smiling face of the most stunningly beautiful woman I've ever seen. Her long brown and caramel highlighted hair is curled in loose waves that bounce as she approaches me. Her skin is flawless and done up with makeup that I know she doesn't need in the least to be beautiful.

"Tessa." She smiles wide, showing me a set of perfectly straight, white teeth. "Hi, I'm Katarina. Or Kat. Either is fine." She shrugs casually.

"Hi," I manage to get through my tight throat. "It's nice to meet you," I add with a nervous smile.

"I love your outfit," she comments right away, eyeing what I have on speculatively.

"Oh, well, it's actually—"

"Don't worry," she interrupts with a knowing grin. "I already know it's from my closet in the guest room. But I don't care. I promise," she assures me. "Please feel free to wear whatever you want. All of it is just stuff I've bought when I'm down here but never get to wear. But I would say we should go shopping together some time."

I can't afford anything I'm wearing, so I know shopping with her will just involve me watching her buy everything while I trudge along for the ride.

"Katarina," Alec interjects, his voice firm. "I couldn't stop you from coming here, but don't think I won't tell you to leave."

"Relax, Alec," she sighs, rolling her eyes. "I'm being nice. Don't hog her when she's the first girl to give one of my brothers a chance. Although I don't know why," she adds, muttering that last part to me.

"Kat," he warns, his voice dropping to a chilling tone that would have any grown man shaking, but not his sister.

"Fine," she huffs, and I see her face drop when she turns from him. Her carefully crafted mask she wears slips before she rights herself and smiles at me again. "It was nice to meet you, Tessa. I hope I get to know you. It can get a little too testosterone-y when you're with Carfano men for too long. So, I'll be around to take you away from them any time you want."

"Thank you," I say with a little laugh.

"Now," she says, clapping her hands together and facing Alec. "I hope you're throwing me an over-the-top birthday party."

"I wouldn't think you'd be happy with anything less," Alec tells her.

"When's your birthday?" I ask.

"In about a month. Oh! Please come to the party!" Her eyes widen and then dart to Alec. "I mean, if you're free. No pressure."

"Sure." I smile.

"Okay, so I'm going to go. There's a poker table with my name on it."

"Kat," Alec warns again, rubbing his jaw.

"Don't worry." She winks. "I won't take all the casino's money. See you later for lunch?"

Alec nods and opens the door for her. When he closes it, he turns to me and stalks forward, wrapping one arm around my waist and gripping the side of my neck with his other hand.

His lips capture mine in a kiss that has me bending

backward at its force and intensity.

He has the ability to make me go from thinking too much, to my mind being a series of fireworks detonating and showering embers down through every inch of my body.

Licking the seam of my lips, he delves into my mouth, on a mission. I don't know how he knew, but meeting his sister was a lot for me, and he's taking away all of that doubt I had in a matter of seconds with this kiss.

It scares me how well he can read me, but not at the same time. I'd like to believe that I can read him too, but he's hiding something. I can sense it. I can see it in his eyes. Right now, though, I don't care. I don't have the ability to care when he's kissing me like this.

Alec tightens his hand on my neck and I moan into him. My hands slip under his suit jacket and grip his shirt at his hips, pulling him closer, needing an anchor before I completely drift away from who I am.

Tearing away, he presses his forehead to mine and breathes in the air passing between us.

"It's just us, Tessa. Okay?"

I don't know what he's referring to exactly, but I like the way that sounds.

"Okay," I whisper, and he pulls back just far enough to look into my eyes. His are shining darkly – two pools of mystery and danger I want to jump into and dive all the way down to the bottom of. I have a feeling the bottom doesn't exist, though. Alec Carfano is an endless black hole of secrets I want to wade in until I'm fully bathed in it all – my body soaked through with everything he is.

"I have work all day," he tells me, his hand sliding up into my hair. "Enzo will take you back to your apartment to pack a bag."

"What?" I ask, distracted by his hand massaging my scalp.

"You'll pack a bag and then come back to me."

"Why? I'll be fine to stay there. You don't have to watch over me like I'll break at any moment."

"*Potrei romperti così facilmente.*" He bends down and licks the shell of my ear, a moan catching in my throat. "I want you here with me. I want you waiting for me. I want you wet and ready for me when I'm done with work so I can slip right inside of you."

Alec's hot breath sends a chill down my spine and I press myself into him, groaning at his words. My body floods with heat, already ready for him.

"Do you still think you'll be okay on your own in your apartment?" he taunts, biting down on my earlobe, eliciting another moan that rings of victory for him. "I'll see you later, *mia bella rosa.*" His eyes roam over my face before leaving me to just stand here, wishing the day was over so he could make good on his promises right now.

CHAPTER 14

Alec

I've never been so addicted to anything in my entire life.

I crave Tessa like an alcoholic.

Just a taste, and I keep going until I'm drunk on her, always needing more. I won't be satisfied until I fuck her into an oblivion that has me passing out, only to wake up and need it all over again.

I would do anything to keep chasing that feeling she gives me.

I would do anything to keep *her*.

A man who lives a life that I do doesn't get to have something so pure in their life like Tessa. And that purity is like another drug I want to take, use, and destroy. I want her purity to run through my veins until it becomes just as tainted as I am.

I know how sick and twisted that makes me, but I don't give a damn. She's mine.

She's spent every night with me in my penthouse this week, in my bed. It was hard to focus on the work I had to do with her on my mind, waiting for the moment I could call it a day and slip right inside of her and lose myself for a couple of hours. Which is what I can't wait to do right now.

Watching Tessa dance is the biggest fucking turn on, and now that I know what her body can do to me, and for me, it's even more of a turn on than when I only let myself watch her.

She moves like water, her body flowing like a waterfall and then floating through the air like the fine mist that sprays up at the bottom.

Her innocence falls in a rush, and what emerges is my little black rose blooming just for me. Her eyes find mine in the shadows and she gives me a seductive smile. My diamonds around her neck, wrist, and in her ears, wink at me under the stage lights.

She's mesmerizing.

She's the most beautiful fucking woman in the world.

I swirl the whiskey in my glass and shift in my chair, trying to accommodate my cock that's making my pants feel so tight I might bust through the zipper.

I've yet to explore all the flexibilities of her body, and right now, as she spins and lifts her leg to her ear, I have to hold back a groan.

The images flashing through my head are of her doing that move naked against my wall of windows as my fingers work inside of her, then my cock. She'll hook her leg over my shoulder as I lift her up and press her against the glass, driving into her until she's screaming out and squeezing me with that tight little pussy of hers.

Fuck.

Downing the rest of my whiskey, I watch Tessa seduce the audience. And while I'd kill anyone who tried to touch her, knowing I'm the one who gets to fuck her until she can't remember her name and not any of the pencil dick fuckers in here, makes me want her even more, and I have to hold back from storming the stage and giving the audience a different kind of show.

Red is the perfect color for her – the angel concealing a little devil who doesn't know how much of a temptation and danger she poses to my sanity.

The crystals that cover her fringed skirt dance under the lights as she spins, but my eyes are fixed on the spot between her thighs that I wish my mouth was tasting right now.

With a jump and fall to the stage that has her rolling towards me, she slides her knees apart right in front of me. Her head is tossed back, and when she drags her back up from the arched position she's in, her eyes lock directly with mine.

She didn't have this move in her routine before, and this close, I can see her eyes are swimming with desire.

My little rose is just as turned on as I am dancing for me. I know it's for me.

That's what sets her apart from every other dancer in this show. She lives what she's dancing. It's real, raw, and passionate. She gives herself over to the music, the beat, and the emotions she's too afraid to tap into any other place than the safety of the stage. She can lose control while remaining untouchable.

Not for long, though.

I need this Tessa to come out and play with me.

I could see the innocence she was masking in her eyes, but I never would have guessed just how innocent she was until I entered her and felt it.

New. Unclaimed. So fucking tight.

My cock is the only one to ever know what it feels like when she comes — the way her inner muscles flutter and spasm, squeezing so hard it has a man seeing black spots in front of his eyes before succumbing to her.

I've never been so desperate for a woman in my entire life. She makes me want to forget everything and just spend every minute of every day exploring her. What makes her come harder than anything else, where on her body my kiss makes her give me that breathy sigh that has my blood rushing a little faster, and how many times she can come apart for me before her eyes roll back and she gives in to the bliss only I can give her.

When the song ends and Tessa is down in a split with her back bent so she's looking back at me, she gives me a come-and-get-it smirk that has me on the verge of cutting the show short and taking what I want right fucking now.

But I reign in the urge, signaling the waitress assigned to my table for another drink.

The second the last curtain falls on the show, I stand and make my way to the back, not allowing Tessa any time to change or remove her makeup.

I need that Tessa, and I fully intend on having her finish her little show for me up in my place.

I wait for her against the wall, just out of sight from the fellow dancers leaving. The note I wrote for her after her solo that's accompanying my flowers tonight had very specific instructions I know she won't disobey. I know what she needs. And she needs this. Tessa won't deny herself what she's wanted since I first started coming to see her dance.

A second later, the back stage door opens and Tessa emerges, still in her costume and makeup, minus the feathered headpiece. She looks around, and when she spots me in the shadow of the light above, she walks towards me slowly, her hips swaying with every step. The chandelier necklace that hangs down her entire torso dances on her skin as she moves.

Her eyes burn into mine, and I know she's still in the mindset of her show. Good. That's exactly what I wanted.

When she's close enough, I reach out and grip a handful of red crystal strands in my fist, pulling her towards me. In a little stumble, she lands against me and I grip the side of her neck possessively as my lips fuse to hers in a kiss that promises all the fantasies I have will become reality.

Her glittered lips feel rough against mine, and I fucking love it. I want to feel them wrapped around my cock – a little roughness to go with her hot, smooth tongue. It'll be enough to bring me to my knees right along with her.

"Let's go," I say roughly, taking her bag from her and dragging her towards my private elevator. The clicking of her heels on the cement floor sends little shocks through me, and when we reach the elevator, I don't even wait for the doors to close before I'm dropping her bag to the floor and pinning her against the wall, letting her feel how hard I am.

Tessa groans into my mouth as I kiss her, her hands

gripping the lapels of my jacket like a lifeline, pulling me flush against her.

My hands run up her thighs, feeling the straps of her heels that wrap halfway up. Those shoes are so fucking sexy, and I fully intend on fucking her with them on.

Her red crystal encrusted panties don't allow me easy access to the part of her I crave the most, so I cup her sex entirely, swallowing her moan like the crazed man I am. Everything she gives me is sustenance to live off of. To thrive off of.

As we ascend the entirety of my hotel, I kiss my way down her neck, my tongue running along the choker necklace that graces her delicate throat.

"Alec," she breathes, her voice a mix of wonder and need that has my cock throbbing for her touch.

I take her mouth again, my finger finding a way to slip under the tight hem of her panties to find her soaking wet and ready for me.

"Did dancing for me make you need me, *mia bella rosa?*"

"Yes." Tessa pushes against my chest, her hips moving against my hand, trying to get me to give her more.

"Do you think as much as it made me need you? Crave you?"

"Yes," she pants, her eyes dark and desperate.

"I wanted to fuck you right there on stage." A little moan escapes her and I reward her with a stroke of my finger along her pussy. "Would you have let me?"

"Maybe," she admits unabashedly, and I reward her again by pressing down on her clit. Her head falls back against the metal of the wall, but when her body starts to tremble, I pull my hand away and bring it to my lips, licking her sweetness off like the treat it is.

"I want you to let go with me, Tessa," I tell her, skimming my hands up her bare middle, tugging on a few of the crystal strands. "I want the rose I see blooming on stage to be the you you are with me."

"Alec," she sighs, reluctance flashing in her eyes.

"*Fiorisci per me, mia bella rosa.* Show me how you feel on stage with me. Show me her. Give me her."

The elevator dings and opens to the hall right before my door, but I wait for her to agree. I'm not going to make another move until I know she understands me and agrees to be my little red temptress.

Tessa pushes me away and I take a step back, seeing the change in her eyes. She's looking at me like she did on stage – defiant, dominant, depraved.

Walking past me, she gives me a little extra sway to her sexy hips. The crystals that hit the tops of her ass cheeks make me wish I could pin her down and pull them back as I drive into her from behind. Her restricted airway would give her a heightened orgasm that I know she'd fight at first, but then give in to, and love every fucking second of it.

Picking up her bag, I follow her to my door and open it. Once again, she takes the lead and walks in first, letting me admire the curve of her spine, her tight, round ass in her little panties, and her long legs that I need wrapped around my hips more than I need to fucking breathe.

Tessa walks straight to the bar by the windows and pours herself some whiskey, tossing it back in one shot before turning back to me with a little smile on her lips that tells me I'm going to get everything I want.

I always do.

"Leave on the shoes and necklace. Take everything else off." I move the leather chair to face the windows and take a seat. I want the view of my city behind her as she strips for me.

Her entire costume is made of red crystals. She's dripping in blood red jewels that remind me of all the blood I've shed in my life, and all the blood I'm going to shed for her. I know it's inevitable, and I'd do it without a second thought. I'd even take a little pleasure in it knowing that it was to keep this woman safe.

"Not yet," she says, twirling a few crystal strands around her finger. "You said you wanted the Tessa I am on stage. Well, she doesn't take orders so well."

I tilt my head to the side. "Is that so?"

"It is. And she wants to give you a special dance. For your eyes only."

My jaw clenches and my dick jumps in my pants as she takes slow and deliberate steps towards me. Placing her hands on the arm rests of my chair, she bends down so her face is right in front of mine.

"If you want to see, Alec, then I need a song. I know the perfect one for you."

I hold back from touching her and telling her who's really in charge here because I want her to dance for me so fucking badly. I'd endure endless torture to have this piece of her she's so willing to give me.

Taking my phone out of my inside jacket pocket, I tap on the app that controls the surround sound in the living room and let her take it from me to search for her song.

Handing it back to me, I look down at the title and smirk. "King" by Niykee Heaton.

"Press play when you're ready," she purrs in my ear. "But no touching, Mr. Carfano." Pulling back to look me in the eyes, she flashes me a sexy little grin that lets me know she's most definitely going to torture me before letting me touch her.

We'll see who's going to be begging for it by the time she's finished.

Pressing play, the song begins, and the bass pounds into my veins, my cock throbbing in time to the deep beat.

Tessa pushes off the chair and takes a step back, but remains close enough for me to reach out and touch her if I wanted to.

Her hips sway as she runs her hands up her torso and over her tits. Always keeping her eyes on me, Tessa swirls her hips and then drops low before coming back up to grip the arm rests of my chair. The crystals hanging from her neck brush over the front of my pants, and I hold back a groan at the light touch.

Rolling her body towards me, she arches her back and pushes her tits out. Almost, but not quite touching me. Only the strands of red crystals do that I want to fist so I can pull her down on top of me.

Pushing herself away again, Tessa reaches behind her and unclasps the hooks of her red crystal bra. She slides the straps down slowly, a sadistic little smile on her red glittered lips.

Letting the bra fall from her, her perfect tits bounce free, and I have to fist my hands at my sides to keep from touching her. Hers are bigger than you'd see on a traditional ballet dancer, but she's not huge. Just the perfect amount for me to grip and tease and see bounce as I fuck her hard.

Tessa takes them in her hands and squeezes them, giving me a little breathy groan that has my cock ready to burst as she slides her hands down her stomach to the waistband of the matching red jewel covered panties.

Her hard, puckered nipples peek through the crystal strands covering her and my mouth waters, needing a taste.

My eyes stay glued to her hands as she slides her fingers under the fabric of her panties. But instead of sliding them down to show me her pretty little pussy, she just slides her hands back up to cup her tits again, this time pinching her nipples.

Biting her lip, she moans, and my eyes flash up to hers, seeing the desperate need in them that I'm holding back from having.

Tessa repeats the same sexy body roll towards me as she did before, except this time her hardened nipples come right up in front of my mouth, and my jaw clenches. I've never had so much fucking restraint in my life as I do right now.

Spinning around so her sexy ass is right in my line of sight, she swirls her hips and drops down again, this time rocking her hips from side to side before slowly slithering herself back up to standing. Turning to look at me over her shoulder, she gives me a little smirk as she slowly, so slowly, starts to slide her panties down.

The red crystals frame her ass so beautifully, and just as her panties fall to the floor, she does the same to the red thong she had underneath, then steps out of them both. Looking back over her shoulder at me, she starts to bend over, sliding her hands down the backs of her thighs as she goes.

The pounding of the song's bass drum lives inside of me

as all of my blood rushes to my already throbbing cock.

My eyes stay glued to the apex of her thighs as she bends, her pussy on full display as she holds her ankles. With her legs slightly spread, her pink folds are open and glistening.

So ready for me. Always ready for me.

Smoothing her hands up the insides of her thighs, she slides a single finger through her wet center before spinning to face me and holding her finger up to her red lips, sucking it clean.

Fuck. Me.

My jaw ticks as I grind my teeth together, my eyes shooting fire into hers as my control finally snaps, and I grip her hips and pull her forward. She falls into my lap as my mouth latches onto her nipple peeking out from the crystals, swirling my tongue around the hard peak.

Tessa's groan is deep and throaty, and I let my teeth rake over the peak as she braces herself on my shoulders, thrusting her chest at me.

Running my hand up her inner thigh, I slide a single finger through her wet folds and drag it up her stomach to circle her nipples with her own juices.

Tessa's hazel eyes stay locked on mine as I repeat the same course and then swirl my tongue around each nipple to lap at her taste of arousal, sucking them deep into my mouth until each is red and swollen.

I know that every time the crystal strands hit them now, she'll get a jolt straight to her clit.

"Go to the windows," I instruct, my voice rough from holding back. It's my turn now.

Climbing off of me, she pivots, and the crystals fan out

around her as she walks straight to the windows. They're all tinted so you can't see in, but she doesn't know that, and her confidence and uncaring that someone could see her has me hardening even more.

"Put your hands on the glass and spread your legs. Let me see that pussy drip for me."

She looks at me over her shoulder in a defiant way, but does as I say, even bending over to give me better view.

It only takes me three long strides to reach her, my hands skimming up the backs of her thighs to palm her ass in both of my hands. Squeezing, Tessa groans and pushes back into me.

Bending forward, I lick the length of her spine, and her back arches with me like a cat before I bite down on the spot where her shoulder meets her neck, eliciting another groan.

Undoing my belt and pants, I shove them past my hips and free my cock from the prison it was in. Sliding it between her wet folds, Tessa moans and tries to grind against me, but I grip her hips in a clutch I hope leaves marks.

"I hope you enjoyed that little show of dominance, *mia bella rosa*. Because it'll be the last time I'll ever show that kind of restraint for you," I tell her as I align myself at her entrance and thrust up inside of her in one swift motion that has the both of us groaning.

With her heels on, she's at a height that gives me more leverage, and I take her without mercy.

When her arms lose their fight, she presses herself fully against the windows. Every sound coming from her makes me move faster, harder. I feel her getting close, and I give her no mercy in my savagery. Like I wanted to, I fist a chunk of crystal strands in my hand and pull her neck back, her initial gasp of surprise turning to a deep moan as her pussy starts to flutter.

Releasing the chains, I pull out and spin her around so her ass is pressed to the glass. Crying out at my leaving her empty, Tessa looks up at me with a fiery anger that has me giving her a teasing smirk.

"Did you want me to let you come, *bella*?" I taunt, and she huffs, her anger evident, which only turns me on further.

"Yes," she hisses, reaching between us and gripping me in her hand. Her juices coating my cock give her the lubricant she needs to slide her hand easily up and down my length, squeezing hard. "Take the rest of your clothes off and get back inside of me," she demands, and I flash her a predatory smile that's all teeth.

Kicking off my shoes, I step out of my pants as Tessa makes quick work of shoving my suit jacket off my shoulders. I take my cuff links off and toss them on top of my pants as she unbuttons my shirt. Her nails graze my skin as she goes, and my cock jerks against her leg with each scrape.

Tossing my shirt to the floor, she runs her hands greedily up my chest.

"Lift your leg up." I tap her right leg, but she just blinks. "Lift. It. Now."

Doing as I say, she braces herself on my chest and kicks her leg up. I grip it in a flash and hook it over my shoulder as I lift her up and press her against the glass, entering her again in a swift push. She screams out at this new position, that sexy mouth of hers no longer trying to defy me, but instead giving me my favorite music that has my control breaking, and I fuck her like the beast I am. The beast she coaxes out of me every time I'm inside of her.

The clinking of her crystals against the glass to the tempo of my thrusts creates a rhythm that mirrors my heartbeat.

It's too fucking good to end, but I can't slow down. Hooking her other leg around my hip, Tessa uses the leverage to pull me in tighter with every thrust. Growling, I pick up the tempo until her cries and pleas fill my ears at a deafening level.

She starts to flutter around me, and just when I know she's about to explode, I press my thumb to her clit and capture one of her nipples between my lips, sucking hard before biting down. Spasming, Tessa screams out her release as her body clenches around my cock like a fucking vice, pulling my release from me with a shot of fire down my spine.

Filling her, I coat her inner walls with my seed, her pussy greedily taking it all. So much so, I feel our combined juices leaking out when I slip out of her.

I slide her leg from my shoulder to around my hip with the other and carry her down the hall to my bed.

I find the clasp to the necklace at the nape of her neck and release her from it as I lay her down. She groans at the feel of the soft bed, making my cock twitch back to life, but I tell myself she needs a break. Her eyes fight to stay open, then give up and close. I'll wake her in an hour with my mouth between her legs, lapping at her sweet center.

Standing back, I place her necklace on my dresser and look down at her. She's so fucking beautiful it almost hurts. But I can't *not* look.

Undoing the knot ties of her heels around her thighs, I

unwrap the straps from around her legs like the gift that they are. Then I cover her with the comforter and leave her to rest before coming back for more. If I join her now, I know I won't keep my hands to myself.

Putting my clothes back on, I bring her uniform back to my room and then head to my office to check in with my captains on the progress of locating the Triads new gambling dens. I know they've set up shop somewhere new already, hoping to fly under my radar. But that will never happen.

I know everyone in this city, and I control everyone in it. No one does anything without asking my permission and paying their dues if I agree. And none of my people would dare keep anything from me if they valued their life.

Leo is setting up a meeting with their leader, but I know that I still have to crush them down with my heel until things are civilly worked out. Or uncivilly if necessary. I'm not partial to either tactic.

CHAPTER 15
Tessa

Waking up, I roll over to find myself alone in Alec's bed while last night floods my memory. Biting my lip, I roll my face into the pillow.

He wanted the Tessa I am on stage, and I let myself be her past the final curtain closing.

I let myself be free. I let myself be the Tessa he needed me to be. He craves her just as much as I crave being her every Friday night, and that makes me feel way more than I'm willing to admit.

He can see the difference between us, and he wants both of us. The sweet and innocent Tessa that walks in the light *and* the seductive and wicked Tessa that has needs beyond her control. Until now. Alec has the power to control, use, and fulfill my every desire that lives both in the bright light of day and the shadows cast in its counterpart.

When I had gone back to my dressing station last night and found my usual bouquet of black roses and black velvet box with a note, I didn't even open the box to see my gift because after reading his note, I packed my bag quickly and walked right out the back door, needing him desperately.

Last night felt different while I danced. I gave in to the music more. I gave into the feelings swirling through my veins more. I gave in to the desires I felt pooling in my core as I took every chance I could to look at Alec in the shadows.

Even his eyes on me were different. More heated. More possessive. More needy.

My entire solo performance was foreplay for the both of us, and while I've seduced an audience with the way I give myself over to the music before, I've never seduced myself. But last night I did.

Suddenly feeling hot and needy, I climb out of bed and walk straight into the massive bathroom and into the black marbled shower. I let the hot water beat down on my sore muscles, and when I wash the sensitive flesh between my thighs, a shiver racks my body. Alec is relentless in his need for me, and while I feel spent and used every morning, it's in the most delicious of ways knowing that it's because he can't get enough of me.

I spent this past week with Alec in his penthouse, but since I was able to pack a bag for myself, I made sure to include all the essentials, plus a few outfits that are actually mine that I can wear.

I pull out a pair of high-waisted cutoff jean shorts that

are frayed around the hem and hit me right below my ass cheeks. Tucking in a white t-shirt, I leave my hair to air-dry and apply a little mascara and blush to give myself the illusion of makeup.

I go to close my dance bag where my makeup was, but the jewelry box I never got to open last night sits on top of a spare t-shirt, and I pull it out, the velvet soft beneath my fingers.

Opening it slowly, I cover my mouth in surprise. Nestled inside is a bracelet to match the earrings he gave me. Deep red rubies are strung together on a gold chain inside of gold settings with little diamonds at the point of each prong that holds the gems. I run my fingers over the rubies, turning it this way and that so I can see the morning light catch the facets and cast flashes of red around the room.

He doesn't have to give me gifts like this. It's too much. I don't need them to know that he likes watching me dance.

Closing the box, I tuck it back in my bag and make my way into the kitchen. I pour myself a cup of coffee and lean against the counter, closing my eyes as the hot liquid slides down my throat and wakes me up.

I don't have to work at the diner today, and I haven't since Alec stormed into Lucy's last Saturday. I went in to explain things to my boss a few days ago, telling him that I was going to be focusing more on my dance classes, and he was so happy for me, knowing that's what I truly love to do. After working there for six years, I owed him more than just a walkout from my shift with a quick, "I have to go. I have a personal emergency." I wasn't going to tell him that the emergency was Alec's burning anger at my uniform and my sudden need to have that fiery rage blanket me in a passion that would have my anger at him simmer in its wake.

I like stoking that fire in him.

"Morning, *bella*," Alec says smoothly, in his deep, seductive voice. He takes my coffee cup from me and places it behind me as his pins me against the counter with his hips. Moving my wet hair over my shoulder, he plants kisses up the side of my neck. "Mmm, you smell so good," he practically purrs, the low vibrations of his voice reverberating through me. His tongue licks the spot behind my ear and I sigh, tilting my head to the side so he has better access. "It's too bad I have to go, or I'd lick you all over to make sure you taste just as good everywhere."

His dark promises make my knees wobble and threaten to give out.

"What are you going to do while I'm gone?" he asks, a hopeful, dirty questioning tone to him that suggests he wants me to sit here and think about him all day. He lazily strokes his fingers up and down my bare thigh, and while I will no doubt be doing that, it won't be here.

"I have classes to teach this afternoon."

Pulling back, he grips my chin and forces my eyes to his. "What are you talking about?"

"I took on two Saturday classes at the studio."

"You didn't tell me that," he says, a hard edge to his words.

"I know. I was going to. It just happened a couple of days ago. Since I'm not at the diner anymore..." I trail off, and his eyes lose a little of their hardness, knowing I agreed to not work there anymore. For him. Something I didn't do lightly.

"What classes?"

"Ballet for ages 5 to 8."

"I bet you look so sexy in your little ballet teacher outfit," he murmurs close to my lips, pressing his hips against mine so I can feel his hard length.

"I don't *not* look sexy," I say back, leaning into him so my lips brush his. Kissing me hard, Alec licks the seam of my lips and bites down on my bottom lip, making me groan.

"Now, all day I'll be picturing you stretching and getting limber for me for later."

"Maybe that's exactly what I'll be doing. And I'll be picturing you when I do." I smirk, and he pulls away, shaking his head slightly like he can't believe I'm real. "I finally got to open my gift from last night," I tell him with a smile. "I was a little too distracted to do it after the show when I read your note."

Alec's eyes turn stormy at the mention of last night, and my body floods with heat that I have to ignore.

"I love the roses, Alec, but you don't have to give me anything else. The bracelet is beyond beautiful, but I don't need such expensive gifts."

Alec cups the side of my neck and brings his face close to mine, forcing my eyes up with our lips so close. "I'll get you whatever I want, *mia bella rosa*. I know you aren't the kind of woman to need such things, but I like giving them to you. I like seeing you wear them on stage. I like the little smile you wear that's just for me. Our secret."

Stroking my neck, I arch back, exposing more of my delicate flesh to him like prey offering up the kill shot for the predator. And willingly so.

His hand tightens around my throat and I sigh, that little breath all the invitation he needs to capture my lips in a kiss that I feel spread through me like a wave – every inch of me covered until I'm drowning in the thick emotions I don't know how to surface from. I don't know if I even want to. They're filling every empty place inside of me that I never thought could be.

Smoothing my hands up his chest, I circle his neck and kiss him back, pouring everything I can't say into him, hoping he'll take it without throwing it back at me.

Untangling from each other, Alec kisses the spot below my ear and inhales my scent before pulling back.

"Have a good day at work," I whisper, biting my lip.

Something flashes in his eyes, but it's gone just as quickly as it came. "I will," he says, giving me one last kiss before leaving me.

With a shaky hand, I reach back for my coffee cup and take a sip, the caffeine making my already on edge nerves because of Alec, even more frayed.

When the door opens again and Enzo walks through, I jump a little, startled out of my thoughts of Alec.

"Did I scare you?" he asks, giving me one of his boyishly handsome smiles that makes him look a lot less deadly than when he's in bodyguard mode.

"No," I say through a laugh. "So, I'm teaching two classes today from 12 to 2. I don't think Alec had time to tell you since I just told him a few minutes ago myself."

"No worries, T. He texted me on his way down. Plus, that other dance teacher who's there a lot," he says, humming. "She's fine. A work of art."

I roll my eyes, knowing exactly who he means. "Her name is Claudia. But don't even go there. She has a boyfriend."

"Not one like me." He smirks, making me laugh at his cockiness.

"I'm more than sure he's not like you. He's an accountant."

"Oh," he scoffs. "How boring."

"Yes, not as exciting as following around some random woman, but…" I shrug.

"You're hardly random. You're the boss's girl. That means something."

"The boss's girl?" I question, pausing at that phrasing.

I like the way it sounds, but I don't take Alec as a man who labels his relationships with his women. He wants me, yes. But beyond our powerful chemistry…I don't know what he's thinking. He's still too much of a mystery for me to even have a semblance of an idea as to what he's thinking in terms of me and him, long term.

"What's that look for?" Enzo tilts his head to study me.

"Nothing," I say quickly, schooling my emotions. "I have to go home to grab the clothes I'll need for class."

"Alright." He nods, holding the door open for me.

CHAPTER 16
Tessa

"Thanks, Miss Tessa," Emily says in her cute little high-pitched voice.

I smile down at her. "You're welcome, sweetie. See you next week."

"See you!" she exclaims, running over to her mom.

I smile at the rest of the kids as they change their shoes and meet their parents out front. I'll admit that this was way more fun than working the lunch shift at Lucy's.

I love the excitement on the faces of the kids, ready to practice and show me what they can do and what they've been working on. The woman who used to teach these two classes is out on maternity leave and the other instructors were being stretched thin trying to cover all her classes. They were relieved when I asked if I could take these two.

When all of the kids are gone, I send Enzo a text telling him I'll be a little longer. This room is open for another hour before the next class, so I thought I'd use it for myself.

Ballet has always been my favorite to teach. It teaches discipline, lines, flexibility, grace, and love. Love is the only way a dancer can survive. Without it, there'd be no reason to push our bodies the way we do, and there'd be no drive or emotion behind our movements. The audience would lose interest pretty quickly.

Stretching my neck out, I press play on the stereo and take a deep breath, closing my eyes as I let the classical music flow through me.

Tears prick the backs of my eyes. I don't know why I chose this song. I don't know why I'm dancing this routine. But it feels important somehow. I have to. I need to.

I haven't danced a full classic ballet routine in years, but before I know it, the song is over and I collapse to the floor, exhausted with tears falling down my cheeks.

"Tessa." Alec's voice floats through my hazy brain like I manifested it myself from wishing he was here. Then his warm hand touches my shoulder.

Looking up in surprise, my eyes meet his in the mirror, and when he sees my face, he steps in front of me, holding his hand out for me to take.

"What's wrong? You were so beautiful, *bella*."

A sob escapes my lips and he pulls me against him, his solid body a welcome comfort. I soak in his strength and power, letting it replace what I lost.

"That was the dance I performed the night my parents

were killed. The routine is burned into my memory. Everything about that night is."

"I'm sorry, baby." Alec rubs my back in soothing circles.

"No, I'm sorry." I sniff and try and step away out of embarrassment, but Alec just tightens his arms around me so I can't move an inch.

"You don't ever have to apologize to me for showing your emotions," he says, cupping my face. "You dance what you feel, and I've never seen anything more beautiful."

Swallowing the lump in my throat, I look away for a moment. "Why are you here? I thought you had work."

"I do. I just wanted to see you."

"Oh," I breathe, surprised, and Alec's dark eyes float over my face. "I'm glad you came," I admit softly.

"Good. Let me take you home."

"I don't want to go home."

"Then where do you want to go? I'll take you anywhere."

"I know a place."

Changing my shoes, I untie my skirt and pull on a pair of sweatpants. Alec takes my bag and guides me out of the studio with his hand on my lower back – a comfort that eases the pain of the flashbacks racing through my mind.

Alec's car has fully tinted windows, and it feels like we're in our own little bubble with just us in the small space.

I give him directions to my favorite spot and we ride in silence as I watch the afternoon sun glint off the ocean next to me.

Parking next to the large rock wall that's meant to help ward against hurricane storm surges, I get out of the car and start walking, not even waiting for Alec. I feel his presence behind me as I step up onto the jetty that extends out into the ocean.

I keep walking out farther and farther, my eyes only focused on where I'm stepping.

Luckily, there's no one else out here right now, and when I'm about three quarters of the way out, I stop on a relatively flat rock that's able to fit the both of us.

Alec hasn't said a word. He just followed me silently, knowing I needed this.

The wind whips all around us as the waves crash up onto the rocks, sea mist coating my face. Shivering, Alec's arms come around me instantly, wrapping me in his warmth from behind like a blanket of security. I haven't felt safe like I do with Alec in far too long, and because of that, I find myself telling him things I haven't told anyone before.

"My brother moved us here from northern Jersey after my parents died," I start, and Alec begins to stroke my arms. "I found this place on my second day here when I was feeling too much and needed space. The apartment felt too small, so I got on my bike and just rode, needing someplace big. A place that felt bigger than everything I was feeling.

"I come here when I feel like I do now. When every breath feels like too much of an effort and the memories find their way to the surface and I can't push them back down."

I have the sudden urge to tell him everything. To give Alec what I've been carrying around with me for six years. He's strong enough to carry it along with me, and I'm strong enough to let him.

"My brother was all I had after my parents. But then he was taken from me too. He was murdered right in front of me." Alec's release of breath at my confession blows across my exposed neck, sending another chill through me.

"James was only 19 when my parents died, but he wanted me to stay with him, which is why he moved us here. He said there was always money to be made in AC. He was lucky to find a construction job during the day and then he worked in the casinos at night. Two of them on rotation so he could get more hours." My voice shakes, thinking about how hard he always worked. For me.

"I didn't get to see him that much with me still being in high school and the hours he worked, but he did anything and everything to make sure I could still dance. He knew it was all I had besides him in my life." Tears slip down my cheeks and I blink slowly, the wind drying them almost instantly.

"What happened to him?" Alec asks me, his arms tightening around me. "Who did it?" he asks a little harsher.

"I don't know," I whisper. "It all happened so fast. All I saw was my brother crumbling to the ground. And blood. So much blood," I choke out, my voice breaking at the end as images of that day flash in my mind.

Spinning me around, Alec keeps one arm wrapped around my waist to steady me, and grips my chin with the other. I allow myself to get lost in his eyes as tears fall from mine. He gives me strength. He's anchoring me to him so I don't just let myself blow away in the breeze.

"I'll take care of it, Tessa," he tells me with all the confidence in the world.

"What do you mean?"

"I'll take care of it," he repeats.

"How?"

"My men will find him."

"It's been six years," I whisper.

155

"That doesn't matter. He'll pay. No one gets away with hurting you or those you care about. Never again." I can see the absolution in his eyes. The determination to exact vengeance for me and my brother.

I don't know how he'll find out who did it, but I don't have the energy to question him right now. Because somehow, I know that if Alec says he'll find him, then he will.

"I'll always protect you." Cupping the side of my neck in the possessive way I love, Alec kisses me softly, slowly deepening it until all that's on my mind is him.

My hands slide up and around his neck, my nails scratching at the base there. Rumbling his approval, he holds me even tighter, pressing me so close that I have no room to breathe. But I don't need to. I just need him. He supplies me my oxygen.

I don't know when it exactly happened, but I need him. Since the moment I first felt him there in the shadows watching me, his complete and utter attention on me, I think I've needed him.

"Take me home with you, Alec," I whisper against his lips when we separate.

With a groan, he kisses me, his thumb stroking the front of my neck as the pads of his fingers dig a little deeper in the back.

I lead the way back across the rocks, careful to not slip and fall between them since my brain is a mess of too many emotions I'm trying to filter through.

Where the inside of his car felt like a hidden sanctuary on the ride here, it now feels as if it's too small. It's suffocating. The air is thick with all that's been said and unsaid between us. All the questions I didn't want to ask him out on the jetty are now flooding me like a broken dam.

What did he mean his men will find the man responsible? How? Who are his men?

Just like when Enzo said I'm *boss's girl*...

He makes it sound like...

I play with the ring on my middle finger as a tingling sensation creeps down my spine. My eyes dart to Alec's hand on the gearshift and I see the faint lines of scars on his knuckles and fingers.

He's more than he says he is.

I've felt his danger and power from the beginning, but I didn't want to think too much into why. Why the owner of a hotel and casino would instill fear in everyone around him. Why he talks of an army of men so casually. Why I have a bodyguard. Why the security at The Aces seems to be military grade. If I stopped to wonder, then I might have run in the opposite direction instead of straight into his arms.

I try to discretely take shallow breaths to rid my lungs of the constricted, oppressed feeling they're in, but he notices. He notices everything about me. His attention is always zeroed in on my every move.

"Relax," he soothes, his voice dropping to that octave that makes my stomach simultaneously twist and melt.

"I am," I tell him, but my voice is far from sounding relaxed.

"Don't lie to me, Tessa. Never lie to me," he says with an edge.

Biting my lower lip, I turn to face the window so he can't see my reaction to him.

I'm not scared of him for myself. I know deep down he

would never hurt me. Not physically at least. But hearing him threaten the life of a man who's haunted my nightmares for six years, and who's had me checking every shadow wherever I go, makes me realize just how deadly Alec is.

He said he took care of the man who attacked me...

That scary guy dragged him down to the basement. The basement...

What's in the basement?

Swallowing hard, I smooth my hands out on my pants as we pull into the parking garage of The Aces.

Grabbing my dance bag from the trunk, Alec places his hand on my lower back as he guides me towards the elevator. I avoid the eyes of the man standing guard next to it, his presence suddenly holding more meaning than I let myself see before.

Walking me straight to his room when we get inside his penthouse, Alec places my bag in the closet. "Take a hot bath. Relax. Take as much time as you need." Tilting my chin up so I'll look at him, he says, "I'll be in my office making a few calls if you need me."

"Okay," I whisper, and he nods, leaving me alone to collect myself. I don't know how he knows I need to be alone, but I'm grateful.

I soak in a hot bath filled with lavender salts to relax, and when the water turns cool, I reluctantly drain the tub and shower off.

Putting on the extra leggings and t-shirt I had in my dance bag, I head into the kitchen to make myself a cup of tea. But when I reach for a cup up in the cabinet, I hear Alec's raised voice floating down from the hall on the other side of the dining room where I know his office is.

I've yet to venture over to that side of his house, and my curiosity gets the better of me when he keeps yelling. Tentatively, I make my way towards him. I know I shouldn't be eavesdropping, but I feel like this is my chance to discover if what I think is true.

I need to know.

Rounding the corner, I inch my way down the hall, his muffled voice through the closed door at the end of the hall becoming clearer the closer I get.

"Leave her out of this," he growls. "Her safety is my priority along with the family's. Don't ever fucking question that again, brother."

My heartbeat is in my throat as I stop right outside his office door. Is he talking about me?

"My men are gathering intel on the Triads every day, collections from the other casinos have been picked up, I have a man working on Katarina's party, and The Broker's party next weekend is mapped out with contingency plans in place. I have everything under control. And next time you want to question my loyalty, *don't*," he emphasizes. "You know I'd never jeopardize us. Any of us. Including myself."

The Triads? Collections? Loyalty?

My breathing quickens as it hits me that my suspicions were right. I've lived in Jersey my entire life. I know what that all means.

He slams the phone down with a snarl and I hear the sound of glass shattering like he threw his drink against the wall. His fast approaching footsteps give me little warning, and before I have the chance to move, his office door flings open. Alec's eyes widen and then narrow when he sees me standing there. They're so dark and angry that I can't even see any good within them at the moment.

"What're you doing?" he asks, his voice hard and full of suspicion. "Were you listening to my phone call?"

"No," I say quickly, taking a step back. "I heard you yelling..."

"So, you stayed to listen? How much did you hear?" He takes another step closer.

I debate whether or not I should play dumb, but I need to know. I need to know who he is. "You don't just own The Aces, do you?"

"I told you my family has a lot of businesses. The Aces I claim as my own."

"Your family..." I start, trailing off, not wanting to say what I think out loud.

"My family, what?" he asks, tilting his head to the side, gauging my every reaction.

"Nothing," I say quickly, shaking my head.

"Tessa," he says firmly, caging me against the wall with his hands on either side of my head.

"Alec, please," I whisper, so softly I can barely hear it.

"Are you afraid to say it? Are you afraid of me?"

"No," I breathe out with a little shake of my head.

"Are you sure? Your eyes are saying the opposite, *bella*." The roll of his tongue on the sweet endearment makes my heart skip and makes me wish he was using that skillful tongue to bring me to heaven instead of asking me the hard questions.

"I'm not afraid of you," I say a little stronger, my voice surprisingly never wavering. I've never been afraid to be with him. I've only ever been afraid of how I feel about him. Of what he makes me feel about myself.

"No?"

"No. But the reason you're so concerned for my safety…that has to do with your family."

"Yes."

"Because your family is involved in things that aren't legal." I say it as a statement, already knowing it's the truth.

"You could say that."

I swallow the lump in my throat. "Your family…you… you're in the…" I don't know why I can't say the word.

Mafia.

I can think it, but it won't form on my tongue, knowing that it's never actually talked about if you're in it.

He flashes me a wicked grin that isn't a smile, but rather a baring of teeth like a wolf to its prey. "I'm not just in it. I am it. *My family is it,*" he emphasizes, running a finger down my jaw and across my bottom lip. "Does that change anything for you?" he asks, almost a threat – daring me to say it does so he can prove to me just how easily it would be for him show me why it shouldn't. How he could make me stay even if I didn't want to.

I'd like to think that him being a part of the mafia would make me run in the opposite direction, but I can't. Doing that would tear me apart. I'd never be able to be the Tessa I am on stage ever again. I know that, and I can't lose that.

"No," I say finally, a little breathless. "It should…but–"

"But what?" he prompts, his eyes flaring with heat.

"I just want you. Anything else…it doesn't matter."

Just as I get the last word out, he slams his mouth down on mine, silencing me with the heat of his lips – searing me, possessing me, claiming me.

This kiss is deep, messy, and fueled by pure passion and

need.

"*Sei la cosa migliore che non avrei mai pensato di poter avere,*" he rasps against my lips, then goes back to kissing me breathless – across my jaw, down my neck, back to my lips. None of it's enough, though.

Tearing his lips away, I whine in protest until he drops to his knees to slide my leggings down my legs, kissing, licking and biting as he goes. Moaning, I sink back against the wall, needing it to hold me up.

Stepping out of them, Alec slides his large hands up the front of my legs and grips the red lace thong I have on and rips it from my body like it was nothing, the material giving way to his need to have me bared to him.

I look down at him, and seeing him on his knees in front of me, his dark eyes full of sinful promises burning up at me like an offering, is something that will always be imprinted in my mind.

Reaching down, I run my fingers through his hair and his eyes darken even more. I grip the dark silken ends and push him forward to where I need him to kiss me.

Taking my direction, Alec buries his face between my thighs and I fist his hair, crying out when he sucks my clit between his lips straight away, not gentle in the least. But that's how I want it with him. I don't want him gentle. I want him to give me the beast he has simmering just below the surface of his barely contained control.

Just as quickly as he took me in his mouth, Alec easily escapes the harsh grip of my fingers and stands. Towering over me, he captures my lips in a bruising kiss, his tongue demanding entrance so I can taste my arousal on his.

Moaning, I tear at his belt, and manage to unzip his

pants so I can slide my hand inside to grip him. He groans into me, his cock jumping in my palm as I squeeze and stroke him, loving the feel of him. Long, thick, smooth, and heavy. A king's dick that reigns over me, making me feel like a queen every time he enters me.

Pushing his pants down just far enough to free himself, Alec lifts me up and I wrap my legs around his hips. My head hits the wall with a gasp and a moan when he enters me in one swift motion.

"So fucking good," he rasps into my neck, licking his way to my ear. "*Sei così fottutamente perfetto.*"

Taking me quick and hard, every thrust sends sparks through my body, my nerve endings alight as fire rages through me.

Alec sets me on fire.

He strokes the demons I carry with me like a pet, and I arch into him, wanting his affection, and loving that he likes my demons because I think they resemble his own.

Grabbing his face, I make him look at me, his eyes flaring each time he fills me so fully. I kiss him hard, biting his lower lip and then smoothing it out. His answered groan brings me higher, so I do it again, and the vibrations of his groan running through me is enough to push me over the edge.

My orgasm hits me like a bomb. So powerful, the scream coming from me is unlike anything I've ever heard. I shove my face into the crook of his neck, biting down hard, needing to give him some of what I'm feeling because I can't hold it all to myself. It's overflowing, and I need to release it all. I need him to feel it all with me.

Alec's deep groan as he fills me with his release falls on

deaf ears with all the blood rushing through my head. But I feel it against my skin, and it sends another wave through me.

Feeling him come inside of me, marking me as his in the most primal and raw of ways, makes me feel like even more of a queen. I make him lose control. I make him fuck with absolute abandon. I make him come like he's putting out a fire.

Panting, we breathe each other in until our hearts calm down. Our chests are pressed so tightly together it's as if our hearts were one.

Unlinking my legs, Alec lets me slide down the wall until my feet touch the floor, and then he lifts my chin so I'm looking at him.

Rubbing his thumb back and forth across my bottom lip, he doesn't say anything for a long moment. Lost in his own thoughts, his eyes are swirling pools of darkness like a lake at midnight. I don't know everything that lies beneath the surface, but I'm still willing to jump in. And even if I drown, it would be a death that comes after knowing the greatest euphoria.

"What're you thinking?"

"Nothing," I say with a shake of my head.

"Tell me," he urges.

Swallowing, I lick my lip where his thumb is still stroking, and while his eyes narrow and darken, I try and find the right words. "I was thinking how I should have known from the beginning. But it wouldn't have made a difference."

"I can't share a lot with you, but I promise it'll never have to be something you have to be concerned about. It'll never touch you. No one will ever touch you," he says fiercely. "My family is all I have, but you..." He pauses, his eyes searching mine. "You matter. Don't ever think otherwise."

Blinking away the urge to cry, I give him a small nod.

No one since my brother has ever made me feel like I mattered.

Although Alec didn't even have to say the words. I already knew. I already felt it.

CHAPTER 17

Alec

I haven't seen much of Tessa this week besides falling into bed with her every night and waking her up with my mouth on her sweet pussy or slipping right inside of her so her beautiful eyes fly open to see mine above her.

She's always wet and ready for me as if she was dreaming of me, waiting for me, and knowing I'd be around soon to take care of her. She always gasps in surprise, and then moans out long and low for me – the two sweetest sounds in the world. Which I won't deny is fucking amazing, but I also want to just be with her, something I've never needed or wanted from a woman before. They always serve their purpose for a good fuck and then they're gone, their names and faces quickly fading from my memory.

But with Tessa, I want to come home and have dinner with her. I want to take her out and show her my city from my eyes, taking her places she never even knew existed. I want to hear her voice as she tells me about her day. I want to see her smile, giving me a little light in my chest to keep some of the darkness at bay.

This week has been a busy one. I've spent my days in meetings, on the phone, and on the road. I had to drive into Manhattan twice to talk with Leo about our meeting with the head of the Triads in two weeks, as well as our plans for the party we're attending tonight. I normally would have just stayed with him in the city until it was all worked out, but I couldn't leave Tessa. I couldn't go a night without her.

Leo, Luca, and I had to go over detailed safety measures and escape routes for both events in case things go south. I don't think they will, but we've stepped up our security since our father and uncle were killed. They were too confident that no one would ever try to take them out. They were too comfortable in their neighborhood.

Not us.

My brothers and I know that anything can happen — anytime and anywhere. We don't cut corners and we always make sure each of us has a man with them when we go out.

That's why I've been so protective of Tessa. I should've been more careful on the phone with Leo last weekend, but he got me so fucking mad that I didn't even think about Tessa overhearing what we were talking about.

She didn't know there was more to me than just owning and operating The Aces, but she does now, and she took it like the woman I know she is — strong and mesmerizing.

A true fucking queen.

I knew the moment I saw her she could handle anything. Especially me. I just didn't know when, or how, to tell her. It's not something you just come out and say, and I didn't want to give her the choice to run. I wanted her so deeply embedded with me that she couldn't leave me. I'm both an asshole and a genius, because she decided she doesn't care. She just wants me. And what that makes me feel is unlike anything I've ever felt.

It was a wave of euphoria that morphed into a deep craving that hasn't left me since she said the words.

I crave her.

Every minute of every day.

I need her.

I want her by my side. She's not a woman you keep in the shadows hoping no one notices her. She's the woman you place center stage for all to see, but never touch.

Mia bella rosa may not know it yet, but she's going to be mine in every sense of the word.

She's stronger than she thinks, and I plan on making sure she knows that.

My phone starts buzzing on my desk, pulling me from thoughts of testing not just her mental strength, but her physical strength. I want to fuck her against the wall with both her legs hooked around me under my arms so her hips aren't touching the wall at all, only her upper back. She'd have to use every muscle to stay where I want her, and it'd be the sexiest fucking thing in the world to see her do that for me. Because I need her to.

"Is everything good for tonight?" Leo asks right away when I pick up the phone.

"Yeah, we're good."

Tonight at Sahara's, a hotel and casino on the other side of the city, a private party is being held that will have all the major players in New York and New Jersey attending. Each of the five families will be represented –Carfano, Cicariello, Melcciona, Capriglione, and Antonucci– as well as the Triads, Yakuza, Bratva, Armenian, and Irish families.

There'll be politicians, CEOs of fortune 500 companies, presidents of unions, police chiefs, and a shit ton of every other higher up in the dirty world we all live in.

It's a show of power.

Having all of us in the same building is a show of power for the man known only as The Broker. He has his hand in every aspect of illegal trades around the world, which is how he got his name. He can broker any deal you need, from anyone, anywhere. Nothing happens in the illegal trades game without him knowing about it. Even if he doesn't have anything to do with it, he always knows and keeps track. Weapons, drugs, women, cars, passports, new identities, hit men, mercenaries, organs. Anything you can imagine.

He can supply safe transport for products and people, and extraction for the same from any situation.

If it's needed, he can supply it.

He's an elusive man who runs his empire from the shadows, sending his people to do the work. He's never seen by those outside of his close circle.

Even tonight, I know he won't be there. He's showing his power by not even attending. That's why my family doesn't like to use him, knowing the price is too steep. Not in money, but in the information he gathers on you and the secrets revealed that he then uses against you if you ever cross him.

The Carfanos will be the most powerful in the room tonight by far, but because of The Broker's way of business, he'll always be a step above us all. And that makes me burn on the inside like no other. Just like knowing the family who ordered the hit of my father and uncle will be there tonight. That makes my blood burn and boil like the river Styx.

If I had it my way, I'd drag every last one of those Cicariello fuckers into hell and watch them suffer for all eternity. Even if I was in hell right along with them, I'd wear a grin so fucking wide knowing my vengeance was exacted.

But I can't. The Cicariellos keep a tight security at all times. The core family, the ones I want obliterated, not their blind soldiers, have stayed locked behind the walls of their compound on Long Island since the hit on my family was made. They thought they could take over our territory and our businesses afterward, leaving us weak and vulnerable, but they didn't know our father. Michael Carfano was a man never to be underestimated, and the Cicariellos did just that.

He and my uncles trained their sons to take their place in the family since we were ten. On my brother's, cousin's, and my own tenth birthdays, we didn't have parties. They were spent in my father's office as he explained the family business to us. Then he took us to the family gym and we started our training. It was equipped with weights, boxing and sparring rings, grappling mats, a shooting range, and knife throwing blocks.

We were made to be strong. Capable of handling ourselves in any situation, ruthless in handing out and receiving punishments, protective of our family, and ready to take over and run the business when we were needed.

That came sooner than my brothers, cousins, and myself would have wanted, but we were ready nonetheless. And that's what the Cicariellos didn't know.

We'll find a way to exact our revenge one day soon. Focusing on maintaining the Carfano name and business dealings was our first priority before we started plotting on how to get at them.

We took care of finding the hitman they hired first and foremost with our own man who is capable of finding those who never intend on being found. Now, over the past few years, we've slowly sabotaged their businesses, trying to draw them out of their fortress, but they've remained strong in there. Such pussies. They don't have the balls to face us. They only send their highest trusted men to events and out to do their business while they live like kings behind those high walls.

The hatred we all feel hasn't dimmed in the least in the past five years, and no matter how long it takes, our justice will be served. A death they'll beg for when we get our hands on them. All of them.

The Cicariellos will send someone close to the family tonight at The Broker's party, but not the ones we want. They know we would find a way to get to them before, during, or after the party, and the only way such powerful people can all gather together in the same place is with the knowledge that if anything were to happen, then an all-out war would rain down on all of us from every direction. None of us wants that. No one could survive that, especially when the war would involve The Broker.

"No talking to Lin tonight. We wait for our meeting," Leo tells me, like he has three times before.

"I know," I say impatiently.

"Alec," he starts, a warning. "You're my brother. I know you. If you get the chance, you'll say something. He's targeting you and your business specifically."

He's not wrong, but I have more than just my business to worry about now.

"Not this time," I assure him, and I hear Leo's audible sigh through the phone. "Don't start again, brother."

"She's a risk you're not ready or prepared for."

"How would you know?" I snap, hating that he thinks he knows everything. "And that's starting again."

"I'll be there at 8."

"Can't wait," I say dryly, hanging up before he can say anything else.

The rest of my day is spent on edge. I haven't seen Tessa since this morning, and knowing Leo will be here soon, I pour myself three fingers of whiskey and sit and wait.

It slides down my throat smoothly with a slight burn that I always welcome. I need Tessa's taste as badly as I need this whiskey.

This morning, before leaving for the basement, she was half asleep as she mumbled something about her show manager booking them an extra performance tonight for a special occasion. It didn't register fully into my otherwise preoccupied brain considering she was naked and her morning voice was sexy and raw like I had just shoved my cock down her throat. I couldn't resist pressing her back into the mattress and kissing her hard while my hand found its way down her body to give her a goodbye worthy of its name.

Now, I wish I had asked a few questions. But right as I

take my phone out to text Enzo, my door opens and in walks Leo with two of his most trusted men, Alfie and Richie.

I slip my phone back in my jacket and down the rest of the amber liquid in my glass. I'll check in with Enzo later. I know he's going to make sure my woman is safe. He knows his life depends on it, and I have to focus on making it through this party.

Standing, I button my suit jacket and give Leo a nod.

"Let's go," is all he says in response.

Only Leo and I are going to the party, not wanting all the Carfanos present in case something goes sideways.

"You look tired," I tell Leo as we're driven across my little island to Sahara's. Alfie drives us with Richie in the SUV in front of us and my two men in the one behind.

"I am," he says in a clipped tone.

"What's going on?" Leo is rarely tired. He's more of a machine than I am. He rarely sleeps.

"The Cubans in Miami have decided to go back on our already agreed upon importing costs, the Armenians have been dropping too many bodies in our territory and not cleaning up after themselves which makes it look like we're taking their enemies out, and you have the Triads who won't just fucking stay down when we put them there. Add in that both the Armenians and the Triads will be in the same room as us in less than a half hour as well as the Cicariello scum lackeys who will be standing in for Joey and the rest of them, and I'm fucking tired. Just tell me you won't be distracted by *anything* for the next few hours."

"Jesus fucking Christ, Leo, you make it sound like I'm some pussy who can't do my job."

"Just checking."

"You don't need to," I grit through clenched teeth.

He looks out the window. "A woman can ruin men like us. Men who do what we do, are who we are. She'll make you think twice before making a decision that you never would have before, risking your life in that split second. She'll change you. She'll give you a weakness where you had none before."

I've never heard him talk like this – lost in a memory he's never shared. I want to ask him more, but decide to lay it all out there on my end for him to know.

"Her name is Tessa. I want you to meet her. I'm not letting her go. I probably never should've gone back to see her dance after that first time, but the moment I saw her…" I trail off, not knowing how to put it into words. "The thought of her out there with another man burns me from the inside out to the point where I know I'd burn the fucking world down before that ever happened."

"She's a fucking stripper?" Leo shakes his head and rubs his temples.

"No, she's not a fucking stripper," I growl, fisting my hands so I don't strangle him. "She's a dancer. Ballet and shit. She teaches kids at a studio in town and is in the Friday night show at The Aces. That's where I first saw her."

"Oh," is all he says.

"What?" I snap, knowing he wants to say something.

"Nothing, Alec. I just didn't expect that."

Releasing a rushed breath, I drop it because I don't know what he means by that and we've just pulled up to Sahara's.

Leo and I lead the way to the door with our men flanking on the side and behind us. The bouncer checking off names doesn't even bother asking for ours, already knowing who we are.

Sahara's is known for their massive midnight pool parties, and as we enter the glass dome structure attached to the hotel that encases the pool area, my eyes immediately scan those who have arrived before us, assessing the threat.

Palm trees rise high from areas around the lagoon styled pool which has women floating in it with their tits out, sipping on cocktails. They no doubt were hired to be something to look at by the men in attendance.

A stage is set up at the far end next to the DJ, which will more than likely have a well-known artist performing on it sometime later in the night. Bars are set up all around to keep the liquor flowing. Private lounge and cabana areas extend off from the cement paths that weave around the pool and surrounding area. A sand beach area to my left has beautiful women waitressing trays of both liquor and cigars in string bikinis that leave little to the imagination.

The stairs leading to the second level are flanked by bodyguards, the private rooms up there where some will go to conduct business or drag one of the many hired women here for a quick fuck.

"I need a drink," I tell Leo, walking us over to the nearest bar.

"I can already tell this is going to get wild pretty soon," he says.

"I know."

The Broker always has surprises throughout his parties. Last year, he had naked women come down from the glass roof, twisting and turning on silk ribbons that had every man in the place completely fucking entranced. Another year there was a sex show on stage that when over, had everyone breaking away to find any semblance of privacy in the cabanas with whichever woman they could claim first. The Broker always hires call girls to walk through the crowd and give the men whatever they want.

I wonder what he has planned this year. He hosts these parties for the areas around the country and world with the highest concentration of his clients, and he doesn't spare any expense.

Moving around the room for the next hour, Leo and I make small talk with politicians, including the mayor of Atlantic City and New York, police chiefs from precincts all around the tri-state area, and presidents of the unions we control. It's always important to show them your face every so often to remind them who owns them. Let them look us in the eyes so they know what's coming for them if they decide they want to go back on any of our agreements and try to fuck us over.

Nothing instills fear in a man who thinks they have a powerful position in life more than when you come around to remind them it can all be taken away in the blink of an eye.

We avoid who we need to, and our men make sure none of them get too close to us either.

After my third whiskey, and while in the midst of telling Leo how bored I am of these people, the lights dim, and the DJ's music morphs into something slow and sexy – a song I recognize.

Three women take the stage and start to dance a routine I've become all too familiar with over the past two months.

My eyes search the dark area surrounding the stage and in between all the guests, hoping it's just the liquor making me realize what I'm seeing.

The song eventually fades out and the women leave the stage, the men all around yelling their praises and vulgarities after their retreating figures.

I'm vaguely aware of Leo saying something next to me, but when the next song starts, and it's one I know better than any other, I throw back the rest of my whiskey and shove it at a waitress passing by before pushing my way forward.

Leo yells at me, but I ignore him, letting him and our men find their own way through the crowd, not caring in the least that I'm exposing myself. My eyes stay glued to the spot I know she'll emerge from any second now.

CHAPTER 18
Tessa

My emerald green skirt fans out around me as I spin out onto stage. My costume tonight for this party is different than my others, but my manager insisted, saying it would go well under the dim colored lights reflecting off the glass dome and pool. He told all of us performing that we needed to elevate our look, and even tweaked our routines slightly to make them even more sensual and eye catching than before.

I got a glimpse of the party through the curtain when Jenna, Kayla, and Gina took the stage a few minutes ago, and all I thought was, *holy shit.*

I'd always wanted to see one of Sahara's midnight pool parties, but this is something else. Something more than I think they usually do. And I know the guests here aren't of the garden variety kind that are typically in attendance either.

I can feel a mixture of fear, power, rage, and a simmering of sinister energy swirling around the room. I don't know who's here, but I know they're all dangerous.

Amongst all of them, though, there's one energy in particular that I feel caressing my skin like a black rose – soft velvet petals before the thorns cut me deep. Gently seductive, yet possessively scarring.

I know that caress. I've come to crave that caress. I've come to need that caress.

On my next pirouette, I stop with a pose center stage, and my eyes lock with a pair of dark and angry ones that I've been drowning in since they first met mine.

The show's manager, Dan, only told us a couple of days ago about working this party. I've barely been able to talk to Alec this week with how busy he's been, and telling him about working some party I was given no information on for privacy and anonymity reasons because of whoever is hosting it, was the last thing on my mind. I was only able to tell him in passing this morning before his hands on my body distracted me, and then he left me in my post orgasmic haze for work.

Alec's eyes look like they could burn all of Atlantic City to the ground right now, and after what feels like forever, but is really only a second, I'm moving away from him, my body following the music as it carries me around the stage – controlling me, guiding me, embodying me.

Alec remains where he is. Under the burning rage, I can still see his desire for me like a flame in the distance of a black tunnel, and I go towards it until it's front and center and I'm blinded by the blaze.

Something comes over me, and without consciously knowing it, I change my routine, my own desires fueling me to do as they please – enslaving me to their needs.

Before I know it, the song is over, and I've danced a routine I've never done before. I don't even hear the audience's response. I only see Alec. He's the only one that matters. He's above them all. He's the reason I can do what I just did.

When the music morphs into something more upbeat, I blink out of my daze and fade back into the shadows so Daphne and Jen can take the stage.

"What was that?" Dan asks me.

"I…I don't know. I'm sorry…I just…I don't know what came over me. I saw him, and…"

"Who?" he asks, perplexed, his eyebrows coming together.

"No one," I say quickly, and he looks even more confused, but he just shakes his head.

"I should be mad, but that was amazing, Tessa. Beautiful."

"Thank you," I say shyly, not even knowing what I did out there.

"Alright, go change for your dance with Jeremy. No changing anything there. You have a partner."

"Of course," I assure him, hurrying off to the makeshift dressing area that was made for us behind the DJ's both with a few well-placed black curtains.

Shit. My dance with Jeremy.

Alec is *not* going to like that.

Dan has had us paired in practices for the past few

weeks to see if we'd be a good addition to the show, and during rehearsals on Wednesday, he told us we'd be added to the lineup in next Friday's show. But today when we arrived, he said tonight would be good practice in front of a crowd before we debuted. I hadn't even given much thought to what Alec would think when we performed before this moment, but now I'm worried.

Our dance is *definitely* on the sexier side, but I've been okay with it since I know Jeremy isn't at all interested in having sex with me. I think his boyfriend would have an issue with it if he were. But Alec doesn't know Jeremy. He's going to see us on stage and think that it's all just foreplay and borderline cheating.

Fuck.

He's going to kill Jeremy.

It's too late now to do anything about it, or warn Alec somehow since we all had our phones confiscated when we arrived for privacy's sake. This party is meant to stay in this room.

Changing into another new-to-me costume, I re-curl a few pieces of hair that have fallen flat and touch up my makeup to make it more sensual and smokey. Swiping on blood red lipstick, I stand in front of the mirror and make sure everything is in place.

Jeremy comes up next to me and catcall whistles. Laughing, I slap his chest and adjust my boobs. The black-on-black jewel encrusted bra I'm wearing has extended straps at the bottom that crisscross down and around my waistline with some good padding that pushes the girls up. The matching high-waisted cheeky briefs show quite a bit of ass as well, and as I turn this way and that in the mirror, my heart rate kicks up. I know Alec isn't going to like this.

"You look hot. Don't worry, Tessa," Jeremy assures me.

"I'm not worried," I lie, and he gives me a look. "Fine," I sigh, "there's someone here tonight that isn't going to like seeing our performance."

"What?" He smiles wide, his whole face lighting up. "A man? You have a man? How come you haven't told me? And he's here?" His eyes widen a fraction before he composes himself again. "The men here tonight...they're all..." I know what he's trying to say. They're not *regular* people. They're the men who rule over their empires us normal people have no idea even exist.

"I know," I finish for him. "And he's really not going to like us dancing together. I already saw his face when he realized I was even here."

"He didn't know?"

"No. All I knew was that we were booked for a special event, and he's been really busy this week. Shit," I groan, rolling my neck around to loosen my suddenly tight muscles.

"You need to relax, Tessa. We're going to dance. He's going to watch. What's the worst that can happen? He can't storm the stage and take you away," Jeremy says, rolling his eyes. Little does he know, that's exactly what I think Alec will do. Especially because Jeremy is only wearing loose black pants and that's it. He has a lot of muscles and skin on display that I'm going to be all over in a few minutes.

"Yeah. You're right," I tell him, bending to tie my black pointe shoes. I don't want to put my worries of a highly probable scenario onto him.

"I know," he gloats. "Now, let's get your fine ass over to the stage so we can make the audience wish they were us."

He blows me a kiss and I laugh, some of my worry fading for the moment.

I can't let Alec make me doubt myself or make me doubt what I'm about to do. Jeremy and I have an amazing routine together, and I know the people watching us tonight really will wish they were us. Or wish they could join us on stage.

The lights over the stage go dark, and that's our cue. Taking my hand, Jeremy walks us out to center stage, and we stand face-to-face with my back to the audience. He loops his arms around my hips, gripping my ass.

I really hope Alec doesn't kill us.

We remain in the dark as the beginning of the song plays, the guitar's bass low and vibrating, preparing the room for us. The volume steadily increases until the lights flash on and the lyrics start.

Jeremy grips me harder to support me as my body bends backward in a sweeping motion, my hair brushing the floor before I'm snapped back up against him, the guitar and drums thrumming through me.

Lifting my leg to hook around his hip, Jeremy drags me across the stage, spinning me around before I hook my other leg up so I'm straddling him and repeat the same back bending sweep. The audience starts yelling all sorts of dirty expletives at us, but I push them away as the electric guitar vibrates through my blood.

This song is perfect. It's dirty rock and roll at its finest, adding a little energy to our performance to get everyone's blood pumping.

Holding on tight around his shoulders, I swing my legs out and around and Jeremy catches them, swinging me around his body like I weigh nothing at all and then placing me down in front of him where he pushes me away and I spin out on my toes fast and tight.

I do a slow walk back to him up on pointe, circling him, assessing him like he's my prey. Jeremy catches my hand after my first pass and twirls me, lifting me off my feet.

It's a tease back and forth between us. I'm seducing him while he's trying to resist, but ultimately can't.

Even as the drums and guitar beat loudly at my system, I can still feel the rage rolling off of Alec from his place in front of the stage. I refuse to look out to him or any of the other people around us. I'm not supposed to anyway. It's supposed to be just me and Jeremy in our own little bubble.

On the next chorus, this complete sense of freedom comes over me, and I use the rage being directed at me to fuel the passion I'm meant to embody – my body moving that much more alluringly.

When the song ends, I'm down in a split at the feet of Jeremy facing the crowd, keeping my eyes up at him while he holds my hands.

But just before the lights fade out, I bring myself to look down in front of me, and my eyes lock with a pair that are cold and distant.

I'm in trouble.

CHAPTER 19
Alec

Red.

Black.

All I see is both of those colors as my vision blurs and clears in and out of consciousness.

What the fuck was Tessa thinking?

I'm going to kill that fucker who had his hands all over her. Slowly. Taking him apart piece by piece until he's begging me to end it. But I won't. Not until he thoroughly regrets ever touching what's mine and then spends an eternity reliving the nightmare of his almost death as further punishment.

"You need to calm down, Alec. This is not the time or

place." Leo grips my arm, holding me back from shattering this whole fucking glass dome to end this party. "Not here. We're leaving." He says something to our guards, and the next thing I know, I'm being dragged away from my spot in front of the stage with everyone parting for us like the red sea.

Red. Blood. I need to see that motherfucker bleed.

"No. We're not leaving." I pull myself from his grip and stand my ground. "If you think I'm leaving her here with the people that are in this room, then you're fucking crazy."

"I'm not the crazy one here, Alec," Leo says calmly as he fixes his tie, trying not to draw any more attention to us than I've already done.

"No, that would be Tessa for thinking she could do that shit without me knowing." Sliding my hand down my sleeve where Leo grabbed me, I order another whiskey from the bar and toss it back in a single swig. Slamming the glass down, the bartender quickly pours me another.

When I toss that one back too, Leo just shakes his head, not bothering to say anything else. He knows I'm beyond the point of listening to reason.

"Fuck," I growl, the images of her straddling that half-naked motherfucker as he gripped her ass –*my ass*– with his hands touching her everywhere. It was like sex with clothes on. *Barely any clothes on.*

Feeling my control snap, I turn back towards the stage and push my way through the perverted assholes who have their eyes glued to the stage, and my anger boils over.

Leo calls out behind me, but I escape the grip of him this time, and my men know better than to ever touch me or stop me, so I make it around the DJ's booth and through the black curtains before Leo can stop me.

Eyes swing to me as I search around the makeshift dressing area until I find her.

I know she can sense me before seeing me because her back stiffens and her hands shake at her sides. Taking a breath, she slowly turns to face me. Her eyes are full of fear, anger, and defiance, but it's the first one I'm going to use to my advantage so she remembers who I am and who she got involved with. She can't act like that and think I won't one, find out, and two, let it go quietly.

I keep my eyes on her as I take slow and deliberate steps forward, her eyes growing more fearful with every stride.

Tessa opens her mouth to say something, but then quickly closes it when I tilt my head to the side.

Blinking, she looks around the room and then past me where her eyes widen, no doubt at seeing Leo and the four bodyguards flanking me. But they're not who she should be worried about. They're here to make sure I don't do something as crazy as actually kill someone in front of so many witnesses.

When my eyes slide to the man Tessa was dancing with who's standing a few feet behind her, my nostrils flare as I suck in a deep breath and resist every urge I have to take my guard's gun and blow his fucking pretty-boy head off. He at least has the decency to look afraid of me.

"Get your things. We're leaving," I direct at Tessa, and she flinches, my voice cutting her. She recovers quickly though, and pulls her shoulders back, leveling me with a look I'm sure is meant to show me she's not going to come willingly. But all it does is make my lips curl up in a sardonic smile.

"You going to challenge me here?" I ask, and her chest starts to rise and fall in heated breaths. "Let's go." My voice drops even lower, and I can feel the fear of everyone in the room ricochet, filling me with a twisted sense of happiness.

Tessa's eyes stay on mine for a beat longer until she blinks and looks away, turning to her dressing table to gather her things. That's when dancer boy decides to lean in and whisper something in her ear.

"Step *the fuck* away from her," I snarl, and I feel Leo and my men take a step towards me.

"Enough," Tessa says sharply, her eyes swinging back to mine. "Just...enough, Alec. I'll meet you out there in a minute."

"I'll wait." I refuse to let her leave my sight for even a second in case she decides it's a good idea to find another way out of here.

I'm not taking any chances with the men that are in attendance tonight and risk any of them taking her for themselves.

Sighing, she throws her makeup and hair things into her gym bag and then shoves her clothes on top of it all, not bothering to change.

"Tell Dan I'll return the costume at practice and that I had to leave early," Tessa says to dancer boy, and he just nods, knowing that words are dangerous for him to speak right now. Or ever again.

Hoisting her bag over her shoulder, she pushes past me and eyes my brother and bodyguards for a split second before slipping through the curtain.

"Tessa!" I yell after her. Throwing the curtain open, I stride after her, gripping her arm and spinning her to face me.

"What the fuck are you doing? You can't walk through a room like this alone." My eyes dart down her body. *"Dressed like that."*

"Like what, Alec? What am I dressed like? I always wear outfits like this on stage."

"Not here. Not with these men watching."

"Who?"

"Men who won't hesitate to take you and do whatever the fuck they want with you before either killing you or leaving you so broken, you'll wish they had."

Her gasp isn't audible with the music blaring, but I see her sharp intake and bend so my face is right in front of hers.

"Would you like that, *mia bella rosa*? Should I leave you here to be picked apart by the wolves?"

"Fuck you," she spits, her rage winning out over any fear she feels. "You have no right to treat me like this. You've known from the start that this is what I do, and if you don't like it, then go fuck yourself, because I'm done."

"What the fuck did you just say?" I seethe, my vision blurring with anger. Grabbing her chin, I force her head back. "Don't throw threats around you know you can't keep, Tessa. You're *mine*, and I have every right to treat you like this. You were dancing like you were fucking. Why did you feel the need to hide this from me? It looked like that took some practice."

Tessa tries to pull away from me, but I just grip her arm and chin harder.

"You can struggle all you want, but I'll always win. You're lucky I didn't kill your little dance partner for touching you like that. And if you want it to stay that way, you won't do that sex show ever again."

She remains silent, but her hazel eyes are blazing with anger. Releasing her chin, I start to drag her through the crowd, feeling the eyes of everyone around us.

Our SUV is already waiting for us when we exit and I open the door, lifting Tessa up and all but throwing her inside, ignoring her grunts and huffs of protest.

CHAPTER 20
Tessa

Alec has no right to treat me like this. Crossing my arms over my chest, the man who was with Alec climbs in after him and closes the Range Rover's door, the small space suddenly feeling like a tin box with barely any air for me to breathe.

I'm beyond mortified that Alec just dragged me out of there like a petulant child he thinks he can control like a mindless doll. Like one of his men he barks orders at and expects obedience like a fucking well-trained dog.

I was humiliated.

Looking out the window as we fly down the streets, I shove my body as far away from Alec's as I can. I don't want a single part of him touching me right now.

The car air is swirling with a cloud of emotions so thick, I can barely decipher my own from the others.

The driver pulls directly into the underground garage of The Aces, and when the engine cuts, the sudden silence is like a bucket of cold water dumped over my head – pins and needles stabbing me without leaving any marks. But I can feel them just as I can feel Alec's silent punishment he's dishing out to me now.

I honestly can't tell if he genuinely wants to hurt me or not.

Alec climbs out first and paces the cement a few feet away.

"So, you're Tessa," the mystery man says from the seat behind me. "I'm Leo, Alec's older brother."

Oh, shit.

If he's his older brother, then that makes him head of the family…

I should have seen it sooner. They look so alike, but where Alec walks around like a bomb waiting to detonate, Leo seems to have a more silent, but still deadly, air to him. Like a poison waiting to be released into the air – properly contained until released, and then everyone in the vicinity is taken out. Quickly. Quietly.

Climbing from the back to sit next to me, he closes the door and tells the driver to lock the doors, shutting Alec out. He turns back abruptly at the sound of the door closing and tries to open it, but can't.

"Open the fucking door, Leo!" Alec yells, pounding on the window.

"Give me a minute!" Leo yells back, making me flinch.

My hands shake on my lap, but I turn them to fists before he can notice, trying not to show him that I know exactly who he is and what that means.

Leo stares at me for a moment. "My brother hasn't been acting like himself lately."

I open my mouth to respond, but he holds up a hand. "Do you know who he is? Who I am?" The inside of the Range Rover is only dimly lit by the florescent lights that manage to seep in through the heavily tinted windows, but I can see the flare of his eyes as if he's excited by the prospect.

"Yes," I whisper, hoping he can't hear the trepidation in my voice.

"Then you know how dangerous it is for him to be so distracted by you."

"I…"

"I can't stop him from being with you. But if you're going to be his woman, then you need to learn what that role means and entails. You need to be sure of it all before he's so far gone, you'll bring down everything we've built by walking away when things get to be too much and you see or learn of something you don't like." His eyes are penetrating mine, his calm voice edged with warning. "Do you know what I'm saying?" he asks, urging me to answer him.

"Yes." I swallow. "I understand what you're saying."

"Good." He nods. "Alfie, you can unlock the doors now," he instructs the driver, the resound shifting of the locks filling my senses as I repeat Leo's words over in my head.

I don't even notice when he climbs out and Alec's face fills the doorframe. "What did he say to you?" he demands.

"Nothing," I whisper, sliding out of the car. I don't want

to talk to him right now.

Tires come to a screeching halt behind us and I turn to see Enzo jumping out of his SUV and walking briskly towards us. His eyes run up and down me to make sure I'm okay before looking at Alec, and when he does, it's like Enzo actively clears his face of all emotion. He stands tall, waiting for Alec to say something.

He doesn't, though. I watch with wide eyes as Alec holds his hand out to the man next to him who pulls a gun from his shoulder holster inside his suit jacket and places it in Alec's waiting hand.

I stand frozen, not sure if what I'm seeing is the truth.

He flips the safety off and holds the gun up to Enzo, who doesn't seem at all surprised. Alec's face doesn't give anything away. Only his cold, dark eyes show the anger he's holding.

"You shouldn't have let her step foot in there. You know that, don't you?"

Enzo nods once, not showing an ounce of fear. He expected this.

"I trusted you to keep her safe. This is the second time you've let me down." Alec's cold voice is devoid of all emotion. No anger, no remorse, no disappointment. Nothing.

Then it all happens as if in slow motion. The deafening sound of the gun goes off and Enzo's torso is thrust backward. He staggers a few feet and then falls to his knees.

Dropping my bag, I run to him. Kneeling beside him, I press my hands to his wound that's bleeding out profusely.

Tears blur my vision, but I murmur words of encouragement to the man who's done nothing wrong in my eyes. He's followed me, driven me, watched over me, and saved me when I needed it.

"Lay back," I tell him, and he actually listens. "You'll be fine, E. You'll be fine."

I press harder against his wound and look up at Alec who's staring at me with those same cold eyes.

"Alec! He needs help!" I yell, my voice breaking at the end. He doesn't do anything, though. He just stands there holding the gun at his side. My eyes sweep around the group of men behind him, all of them with the same blank, emotionless expressions.

I look Alec in the eyes again. "Alec," I repeat, "if you don't get him help, I'll never forgive you. I trust him to protect me. I don't give a damn if you think you need to prove anything to these men."

"I'll be fine, T," Enzo says weakly, blood spurting through my fingers as I try and keep the pressure.

"Yes, you will be," I tell him. "Alec!" I yell, but he just turns and walks away, handing the gun back to the man and telling him something in the process.

The guard takes his phone out and dials a number. A few minutes later, Joe, the doctor who checked me over after I was attacked, comes running from the other side of the garage.

"Please help him," I beg. Looking down at Enzo, his eyes are closed, so I slap his cheek softly. "No, wake up! Stay here, E!" I keep patting his cheek, then slap him harder, and he groans, opening his eyes.

"Jesus, T. Ow."

I give him a smile as Joe gets to work. He digs in his bag and comes out with a wad of gauze and replaces my hand with his.

"We need to get him up to the room. Help me with him," Joe orders, and three men step up to lift Enzo from the floor and carry him to the elevator.

"Is he going to be okay? Where are you taking him?"

"To the medic suite in the hotel where I'll do everything I can to save him."

Sitting back on my heels, I feel the rough cement digging into my legs, and I realize once again that I'm still dressed in my show costume.

I look down at my bloody hands and don't know what to do with them.

"Here," Joe says, handing me a small towel from his bag. "You did good, Tessa."

"Thanks," I whisper, rubbing my hands on it, the stark white turning a vivid red. I didn't do good, though. Enzo is dying because of me.

The elevator dings and the doors open. "I have to go," he says quickly, grabbing his bag and running to the waiting elevator car.

I look after him, and I'm surprised to see Leo is still here, looking at me with what I think is respect in his eyes. But I don't care. I'm done. I want to leave.

"I need to go home," I tell him.

"I'll take you." Lifting his chin at the man he called Alfie earlier, he gets back behind the wheel and Leo opens the back door for me.

Standing on shaky legs, I grab my bag and look back at the closed elevator doors. "Will he be okay?"

"Joe will take care of him." He nods, and I return it with a small one of my own before climbing inside the car.

I give Alfie my address, and when we pull up to my apartment building, I look down at my costume and blood-stained hands.

"Alfie will walk you up. No one will bother you," Leo tells me.

"Right. Sure," I answer in a daze. I don't feel anything right now. I just watched a man who's been with me every day for the past month, or two if you count the one I didn't even know about, get shot in front of me. It was too reminiscent of watching my brother getting shot and bleeding out on the sidewalk.

I couldn't help him.

I couldn't do anything to stop the bleeding from the shot to his chest while people just stood around and watched me scream and cry for help.

Help arrived too late for James.

"Give me your phone," he says, but when I look inside my bag, I realize I don't have it.

"It was taken at the party and I left before getting it back."

"I'll have it brought to you," he assures me. "And my number will be in it when it is. Text me tomorrow if you want to know how Enzo is doing."

"Okay."

"It'll be my private number that only my brothers and sister have," he tells me, and I glance over at him.

"I understand. Thank you."

Climbing out of the SUV, Alfie walks silently beside me up to my apartment, and I give him a noncommittal thanks before disappearing inside and locking the door behind me.

I don't want to be bothered by anyone.

Scrubbing my hands under scalding water for what feels like an hour, Enzo's blood is finally gone, but I can still feel it.

Peeling my costume from my body, I lay it out on the chair in my room, seeing that it luckily didn't get ruined, and then step into the shower, letting the hot spray of water wash away every other trace of tonight.

CHAPTER 21
Alec

Downing my whiskey in a single shot, I pour another, and quickly shoot that back as well.

Tessa shouldn't have been there tonight.

Pulling out my phone, I see four unread texts and one call from Enzo that I didn't see earlier, warning me that Tessa was going to be dancing at The Broker's party tonight.

Fuck.

Pouring myself another drink, I scrub my face with my hand, trying to get the look on Tessa's face out of my head when I shot Enzo.

He may have called and texted, but he should've never let her go inside. He should've locked the fucking car doors and driven her right back to my place to wait for me.

He knew better, and he paid for his mistake.

I should've put a bullet between his eyes for fucking up a second time with Tessa, but like Leo said I would, I second guessed myself and went for his shoulder instead. It may still kill him, but he has a slightly better chance of living if he hasn't already lost too much blood.

Anything could've happened to her tonight at that party. Those men saw her the way only I've seen her, and I know any one of them would love to take what's mine from me as payback for something or other.

Loosening my tie, I sit in my leather chair in the living room and stare out the windows at nothing in particular.

At some point, Leo storms in and pours himself a drink, taking the seat next to me.

"Where is she?"

"I took her home."

"What?" I clip, looking at him. "Why?"

"She needs some time away from you, Alec."

"That's not your call to make. I don't want her alone. She might run."

Leo huffs out a laugh. "I have someone on her. But maybe she *should* run."

My hand tightens around my glass. "Shut the fuck up. I'm not letting her go."

"Well, you better think of a way to come back from tonight."

The image of her kneeling by Enzo, her hands covered in his blood and completely unfazed by it fills my mind, and the corners of my lips lift.

"She was beautiful tonight," I say without thought. "She

handled it so beautifully. Half-naked, her hands covered in his blood and spitting mad. She's the most beautiful fucking thing in the world."

"You're fucking crazy." Leo shakes his head and sips his whiskey. "I know you hesitated from killing him because of her, but I think you made the right choice. She wouldn't forget that image in her head. She might eventually get over it and move on, but she would never forget it."

He's right. But Tessa needs to know that I'm dead serious when it comes to her. And if she's going to hide shit from me, or decide she wants to let another man put his hands all over her, she needs to know there'll be consequences.

I'd kill for her, and already have. But I'd also kill *because* of her.

Wiping a towel across my chest and around my neck, I lie back on the bench and go for my tenth rep of weights.

I couldn't sleep with my mind going crazy over Tessa, wondering if she's alone, if she's mad, or if I should go to her and just fuck the anger right out of the both of us.

With one last lift of the bar, I clink it back into place and sit up.

I take a quick shower, but my cock is still rock hard from the thought of fucking her angry and having her fight me before giving in. My hand isn't an option. Only Tessa's tight little silken pussy will satisfy me.

The next thing I know, I'm dressed and grabbing my keys as I storm out of my house. When I reach the garage, I have to step over Enzo's blood stain on the cement to get to my car, and my anger flares once again.

I don't know why I let Tessa make me this fucking crazy with shit I've never felt before or know how to handle. Obsession, possession, jealousy, a manic need that only grows the more I have her, and this crazed fucking feeling in my chest that makes it seem like that organ in there is pumping harder than usual.

Ignoring the stain, I climb in my Audi and peel out of there. I take the streets of AC at a speed that's more than double the limit.

When I get to Tessa's apartment building, I take the stairs two at a time, needing to get to her quicker. Leo has one of his men outside her door, and he gives me a curt nod at seeing me. For the life of me, I can't remember his name right now, and I'm not in the mood to ask or care.

Knocking on her door, I wait a few seconds, listening for movement inside. When I don't hear anything, I knock again, harder this time, and the door flies open to an angry Tessa.

"What the hell are you doing here? It's four in the morning!" Her eyes are blazing.

"I don't care what time it is." I push my way inside and kick the door closed behind me.

"Get out!" she yells, holding her hand up to try and keep me away.

Pushing her hand aside, I lift her up by the waist and toss her over my shoulder, striding through her living room and into her bedroom.

Throwing her down on the bed, she crawls back up to the pillows. "What do you think you're doing?"

"I'm going to fuck the anger out of you," I tell her as I

grab the back of my shirt and take it off, tossing it to the floor.

"I doubt that's possible," she huffs.

"Is that a challenge, *bella*?" I ask cruelly. "Because you know I always win."

"Not this time," she pushes back.

Tessa goes to climb off the bed and I grab her ankles, dragging her down so her back is flat on the mattress, easily fending off her kicks.

When I release her to push down my sweat pants, she scurries to her knees at the end of the bed in front of me, her eyes revealing the battle she's waging between desire and hate.

Good.

It'll make fucking that hate right out of her all the more sweeter.

CHAPTER 22

Tessa

Staring up at Alec while he strips for me, my mind and body wage an internal war of both wanting him more than anything, and wanting to slap him for being so presumptuous in my need for him.

With his broad, naked chest on full display, my hands itch to reach out and touch him, to feel his warm, taut skin.

My eyes roam down his toned abs that are calling to me to run my tongue between all the defined ridges, and then settle on the monstrously erect cock that's swollen and in desperate need of my touch.

"You can't just think that coming here and stripping so I can see what I'm giving up will make me crumble like some weak woman you're used to controlling."

"Oh, I know you're not weak, *bella*. That's why I know you'll fight me." Gripping my oversized t-shirt in his fist, Alec pulls me towards him and crushes his lips to mine, silencing me from further argument.

My body comes alive with his touch, and I have no choice in whether or not I respond to him. It's like breathing. It happens without me even knowing.

But I don't want to want him this much. It's not going to end well.

Remembering what happened tonight, I push him away, but fall back onto the bed in the process, and Alec flashes me a predatory grin that both sends a chill down my spine and makes my body flood with need.

I'm only wearing an oversized t-shirt and panties, and when Alec climbs up on the bed, he easily opens my legs and occupies the space between them with his large frame.

"I know you're wet for me," he taunts, leaning in close so I feel his breath on my neck. Licking his way to my ear, he bites down on my lobe, and I bite down on my lip to keep from groaning. I will not let him have that satisfaction. "I'll bet you anything you want that your panties are soaking wet. *For me*," he growls, biting down on my neck.

Arching off the bed, my chest collides with his as he snakes a hand between us and runs a knuckle down the seam of my sex through my panties.

An animalistic groan vibrates from his lips into my neck, and I bite down harder on mine to keep from making a sound.

I hate that he can render me utterly powerless with a single touch. He could brush my arm as he walked by and my body would burn for more.

I hate how much I've already fallen for him, and I don't see my need for him lessening. But I can't do this with him if he's going to control every aspect of my life and kill whoever dares to defy him because of me.

Gripping the waist of my panties, Alec literally tears them from my body, the simple black cotton biting into my hips as it rips.

"You won't win, *mia bella rosa*. I know everything you love done to you. I know how to make you come so hard you won't even remember why you're mad at me. Should we test how strong you think you can be against me?" he whispers harshly in my ear, his voice like gravel on my insides – rubbing me raw.

"Making me come doesn't mean you win," I tell him, and he chuckles darkly.

"That's exactly what that means." Entering me in a single thrust, my mouth hangs open in a silent scream as my body adjusts to his size without warning.

Sliding his hands under my t-shirt to palm my breasts, Alec pinches and rolls my nipples between his fingers and I close my eyes to the sensations rippling through me.

"Look at me when I'm inside of you," he demands, but I shake my head, keeping my eyes squeezed closed. Rolling his hips, Alec pulls out almost completely before slamming back inside of me full force.

A little whimper leaves my lips and I can sense the victorious gleam in his eyes without even seeing it, so I use every ounce of strength I have to push him off of me and roll him over, using the element of surprise to execute the maneuver.

I rip my shirt off over my head and sink down on him before he can stop me.

I'm taking back the control.

Alec's deep grunt at my sudden impalement makes me smile condescendingly down at him. "I thought you were going to win."

His dark eyes turn molten black as I splay my hands over his chest and roll my hips, my clit rubbing perfectly against him. I bite my lip and toss my head back as I suppress the moan threatening to explode from inside of me.

Alec's deep snarl, followed by a head-rushing switch of positions, has the breath leaving my lungs in a rush. On my back again, he grips me behind my knees and spreads me open, thrusting into me furiously.

His brows are drawn together as he takes me with a hardened need to fuck the anger out of me.

He doesn't let me move and he doesn't let me challenge him anymore. He just takes what he wants from me, using me for his pleasure in the most brutal and raw of ways.

I want to hate it.

I want to hate how much my body loves it.

I want to hate that the fire running through my veins is because of his unbridled passion.

But I can't hate any of that.

I fucking love all of it.

And I fucking love him.

Even when I hate him, I love him.

"You can't win when it comes to me, Tessa," he says as he thunders into me at an unrelenting pace that I know will have me sore and bruised in the morning. "I fucking *own you*. I own this body. I own this pussy. I own your mind. I own your *everything.*" Each ownership claim is punctuated with a thrust that drives me higher and higher, feeling his words bone deep. They seep into my marrow and take root.

My orgasm comes in a rush and hits me hard and fast, my body shattering off into a million little pieces that scatter into the wind as I ride wave after wave flooding through me.

I had no choice.

I never have a choice when it comes to Alec. He can take and take and take from me and I wouldn't have a choice because he replaces what he takes with himself. And with him comes the most euphoric feelings I've ever experienced, and probably ever will.

Pushing my legs down against me as far as they'll go, Alec somehow finds the ability to go even harder and faster, and the pressure in me builds again in a matter of seconds.

"Again," he growls, and my body detonates at his command. A scream is torn from my lips as I shatter further.

I'm drowning as the waves crash over me and pull me under. I can't ride them anymore. I'm too worn and weak to hold my own, so I sink beneath the strength and power of the waves, subsequently guaranteeing Alec's victory.

Coming to, I roll onto my side and cringe at the soreness between my thighs.

I blink my eyes open in my darkened room, already knowing he's no longer here. I can always feel when he's near, but I'm coming up empty.

He left me here after that…that…I don't know what to even call what we, or rather he, did.

Groaning, I get out of bed and drag my feet to the

bathroom and straight into the shower, the hot water beating down on my skin a welcome relief from the tightness I feel all over.

I'm so tired.

Last night bled into this morning without any recovery.

Leaning against the tile wall of my shower, I close my eyes and drift off until I start to feel myself slide to the side, and I catch myself before I fall. Turning the water off, I wrap myself in a towel and crawl back into bed, not caring that my hair is sopping wet or that I'll ruin my pillows.

The next time I wake up, the sun is bright in my room and I shove my face into my wet pillow. It's a drastic contradiction to how I'm feeling.

So, Alec thinks he can just act like a complete asshole, then come and fuck me like he'll never see me again, and then leave?

My core is still throbbing from how rough he was with me, and he just left me without a word?

My anger from last night flares when my brain catches up with all of the events that led to me lying here alone.

Shuddering, I hug the towel I'm still wrapped in tighter, and my eyes catch on a piece of white paper on my nightstand next to my phone that he must have gotten back for me.

I always win.
-A

His beautiful script doesn't make my heart beat faster because I'm swooning like after my shows, but instead beats faster because I'm fuming. I feel used. And not used in a sexy way. Used in a cheap whore way that has me questioning everything that's happened this past month with him.

Was any of it real?

Does he even like me?

Is he just infatuated with the girl I am on stage and thinks because he gave me gifts, he can fuck me like he bought me too?

Grabbing my phone for a distraction from these thoughts that will only cause me to spiral out of control, I scroll through to find Leo's number he said he would have put in.

Hi, Leo, it's Tessa. Is it possible to visit Enzo today? I don't know where he was taken or if I'd have access to the room on my own.

A message comes in not five minutes later.

No, you can't see him, Tessa. He died a few hours ago.

My head spins.

What? No.

He's dead?

Enzo is dead?

A few hours ago?

Alec was here a few hours ago…

Did he already know? Did he come here knowing?

That fucking bastard.

He killed him and then came here to fuck me before I could find out. Then he left before I could hold him accountable.

CHAPTER 23
Alec

Another death on my hands. Another soul constricting mine. As the number grows, the tighter I feel. Only when I'm with Tessa does it all lift from my chest and I can breathe again.

But when she finds out about Enzo, I know she'll feel the beginnings of the weight I carry every day. And being with me will only guarantee that weight will get heavier.

There will always be more death. More blood. More betrayal.

My world is the dark and dirty side to life that everyone likes to pretend doesn't exist, when in fact they live amongst it every day.

All bright and good things cast shadows, and that's where my family lurks, waiting for those good ones to fall wayward where we'll happily take their demons for them – for a price.

Looking at my phone buzzing on the table in front of me, I pick it up reluctantly. "What do you want?" I bark at Leo.

"Watch your fucking tone, brother."

"What do you want?" I repeat.

"I told her."

My blood runs cold. "Told who, what? You better not mean you told Tessa about Enzo."

"Of course I do. She texted me to ask if she could visit him, so I told her."

"That wasn't your place."

"It is my place," he starts, but I hang up on him before I can hear the rest of his shit.

FUCK!

I got the call shortly after Tessa passed out from coming so hard her eyes rolled back. She can try to fight her need for me, I'll even welcome the fight, but I know what she needs, and I'm the only one who can give it to her.

No other man will ever be able to give her everything that I can. Even the thought of another man trying to take away what's mine has me reaching for my gun in my desk drawer.

I left her before the sun even rose, needing to deal with the Enzo situation while I figured out how I would tell her.

I should've just shot him in the head and been done with it instead of giving her hope that he would survive. Tessa needs to learn that I have no mercy when it comes to her and her well-being. I won't let anything bad from my world touch her. I never want to see her beautiful skin marred again.

Pushing away from my desk, I button my suit jacket and head down to the garage, seeing Enzo's blood stain has been scrubbed clean.

Arriving at Tessa's apartment, I take my time walking up to her room. When I first found out where she lived, I had the building manager make me a lobby entrance key and one to her apartment. I knew I'd need to come and go as I pleased at some point, and he didn't even question me. He wouldn't dare.

"She's in there, sir," Tito, Tessa's new bodyguard I assigned to her tells me. "She's been very loud for the past half-hour," he adds.

"That's my doing. Enzo's dead." Tito's expression doesn't change. No reaction. The word has already spread about Enzo. Good. All my men need to know that she's a priority and I don't fuck around. Watching her isn't a job to take lightly and there will be serious consequences if you fuck up.

"I'll make sure she's safe, sir," he tells me with an edge to his voice, letting me know he's taking it seriously.

I don't say anything. I don't have to. Threatening with words only goes so far. It's when you show what will happen if disobeyed that matters.

Enzo got too close to Tessa. His job was to protect, not befriend her, and because of that, he put her wants and needs above my orders. That can't happen. Ever. My orders are for Tessa's benefit. *Always* for her benefit.

I know Tito won't make that mistake. He's a part of my extended crew for when I need more than two guards with me when I go out. I trust him with my life, so I know I can trust him with Tessa's.

I hear music and the clanging of pots and pans coming from inside her apartment, so I knock hard. The door opens in a flash and I'm greeted to a pissed off Tessa – a sexy fucking sight that has my cock turning as hard as her eyes.

"Are you here to fuck the angry out of me again?" she spits. "Because it may have worked a few hours ago, but it sure as hell isn't going to work now. You killed him. You shot Enzo in front of me, your brother, and your men to make a point. Well, you made it. I'm not allowed to talk to anyone but you. Or are you going to shoot your brother now, too?"

"I might," I clip. "He shouldn't have told you."

"You're not getting this, Alec," she starts, gripping the edge of her front door hard.

"No, *you're* not getting it, Tessa. You're *mine*. And it's my job to keep you safe. He wasn't doing the job, so he had to go. He was never meant to be your friend. He was meant to keep you safe. And he failed twice. Tito here" –I nod at him standing a few feet away– "won't make that mistake."

Tessa pops her head out to take a look at Tito and her eyes narrow. He's a big guy – tall, broad, and all muscle. The epitome of a bodyguard.

"I have no doubt," she says, her voice dripping with sarcasm. "I know I won't be able to convince you I don't need him since you think you know everything that's best for me—"

"I do know what's best for you," I cut in.

"You don't!" she yells. "And you're not coming in here, so go." Tessa starts to close the door on me, but I slap my

214

hand against it to stop her.

"You don't get to slam the door in my face," I growl.

"I can do whatever I want, Alec. Get out of here. I can't even look at you."

My eyes turn to slits. "What are you trying to say, Tessa?" I say slowly, knowing she's not saying what I think she is.

"I'm telling you I need space right now. I don't want you around me." Gritting her teeth, she stands tall with her shoulders pulled back in a stance that's supposed to make me think she's serious.

"You don't get to decide that."

She barks out a laugh. "You thinking I don't just solidifies my issue with you."

I take a step closer to her. "And what's your issue with me? I didn't realize you had an issue with me giving you expensive jewelry and the best sex you'll ever have."

Tessa's pouty sex lips separate as she inhales a small gasp. "Get out," she breathes, blinking rapidly. "We're done, Alec. Thank you *so much* for the expensive jewelry and great sex. I guess I don't need anything else from you."

She goes to close the door on me again, but I push my way past her and slam it closed behind me.

"Get out!" Her eyes are on fire and her body is wound tight, looking like she's ready to attack me if I come any closer.

"You don't get to decide when this is over." Grabbing her around the waist as she tries to back away from me, I spin her around and pin her against the closed door. "It's never going to be over."

Slamming my mouth down on hers, I silence her from

any protests she planned on yelling at me. I know she doesn't want this to be over.

She's mad now, but she'll get over it.

Tessa bites down on my lip hard enough that I taste metal, and I growl, pulling back a fraction.

"Get off of me," she says angrily. "You can't just—"

I silence her again with my lips, the taste of my blood mixed with her anger making me want her even more.

"I can do whatever I want, *bella*."

Her chest heaves against mine with every breath. Her cheeks are flushed and her eyes go through a slide show of emotions before settling on one. Desire.

Tessa digs her nails into the nape of my neck as she fuses her lips to mine.

I know her better than she thinks. I know she can't resist this – us. We're more than our fleeting anger and words spoken as a result of it.

"You're going to have to try harder to fuck the anger out of me this time," she challenges, and I immediately lift her up and grip her tight, round ass. She wraps her legs around me and I storm down the short hall to her bedroom.

Tossing her down on her bed, she looks up at me with slits for eyes and rips her t-shirt over her head defiantly, as if she hates herself for doing it.

She may think she can stand her ground, but I watch her eyes follow my fingers as I undo the buttons of my shirt. Each one I slip free from the loop makes her eyes flare, and by the time I reach the last one, she has her bottom lip between her teeth, scanning the sliver of torso she can see.

The side of my mouth kicks up in the slightest of smirks, making her look back up at me. She purses her lips in what is supposed to be defiance, but it only makes me want to bite them and then kiss them back into the precious pillows that make me believe in something more than life itself.

Seeing my smirk, Tessa purses her lips tighter. That is until I shrug my shirt off and she releases a sigh, as if the sight of me relaxes her. Not for long, though. I plan to work her up into a tight coil before letting her spring free.

"I always win," I taunt, wanting her to get angry again.

"That note made me want to slap you."

"You could try, *mia bella rosa*. But then I'd just tie you up and fuck you." Her breathing quickens, and my cock jerks. "I can see you'd like that. But right now, I want you to have a fair fight."

Tilting her head, Tessa studies me as she reaches behind her and unclasps her bra, freeing her perfect tits, her nipples already tightly pebbled and begging to be tasted.

"I always win, too," she practically purrs, the little devil disguised as an angel that she is.

Shedding my pants and boxers, I take my swollen cock in my hand and look down at Tessa splayed out on the bed, sliding my hand down my length. She licks her lips and I hold back a groan.

"You win because I let you. And by the look in your eyes, I can tell you're dripping for me. Spread your legs for me, *bella*. Let me see."

Running her hands down her thighs, Tessa pries her knees open and gives me a perfect view of her glistening pussy. My cock swells even more and I can't hold back the groan that rumbles from my chest. She's so fucking sexy. She doesn't even realize how beautiful I find her. She'll never fully realize.

"Touch yourself. Show me what you want me to do to you."

Biting her lip, Tessa's delicate fingers trail down her inner thighs and then runs two up the seam of her pussy, catching her sweet cream and spreading it up to her clit. Rubbing circles around herself, her neck arches back and she moans. I feel it as a straight shot to my aching cock.

Yes, I always win, but not before she renders me so completely out of my mind that I take and take and take from her until she has no choice but to give in to me.

Pouncing on her like a fucking lion, I align myself at her core and press into her at an agonizingly slow pace. I want her to beg me to fuck her harder – faster. I want her to be so fucking blind to anything but me that she'll forever and always only see me.

"Alec," she chokes into my ear, and I pull out just as slowly, only my tip left inside of her. Her pussy squeezes me, begging me to stay inside of her.

I repeat the same slow push in and out of her, using every ounce of control I possess to hold back.

She looks up at me with glassy eyes, and I know I've got her.

"Just fuck me already!" she grits, breathing hard.

Giving her a wolfish grin, I pause, just the tip of my cock enveloped in her heat. The look in her eyes makes my gut twist, and I drive into her hard and fast, letting her feel all of me. Her hot, silken tunnel flutters around me after only a few strokes, but I need her to hold out.

Slowing down, I make long and controlled thrusts into her heat. She whimpers and mewls into the crook of my neck, needing more, but holding herself back from asking for it.

She's too strong willed for that and I fucking love it.

Swirling my tongue around each of her nipples, I never give either one my full attention, and as Tessa squirms beneath me, her pussy welcomes me, flooding my cock with her juices. Her inner muscles squeeze me over and over, attempting to swallow me into her tight little body, but I don't let it.

Each thrust into her, I pick up my pace until I'm relentlessly taking and using her body the way I want and need. I can't stop or help myself. I need to show her that I own her. I need to prove to her that me, and only me, can make her come even when she doesn't want to, and even harder than the last time.

Tessa claws at my back, her nails raking into my skin, trying to get even closer to me. And I fucking love that. I want her to mark me like an animal, because Tessa wild and untamed is the most beautiful version of her.

Without warning, her pussy clamps down on me and I see fucking stars clouding my vision. But I push through her orgasm, determined to make her come again.

Tessa's mouth is open in a silent scream, her head thrashing from side to side. Her back arches into me as her nails dig into my shoulders, most definitely breaking the skin this time. The bite of pain drives me past my thin layer of control and I lose my mind.

Pulling out, I flip her on her stomach and lift her hips up in the air. Gripping her ass in my hands, I spread her open and thrust back into her. I go even deeper like this.

Tessa's hands reach out in front of her to press them flat against the headboard, giving me even better leverage to go harder. Her muffled scream into the pillow at my intensity has me slapping her ass, and she squeezes me inside of her.

Fuck.

I slap her ass again and she squeezes me again, her moan my siren call.

It's almost funny that she thinks she can fight me on this. She wants to try to tell me she can live without this? I'll show her just how wrong she is.

Pounding into her, I look down to where our bodies meet and see her juices coating my cock as it disappears inside of her. That sight alone sends sparks running down my spine and I feel her start to quiver again. I reach around her and find her swollen clit and press down hard. Tessa lets out a scream that could wake the fucking dead as she gives into me, and with two more strokes, I let her fire consume me.

She milks my cock greedily, taking everything I have like her pussy is in a drought and she needs every last drop of my come to survive. I'd never let her go without, though. She'll always be full of me – overflowing even.

I pull out of her and she whimpers at the loss. Falling to the bed beside her, I pull her against me. Her eyes remain closed as she tucks herself up against me, her hand resting on my chest, right over my heart that beats solely for her. It only beats when she's around. And when she's not, it's as if I walk around lifeless, only breathing because it's a necessity to get me to the next time she's with me.

If anything were to ever happen to her, I wouldn't survive. *I couldn't survive.*

CHAPTER 24
Tessa

It's been two days, and Alec was right. He always wins. He somehow manages to break through every defense I throw up and then makes it impossible to rebuild the walls before he comes through and tears me down from the foundation so I have nothing and no one but him to be my base.

I've been on my own for so long though, that I don't know how to let someone help me. I'm not used to letting someone else be my strength.

I don't know how to *let* anyone be my strength.

I've lost all my family, don't have any true friends, and I've never had a man in my life. Especially not a man like

Alec Carfano. He demands my everything so he can be my everything. And the craziest, most fucked-up part, is that I want him to *be* my everything.

Slipping a little black dress over my head, I reach behind me and zip it up as far as I can, but I'll need Alec's help for the rest.

Picking out a pair of black Louboutin heels, I slide them on and stand in front of the mirror to admire them. I've always wanted a pair, but they're way out of my price range. I'm still playing dress-up in his sister's closet, who just so happens to be my size in everything.

I told Alec I felt weird about it, but he just brushed it off and said she can go buy it all again if she wants. I don't even know what that would be like. To have a closet full of designer clothes, shoes, purses, and accessories to call my own would be a dream.

Swiping my lips with red lipstick, I run my fingers through my hair to break up my curls a little, and then head down the hall to find Alec. He's in the living room on his phone, but the moment he looks up and sees me, he slips it back into the inside pocket of his suit jacket while his eyes roam the length of me.

"I need help with the zipper," I tell him, turning around in front of him.

Standing, he kisses my bare shoulder, brushing his fingers softly down my spine to where my zipper is half closed. "Are you sure you want me to zip it up and not down?" he murmurs in my ear. His other hand snakes around my middle and splays across my stomach right below my breasts.

"Zip up." I lean back into him. "You said you were

taking me out."

"I would much rather stay in. I can order you food from anywhere you'd like and then I can eat you for dessert."

"Zip me up," I insist, and he surprises me by actually doing it. "Just think about how satisfying it'll be to zip it down later," I tell him, turning in his grasp.

Running my hand up his chest, I cup his cheek. His day-old scruff scratches my palm and I hold back a moan. He looks sexy. More wildly dangerous than when he's clean-shaven and showing off every hard plane and angle of his jaw and cheek bones.

"I'll think of nothing else. You're too distracting, *bella*. Even when I'm supposed to be working, all I think about is you. Especially you spread out on my desk so I can have your taste on my lips and tongue the rest of the day."

Oh, I want that. "You'll have to tell me where your office in the casino is, then." I smirk, walking off towards the door. His rumbling approval follows me, and he catches me around the waist, spinning me around and kissing me hard.

"I'll show you tonight."

Taking my hand, Alec walks us out, and we take the elevator down to the main floor of the casino where I'm greeted with the vibrant sights and sounds of people trying to change their lives with a little risk and a bet.

Like last time, people turn and stare at us as we walk through the casino. Mainly at me though, since everyone who looks at Alec immediately flits their eyes away like they just got burned. They settle on me instead. I keep my head held high and my eyes straight ahead, refusing to shy away from being by his side.

Alec Carfano is a man who instills fear, and now that

I've seen firsthand what he's capable of, I have to come to terms with loving that side of him as well. The side of him that would do anything to protect me.

I'm so far gone at this point that I want his darkness to cover me. It's comforting to slip into the shadows with him and feel like I belong somewhere for the first time in my life.

We go to his family's restaurant again, and this time I'm hoping I get to finish my meal without having another panic attack. The hostess greets Alec like the king he is and politely smiles at me when seating us at a reserved table in the back corner that ensures our privacy.

Alec orders a bottle of red wine for us and I greedily take a long sip to relax when it arrives. Being out with him makes my stomach flutter. I like people seeing us together. I like the jealous glares I get from other women who wish they were me. I like showing everyone that he's mine.

"I want to take you somewhere this weekend," he tells me, his velvet voice making my insides melt and then twist. I'd go anywhere with him.

"I have classes to teach on Saturday."

"It'll be on Sunday."

"Where do you want to go?"

"I want you to meet my family. We used to have Sunday dinners every week without fail while I was growing up. But five years ago, my father and uncle were killed —Vinny's dad— which meant my brothers, cousins, and I had more responsibilities to take on and we let our tradition slip away."

"Oh, Alec, I'm so sorry."

"Thank you, *bella*," he says sincerely, a reflective look in his eyes. "It's a part of the life we live."

Stunned, my mind is suddenly filled with the image of

Alec lying dead on the sidewalk at my feet with bullet holes in his chest that won't stop bleeding. I try and help him, but I can't. There's nothing I can do, and I watch as he dies in my arms.

Clearing my throat, I look down at my lap and twist my napkin in my fingers.

"That won't happen to me, Tessa," he says, and my eyes flit up to his, seeing something in his that makes me want to cry. I can't imagine this strong man in front of me ever rendered weak by death.

"How do you know?" I whisper.

"Because I'd never leave you," he says simply, as if it's a fact I should already know. "My family takes greater precautions now that ensures we all stay alive and well."

"You better." I nod, sipping my wine, and the corners of his lips turn up slightly at my concern for him. He has to know I never want to see him harmed.

"Only maybe a few times a year now do we get together – my brothers and sister, mother, cousins, uncles, aunts," he continues, talking about this weekend. "There's a lot of us, and this Sunday we're gathering at my mother's place on Staten Island."

"Oh," I breathe, completely surprised. "So, you want me to meet your entire family?"

"You've already met Leo, Vinny, and Katarina."

"I know, but…"

"If you don't want to, then we can do something else," he says with a little edge, and I have to quickly recover.

"No, Alec. I want to. I'm just surprised and nervous. I've never met someone's family before," I confess softly, playing with the napkin on my lap.

"You've also never had a cock inside of you before me. But you ended up loving it."

I can't hide the smile that overtakes my face. "Are you seriously comparing the two?"

He lifts his shoulder in a shrug, his eyes dancing with the memories of all the times and ways he's had his cock inside of me. "I'll protect you from them."

My eyes widen. "Do I need protecting from them?"

"They're nosey. Especially the women in my family."

"I can handle my own," I tell him, raising my chin.

"I know you can, *mia bella rosa.*"

"Alright then, as long as you know." I smirk, sipping my wine. "I'd be honored to meet your family."

Alec looks at me for a long moment, his rough edges softening for the slightest of time to show me how much he liked hearing me say that.

We order dinner, and I eat my shrimp scampi like my life depended on it. "That was the most delicious thing I've ever eaten," I tell him, pushing my plate away. "Except for that one other thing," I add, rimming the edge of my wine glass with my nail. Alec pauses mid-air as he was bringing his own glass to his lips. "I'm full, but I always have room for dessert."

His eyes flare with unfiltered heat. Downing his wine, Alec stands, holding his hand out for me to take. He pulls me in close to whisper in my ear, "I'll fill you up, *bella.*" His raspy voice sends electric waves down my spine and I lean into him, my legs suddenly feeling unsteady.

Wrapping his arm possessively around my waist, Alec guides me out of the restaurant. We walk around the outer perimeter of the casino, and when we reach a gold door, he places his hand on a scanner, punches in a keycode, and has his eye scanned before it unlocks.

I step through before him and the lights turn on from motion sensors, illuminating a short hallway with one black door to the left, and another straight ahead at the end. Heading for that one, Alec scans his hand and punches in another passcode.

Stepping through this door first as well, Alec turns the lights on behind me, and I smile to myself. His office here is just as I'd expect. A dark mahogany desk greets me with a brown wingback leather chair suitable for a king behind it. Bookshelves line the wall, where old leatherbound books with gold embossed designs call out to me to inspect closer.

Two brown leather chairs sit in front of the desk for guests, a drink cart off to the side holds an assortment of liquors, crystal glasses, and a cigar humidor, and then lining the wall next to me are rows of flatscreen TVs that I'm sure are used for security.

I know exactly what he wants, so I spin around and place my palms flat on his chest. "Go sit in your chair," I tell him, and his eyes darken.

I give him a little push when he doesn't move at first, and then close his office door. Taking a deep breath, I feel the wine buzzing in my blood, and I use that to slip into the bold Tessa he loves to watch on stage.

Turning to face Alec, I lock eyes with him as he sits back in his chair like the ruler he is. He angled the chair to the side for easier access, and with slow, deliberate steps, I walk towards the only man capable of bringing me to my knees.

When I round the desk, my eyes drop to the bulge in his pants and my core clenches, wanting him inside of me. But this isn't for or about me. This is for Alec. I want him to come to work every day and picture me here on my knees as I take him deep into my mouth. He'll hear my moans as I lick his entire length and suck on the tip like a lollipop I want to savor.

"Are you just going to stare, *bella*? Or are you going to get your dessert?" My eyes flash back up to his and I take another step closer, my tongue peeking out to lick my bottom lip.

Alec widens his legs and rubs his jaw, his eyes slits as they assess me like a prize he just won. He holds his hand out to me and I close the distance between us, his large hand encasing mine in a cage of warmth and security.

His eyes never leave mine as I kneel before him, his hand keeping a tight hold on mine.

Only when I'm between his legs does he let go, and I slide my hands up his thighs, gripping his hard length through his suit pants. Grunting, Alec looks down at me through hooded eyes.

He keeps his hands on the armrests of the chair, letting me do all the work. I undo his belt and slip the button free, sliding the zipper down slowly. I savor this moment. I may be the one on my knees, but he's the one who needs me to take care of him.

Reaching inside of his pants, I free him from the confines of the expensive fabric, and Alec groans at my touch. I scoot as close to him as I can and look him in the eyes as I slide my hand down the length of him, tightening my fist when I reach the base. Keeping it there, I lean forward ever so slowly, breaking eye contact only when I'm staring down the barrel of the gun that has more than enough power to kill me when inside of me – driving me way past my limit on emotions and sensations.

Inhaling his masculine scent, I slide my tongue under his swollen crown that's begging for attention, and then down his entire underside, following the vein that's bulging from his tight, smooth skin.

Alec stiffens under me and I know he's holding back from touching me. He wants me to stay in the lead. And for that, I feel a rush of power.

Tightening my fist, I flatten my tongue and lick my way back up, rimming his head and sliding it between the slit at the tip. Alec's hips jerk towards me with a sexy grunt that fuels my need to make him fall apart because of me. Just me.

Sucking his entire swollen mushroomed head into my mouth, I let it pop from between my lips and look up at him before opening my mouth as wide as I can, taking as much of him as I can at once.

"Fuck," Alec groans, his hands tightening on the armrests, the leather creaking beneath his fingers.

I slide one hand under his crisp white dress shirt to feel his taut skin across his muscles as they flex into my touch. Tightening my fist at the base of his thick cock, I can barely get my hand all the way around him.

Working in tandem, I go down on him as far as I can with my fist moving up to meet me the rest of the way.

I relax my jaw and take him even deeper, and when he bumps the back of my throat, he grunts, and I pick up my rhythm.

Bobbing up and down, the leather creaks again as his grip tightens on the armrest beside my head. I feel him swell inside of my mouth and I moan around him, making Alec groan at my vibrations. I tighten my lips and suck as hard as I can on my way back up his length.

I know he's close.

Picking up the pace, I feel him harden and lengthen further until he can't hold back any longer when I tighten and twist my hand around his cock, swallowing him down my throat as far as I can take him.

Alec groans out long and low as hot spurts of come shoot down my throat, filling me with his seed. He tastes like a man – musky, spicy, powerful. I just took a little of his power, and I can feel it running through me as a new part of my soul – a piece of him in me.

Licking him clean so I get every last drop that I earned, I rest my hands on his thighs and look up at him. His eyes are hooded and his jaw is tight.

He reaches out and grips my chin between his thumb and forefinger. "Are you full now, *bella*? Did I taste better than your meal?" His low, hypnotic voice mixed with the taste of him on my tongue has me reeling.

"Yes, and yes."

"Come here. Let me take care of you now," he says, holding his hand out for me to take.

On my feet, Alec grips the hem of my dress and lifts it above my ass before laying me out on his desk and making good on his promise to take care of me. More than once.

CHAPTER 25
Tessa

Sleeping in, I wake up alone, but I curl into Alec's pillow and inhale his manly scent.

I never knew a man could, or would, be so relentless in his desire for me. It's like Alec can't sleep until he's wrung me out and we both pass out entangled together. I'm not complaining, though. I never would. Because when I'm so tired and laying across his chest, it's in that moment I can feel his steady, thumping heartbeat beneath my cheek and it makes me feel closer to him.

It can be easy to get wrapped up in seeing him as more than a man and capable of things that regular men never could be. But when I'm lulled to sleep by the sound of his heartbeat, I'm reminded that he's real. He's capable of so much more, but he's also a man capable of feeling more than just death and vengeance.

I'm so in love with him, I don't even think the word love is enough to encapsulate how I feel. I don't think any single word can. But love is the only one that comes close to describing the all-consuming burning blaze that lives inside of my heart, soul, and body just for him.

Who he is to everyone else doesn't matter. It's who he is with me that I'll only ever judge him on. He's just Alec to me. *My Alec.*

Slipping on a robe, I head into the kitchen and make myself a cup of coffee. I bring a dining room chair over to the windows and enjoy my coffee with a view.

The mid-morning sun glints off the breaks in the ocean as waves crash against the shore. I've always loved the ocean. There's something so mysterious about it that makes me feel like I can sit and stare at it all day.

There's a whole world beneath the surface – vast, deep, delicate, and intricate. The life of one species is always dependent on the life of another. They feed each other, from the bottom of the food chain to the top. Each serves a purpose and an important role.

But from here, looking at the ocean from the top floor of the tallest building in the city, all I see is a slate of blue. All of that life isn't visible until you dive in and explore. It's like people in that way. You can look at a person and see their beauty, or the beauty they want you to see, but you have to dive beneath their surface to see who they really are. That's when you discover how intricate the makeup of a single person is and why they are who they are. Everything they've done, seen, experienced, and stand for, make up who they are and make them unique and different from anyone else.

I can't even pretend to know everything that lies beneath Alec's surface, but I want nothing more than to have the time to discover as much as I can.

"Tessa," a voice says behind me, startling me from my thoughts. Turning my head, I see Vinny standing by the door.

"Hey, Vinny. I didn't hear you come in. Alec isn't here if you're looking for him."

"He didn't come back here?" he asks, his brows coming together.

"No. Should he have? Is he okay?"

His features smooth out, showing no emotion. "Yeah, everything's fine. I just needed to go over something else with him that I didn't get to this morning."

"If he comes back, I'll tell him to call you."

"Thanks, Tessa." He nods, then adds, "How are you doing?"

I give him a small smile. "I'm good. Thanks for asking."

"If you ever need anything and Alec isn't around, I'm here."

"Okay. Thanks, Vinny." The way he said that was a little odd, like he's hiding something, but I'm sure he's just being nice.

After he leaves, I put my mug in the sink and go and take a shower. I have a class to teach in an hour.

I'm exhausted. Teaching classes after barely getting any sleep from Alec's relentless need for me has me going straight for a hot shower and changing into something simple and comfortable when I get back to his house.

I relax on the couch and watch a little TV for a few hours until my stomach growls. I haven't heard from Alec all day, but he's probably just been busy, so I decide to root around his cabinets and fridge, finding everything I need to make creamy tomato and basil chicken over linguini with a side of homemade garlic bread.

I taught myself how to cook when it was just my brother and I. He was hopeless in the kitchen, and with him working all the time and us on a tight budget, I had to find ways to get creative. I learned to make what was simple taste extraordinary.

When I have everything made, I check my phone and still see nothing from Alec. I don't want to bother him while he's working, so I send him a simple text just telling him I have a surprise for him and to come home soon. But when an hour passes and I still haven't heard from him, I'm beyond starving and decide to not wait any longer. I make myself a plate and eat alone on the couch while I watch an episode of a mindless reality TV show.

Another hour passes, and I'm starting to not be able to keep my eyes open, so I clean the kitchen up and put all the dishes in the dishwasher and the leftovers in the fridge. I leave Alec a note on the counter for when he gets home, telling him to check the fridge if he's hungry, and then head off to bed.

Moaning, my eyes pop open and I grip the sheets in my

fists. Looking down, I can see the shadowed outline of Alec between my legs from the moonlight glowing in from the windows. His tongue is doing magical things to me while I try and decipher if this is a dream or not.

"Alec," I croak, lifting my hips to him. Holding me down, he swirls his tongue around my clit and then presses it down flat as he slides a single finger inside of me. That's all it takes. My mouth falls open as my throat closes around a strangled cry.

Alec crawls up my body and slides right inside of me as he kisses me deep. I'm still in a dream-like state after being woken up in the best possible way, but his kiss feels different. More urgent and filled with a deep need to tell me something without words. But I don't know what that is. I just know he needs this right now and I'm all too willing to give him anything he wants.

He moves inside of me like he's savoring me. He doesn't take me hard and fast like he's chasing off his demons. No, this is different too. It's so unlike him, but deliciously good all the same, and I don't have the brain capacity to analyze it further while he's inside of me.

Picking up his pace, Alec lifts my hands above my head in his and kisses his way down my throat, sucking on my nipples through the silken fabric of my camisole. Moaning, I meet his every thrust with my own, needing him to give me more. I always need more from him.

Alec looks down at me, and in the faint glow of light that reflects off his eyes, I see something in them that scares me. But when he realizes I can see him, he kisses me hard, and I lose all sense of thought.

The pressure builds in me, and when Alec bites down on

my bottom lip, I explode, that bite of pain the tipping point.

Groaning into me, the vibrations travel through my veins and make my inner muscles pulse around him continuously until I have nothing left to give him.

Alec collapses next to me, pulling me against him. I don't say anything, and neither does he. It's just our uneven breaths as we come down from the high and the leveling of our combined heartbeats to fill the silence of the middle of the night.

As my eyes grow heavy again, I'm struck with what this felt like and why I couldn't decipher it in the moment.

I saw regret in his eyes and felt goodbye in his touch.

CHAPTER 26
Tessa

Alec has been avoiding me. I don't know what happened, but something is off. He leaves every morning before I wake up and comes home long after I've gone to bed. Sure, he wakes me up with his hot mouth on my core, or the quick invasion of his cock, but I haven't talked to him for days.

I would never complain about having him like that, but I haven't looked him in his eyes unless it's his in the dark as he takes me. I haven't heard his voice unless it's to command me to come. And I haven't felt his touch unless it's his rough grip on my hips as he pounds into me.

I don't know if I'm reading too much into it, but it feels

like he's pushing me away.

Tonight, though, we're going to his mother's for dinner, and because of how he's been avoiding me, my nerves have been amplified. I don't know what to expect from him.

Do they know I'm coming? How will he introduce me to everyone? Will he hold my hand? Will he act like this week never happened and everything is just fine?

I dress in a flowy navy blue maxi skirt with a slit on one side that goes up to my knee, and tuck in a white short-sleeved top that has little knot ties on the sleeves. Adding a long, blue crystal tasseled necklace and a pair of nude wedges, I curl my hair in loose waves and apply my makeup.

I want to make a good first impression on his family, especially his mother, but I don't want it to look like I'm trying too hard or wear clothes that are too fancy so they think I'm with Alec for his money. I'm just going as me.

Unless I'm expected to wear something fancy?

Mild panic starts to set in, so I quickly gather my purse and head out to the living room to see if Alec is here.

I wouldn't be this nervous if he would've talked to me and maybe given me some direction as to what to expect. But nope, I'm flying blind on this.

"Hey, Tessa," Vinny greets, standing from the couch. "You look beautiful."

"Thank you." I smile. "Is this okay for a family dinner? I've never done this before, but Alec's always in a suit, so am I supposed to wear a nice dress, maybe?"

Laughing, he shakes his head. "You look perfect. Don't worry, Anita will like you."

"Anita?"

"Alec's mom," he says, and I immediately feel dumb.

"Alec hasn't exactly told me anything about her, or what to expect tonight."

"You'll be fine. Just be yourself."

I take a deep breath and let it out in a rush. "Alright." I nod. "How much longer will Alec be?"

"Oh." He frowns. "Did he not tell you?"

"What?"

"He's meeting us there. He had to go into the city this afternoon to talk with Leo and Luca."

"No, he didn't tell me. We haven't really talked in a few days," I tell him reluctantly. "Is he okay? Is something going on? I know you can't tell me much, if anything, but…"

"He's fine," Vinny says quickly. "He's had a lot of work lately."

Yeah, that sounds like a bullshit answer, but I'm not about to tell him that. "Alright, so it's just us?"

"Yeah, and we better get going if we want to be on time."

Heading down to the private garage, Vinny guides me over to a sleek red Mercedes.

"I like this one." I smile, running my finger along the hood. "What is it?"

"It's a Mercedes AMG GT Coupe." Vinny's chest puffs out with pride. Oh, boys and their cars.

"Let's see how fast she can go."

"Get in, gorgeous, and I'll show you."

A little giddy, I slide in and buckle up. The engine rumbles to life and I feel the vibrations in my blood. Vinny takes the streets inside Atlantic City easy, but then opens her up on the Parkway, weaving in and out of cars as we blur by them.

Laughing, I turn and see Vinny with a smile on his face that matches my own. I haven't had a real reason to smile this week. First, Enzo, then Alec. But this? This is fun.

He lets off the pedal after a few minutes and we drive in a comfortable silence for the rest of the way as I tap my fingers to the music playing.

When we cross the Goethals Bridge onto Staten Island, I keep my eyes trained out the window, and Vinny lowers the music when we turn off of the highway. "This is Todt Hill," he says, and my eyes bug out at the massive mansions we pass.

Pulling up to a gate, Vinny rolls down the window and punches a code in a black box, allowing the iron gate to creak open. My mouth hangs open at the beautiful house taking up more than the windshield will allow me to see.

"Our grandfather bought this house out here for our nonna when she got tired of the city."

"I…" I croak, my palms starting to sweat. A massive white stone house that has two large columns on either side of the front door stands before me. There are second floor balconies lining the front of the house that are held up by a set of columns, creating overhangs for porches that line the entire first floor.

A fountain sits in the middle of a circular brick driveway, trees line the front wall of the property to partially hide the house from the street, and perfectly landscaped flowerbeds are everywhere I look.

This is more wealth than I've ever known, and I know the inside will be just as extravagant. I thought Alec's penthouse was the epitome of luxury…well this…this is more.

Vinny laughs at my reaction. "Don't worry, Tessa. It's just a house."

"That's not a house," I whisper.

"It is. Just like this is just a car. A fast car." He smirks. "But a car nonetheless. They're just things, Tessa."

Taking a deep breath, I close my eyes and nod. "Thank you."

"Anytime. I like you, Tessa. I think you're good for Alec. He needs a woman by his side to come home to. I, on the other hand"–he smiles–"have no need for just one woman."

A laugh bubbles up and out of me. "Maybe one day you'll think differently, Vin."

"I don't want to think differently," he scoffs, parking behind a fancy Audi on the circle drive. Checking his phone, he frowns. "They're stuck in traffic."

"So, it's just us again?"

"It'll be fine. Let's go in, I'm starving."

Climbing out of the car, Vinny loops my arm in his and walks me up the front stone steps. For some reason, I'm not totally buying the traffic excuse. Something's going on with Alec.

My eyes widen the moment we step inside the house, and I'm speechless. A massive chandelier hangs above us in the large foyer which is flanked by two curved stairways that lead to the second floor with a balcony overlooking the entire entryway.

Voices and laughter echo through the house, and Vinny walks me further inside. After walking down a short hallway, we turn the corner and stand in the large doorway to the dining room, and all the talking stops as every pair of eyes land on me.

Sitting around a table that looks to fit over twenty are seventeen of Alec's relatives, and I'm struck with panic at the anticipation of having to remember all their names.

"Hi, Tessa," Katarina greets with a warm smile.

"Hi, Kat." I smile back, thankful for her breaking the ice.

A beautiful woman at the head of the table stands and walks over to me. Vinny releases my arm as she takes my hand. "Hi, Tessa. I'm Anita, Alec's mother." Her smile is genuine, but her eyes hold a cautious wariness.

"Hi, Mrs. Carfano. It's a pleasure to meet you."

"Come sit." She waves her hand at an empty seat and then addresses Vinny. "Vincenzo, where are my sons? Or have you decided to take Tessa for yourself?"

"As tempting as that is"–he winks at me–"they're just stuck in traffic."

Mrs. Carfano waves her hand in the air dismissively. "Oh, excuses. Well, we'll just have to get to know Tessa while we wait."

Damn it. I'm going to fucking slap Alec for doing this to me.

"What do you do, Tessa? I'm Gia, and this is my sister Aria. Alec's cousins." Wow, twins. And they're gorgeous. Perfect skin, hair, smiles, and eyes that are this honey brown that I'm sure have drawn in every man they've met. Women, too.

"I teach dance at a studio in town, but I also dance in the Friday night show at The Aces."

Their eyes widen at that, and I'm worried for a second that maybe I shouldn't have told them that? But then again, Vinny told me to be myself, and I don't want to lie to his family. I'm also not ashamed or embarrassed.

"Wow, that's amazing," Gia says with a smile.

"I love it." I smile shyly, my eyes flitting around to everyone.

"I'm Vinny's brother, Nico." A handsome man who looks similar to Vinny stands and shakes my hand. "I work with Leo. Vin likes Jersey more than I do," he jokes, slapping his brother on the back.

"And I'm Mia, his sister." She smiles sweetly.

"Hi." I smile back.

Vinny points at three men who look like Italian models who came straight from an Armani photoshoot. What is it with this family? Everyone is beautiful. "This is Stefano, Marco, and Gabriel," he says, and they nod their hellos, their eyes perusing me as if I were a threat to them.

"Of course he leaves me as the last cousin to introduce," another beautiful woman says, smiling. "I'm Elena."

"Hi." I smile, and Vinny proceeds to finish off the introductions to all of Alec's aunts and uncles, including his own mother, Teresa. Her husband is Alec's uncle that was killed along with his father a few years ago. She and Anita are the only ones on their own and they both share a loneliness in their eyes. I should know. I saw the same look in my eyes every time I looked in the mirror. Until Alec.

Taking a seat next to Katarina, she pours me a glass of wine, and after finishing it, I'm finally able to relax and join in the conversations around me. I discover Mia just graduated high school and isn't sure what she wants to study at University in the fall yet. Gia and her sister Aria are nineteen and models with an agency in Manhattan, but they have bigger dreams of starting their own fashion line one day. Elena is seventeen and everyone calls her the princess of the family because she's the daughter of the only daughter born to Alec's grandparents. The princess of the princess, they say.

Elena has an older brother, Matteo, who works in Miami with Gia and Aria's brother, Saverio. The two of them run a club there, and while Gia and Aria are in the middle of inviting me to join the two of them and Katarina on a trip they're taking there in a couple of months, Alec walks in with his brothers.

"She's not going anywhere with you," he states sternly, his eyes hard.

"Why not?" Gia counters, raising her chin. I like her even more now that I see she's not one to back down from an angry Alec.

"Because I said so."

"Real original, Alec," she says, rolling her eyes.

Alec locks eyes with me and walks over. Placing his hands on my shoulders, he leans down and kisses my cheek. "Hi, *bella*."

At the sound of his smooth voice in my ear, I close my eyes and lean back against him. I haven't heard him call me that in days.

"Hi," I whisper.

He takes the seat next to me and pours himself a glass of wine.

"It's good to finally meet you, Tessa. I'm Luca." He sounds sincere, but his eyes are showing all the skepticism he's not willing to display outwardly in front of Alec.

"Good to meet you, too." I know his family is probably wary of anyone new. None of Alec's cousins have a significant other with them, making it seem like he's the first to ever bring someone here.

That makes me feel slightly better, and gives me hope that whatever is going on with Alec is fleeting and we'll move past it. He wouldn't have still had me come tonight if he was going to end this between us. Meeting his family is too important.

Dinner goes smoothly. I love listening to everyone talk to one another. I've never experienced such a large family gathering like this, and it's not even a special occasion or anything. It's just a Sunday dinner, but to them, it's important to have everyone gather together.

I help clear the table with Alec's mother and aunts, and while they plate the dessert, I start placing the leftovers in containers. While dessert is brought out to everyone, Alec's mom stays behind with me.

"So, Tessa," she starts, turning to face me. "My son seems to be very taken with you."

"Oh, well, yes," I say dumbly, unsure of how to respond to that.

"He's never brought a woman home before. None of my boys have."

Snapping the lid in place on the container of pasta, I take a deep breath and turn to look her in the eyes. "I'm honored he asked me to meet all of you. I know family is important to him."

"It is." Her eyes hold mine. "My family is all I have."

"I understand," I tell her.

She tilts her head slightly. "Do you? Being with Alec is more than just what he can give you."

"I'm sorry, I don't know what you mean." Is she insinuating what I think she is?

"Of course you do," she huffs. "You're not unintelligent.

I also know my son can be distracted easily by a beautiful young woman who dances for a living." She sneers the word 'dances' like it's a dirty job. "Being with him requires more than the ability to be flexible."

Shocked, my eyes widen as I struggle to find the right words to say so I'm not disrespectful.

"Mother," Leo says harshly from the entryway. "That's enough. You know Alec wouldn't like you talking to his woman like that."

"It's okay, Leo. Thank you, though," I say, finally finding my voice. "Mrs. Carfano, I'm not with Alec because he can give me anything other than himself. He knows that. I also know who he is and it doesn't scare me. And yes, I'm a dancer. It's my passion. I wouldn't give it up for anything, and Alec also knows that. He sees me, and I see him."

She just stares at me, assessing me, and when I flit my eyes to Leo, I see respect shining back at me in his.

"I see," Mrs. Carfano says, the same look of respect in her eyes as Leo has in his. "Well, if my sons and nephew are so taken with you, I guess I should get to know you better."

"I'd like that."

"Good." She nods, leaving me alone with Leo as she walks back out to the dining room.

I breathe a sigh of relief and sag against the counter.

"You did good, Tessa," Leo praises. "She was testing you, but you stood your ground, and that's what she respects."

Nodding once, I play with the ring I always wear on my middle finger. It was my mother's, and it brings me comfort to touch it whenever I'm feeling vulnerable. His mom may have been testing me, but she also insinuated that I was a whore who lured her son in with my body so he could buy me things.

"Tessa—" Leo says, but I cut him off.

"It's fine. I'm fine. I just need a minute. Where's the bathroom?"

"Down the hall and to the right."

"Thanks." Turning on my heel, I make a beeline out of the kitchen, but the house is so big, I picked the wrong direction and don't find the bathroom in any of the doors I pass.

I go to turn back, but hear Alec and Vinny's hushed voices yelling at one another angrily from the next door down the hall. I approach slowly.

"Are you going to avoid telling her forever? She asked me if something was wrong with you tonight and I had to lie to cover your ass," Vinny says. "And you had me introduce her to the family? That's bullshit, Alec. You should've been here."

"Don't fucking tell me how to handle this."

"I will, because you're *not* handling it. Grow a pair and tell her. Let her decide your fate. Or are you too chickenshit to find out how she'll react?"

I hear scuffling of feet and rustling of clothes. What are they talking about? What hasn't Alec told me?

"Stay out of this," Alec growls, angrier than I've ever heard him. "Tessa isn't your concern."

When I hear footsteps getting closer to the cracked door I've been standing near, I duck into the room across the hall and hide. Looking through the crack in the door, I wait for the two of them to leave and go back to the dining room before sneaking out to find the bathroom. I lock myself inside for five minutes, needing to get my shaking hands under control.

Alec's been hiding something from me that is clearly going to upset me or Vinny wouldn't be arguing with him on why he hasn't told me.

I can't bring it up here. Not at his mom's house, and certainly not in the presence of almost his entire family. Washing my hands, I take a deep breath and steel my spine before returning to the table. I feel Alec's eyes on me as I take the seat next to him, but I ignore him. If I look at him, I know I'll want to ask him all the questions I have swimming in my head, so I keep my eyes on either my dessert or the other women around the table.

I know he can sense a change in me, but he, too, doesn't dare bring it up now.

When we say our goodbyes, I get hugs from all the women, but his mother just nods respectfully at me. As do the men around the table who are all so serious. They have an edge to them that would make me quiver if I met them under different circumstances. But I think I'm starting to get used to these Carfano men and their constant stern demeanors.

Alec guides me over to a sleek Aston Martin at the back of the car line taking up the entire driveway. He must have driven separately from his brothers from Manhattan since they get into a Mercedes in front of us.

Opening the passenger door for me, I feel his eyes on me as I slide inside, but he doesn't say anything. He also doesn't say anything for most of the ride back to Atlantic City. Neither one of us is willing to breach the subject of his absence and distance this week, I guess.

But when we turn off of the Parkway, I know I have to

ask him while we're still in the car. He can't avoid me or walk away if he's driving. Turning down the music, I look over at him. "Alec, I have to ask you something."

"What is it?" His voice is strained and his hands tighten around the steering wheel.

"What's been going on with you this week?"

"Nothing."

"Don't lie to me," I say, a little more harshly than I intended. "You've been avoiding me, and I want to know why. I heard you with Vinny earlier. What aren't you telling me?"

"You were eavesdropping again?" he asks darkly, the air in the small space suddenly feeling thick.

"I was looking for the bathroom and turned the wrong way. But that's not the point. You're keeping something from me, something big, and I need to know what it is. I can't keep pretending everything is fine. These past few days have been…" I trail off, not wanting to tell him just how much I've missed him, and how I thought every time he came to me in the night it might be the last.

I feel like I'm on a rollercoaster with him and right now we're at the top of a hill. Either we have the momentum to get over the peak and free fall down this ride together, or we get pushed backwards and have to start all over again.

"Have been what?" he urges.

"Just tell me," I whisper, the fight leaving me.

He takes a moment, and just when I think he's going to be silent for the rest of the drive, he says, "I had Stefano, my cousin you just met, look into your brother's death." My heart immediately starts to race. That's not what I was expecting him to say, and I have to remind myself to breathe.

Rubbing his jaw, Alec white knuckle grips the steering wheel. "It was my fault," he says in a detached voice.

I don't think I hear him correctly, but when it sinks in, my ears start to ring as my blood rushes, making me dizzy. "What did you just say?" I whisper, my words barely audible.

"It's my fault. I told my uncle to order the hit on your brother."

My heart twists in my chest. I don't understand what he's saying. How would my brother and Alec even have crossed paths?

"Why?" I choke out, wrapping my arms around my waist, making myself as small as possible.

"I had my reasons," he says coldly, and my blood burns.

"What reasons?" I demand. "Why would you even know who he is?" Alec stays silent, and I yell, "Tell me!"

"He was pushing drugs through all the casinos in town before coming to The Aces. He didn't listen to reason when we asked him to stop, so I made the call."

Drugs?

"Stop lying," I croak, the backs of my eyes stinging. "James didn't deal drugs. He worked construction and as a pit boss in a couple casinos."

"I'm not lying, Tessa. I would never lie to you, and I especially wouldn't lie about this when it means I'm telling you I'm the reason your brother is dead."

"Alec." I choke on his name, and it suddenly feels like acid rolling off my tongue.

"I couldn't have that shit in my casino or the others around town. It would bring too much heat on us. If it wasn't me, one of the gangs in town would've caught up to him. He was taking business away from them by delivering the product right inside the casinos instead of the streets."

"Shut up. Just shut up," I beg, shaking my head. This can't be real.

"I did what I had to do at the time."

"SHUT THE FUCK UP!" I scream, my throat raw. I don't want to hear it – any of it. "Take me home. We're done."

"No."

"No?" I say through a harsh, humorless laugh. "You don't get to decide these things. You killed my brother." Tears start to spill from my eyes and I swipe at them furiously. "I'm alone because of you."

"I didn't kill him," he says through clenched teeth. "And you're not alone anymore."

"You might as well have. And I am alone. Because of you. You took away the only family I had left. And why? Because of your fucking business," I spit, hating, for the first time, that he's not normal.

Alec doesn't say anything in response, he just puts his foot down a little harder on the gas.

I know why he's been avoiding me now. Why he's only come to me at night and fucked me until I fell asleep again. Because he knew it would be his last chance. At least I was partially right to his motives.

Alec doesn't take me back to my apartment, but instead pulls right into The Aces parking garage.

"I'm not staying here with you."

"Yes, you are. Get out of the car."

I know he's not going to take me home, but there is a stairwell just around the bend about forty feet away that will eventually lead me to the casino where I can get lost in the crowd of people. Thinking over the quick moves I have to make before he has the chance to catch me, I climb out of the car and make a break for it.

I'm not thinking of anything besides getting as far away as I can right now.

But all too soon, I hear Alec cursing behind me and his footsteps getting louder as he catches up to me. The wedges on my feet aren't helping my cause.

"What the fuck do you think you're doing?" he growls, grabbing me by the arm and swinging me around to face him. "You can't just run away from me." Alec steps closer so we're practically touching, our chests coming within a few millimeters of the other with each labored breath.

Gripping my chin with his other hand, he lifts my face to his. I defiantly meet his dark, hardened eyes that are flaring with anger.

"You don't get to run away from me. *You're mine.* I don't give up what's mine."

"I'm not yours. Not anymore."

"That's where you're wrong. You'll always be mine. You just need time to see that."

"No, I–" I'm cut off from my retort when the air in my lungs is pushed out in a single breath. Alec hoists me over his shoulder and marches me over to the elevator.

Pounding at his back with my fists, he holds my legs steady to keep me from kicking him.

When the doors close, he lets me fall to me feet, but then pins me against the wall with his larger frame so I still can't escape him. I can feel every inch of him against every inch of me, and while I want to punch him in his overly handsome face and make him pay for what he did to my brother, my body still lights up for him.

It has a life of its own whenever I'm near Alec, and for a moment, I almost let myself give in.

But then the doors slide open to his short hallway, breaking the spell.

"You have nowhere to run, Tessa," he says, stepping back.

I know he's right. I have nowhere to run to. At least, tonight I have nowhere to run. But come tomorrow, or the next day, I'll find a way to leave this fortress.

Alec holds the elevator door open for me as I come to the conclusion he already knows. I walk past him, and he follows, staying close. When he opens the front door for me, I immediately head straight for the guest room. He may have the strength to keep me here, but I'm not sleeping in the same bed as him.

Slamming the door behind me, I turn the lock on the handle, and everything that just happened in the past half hour comes rushing at me full-force.

I sink to the floor. I can't feel my legs anymore. I can't feel anything anymore.

Tears fall down my face in rivers of shame and disdain while my heart squeezes in my chest to the point where I think it'll burst.

I've never felt this...this...burning pain where it feels like my chest is on fire – spreading slowly through my body to where everything goes from numb to intense pain.

Sitting with my back against the door, I wrap my arms around my knees and let myself go. I let out everything, grieving for everything we could have been.

I fell for Alec hard and fast, and he just broke my heart

in the same way.

He has so many secrets hidden beneath layers of lies and more secrets.

I'm so stupid. So fucking stupid for falling for him and thinking that we could even be something.

But Alec Carfano isn't a man you just fall in love with. It's more than that. He was a wildfire that took over every aspect of my being and my life until every thought, every feeling, and everything was him.

It's a fire that's still burning inside of me, only now that burning is restricted to my chest and my heart that seems like it may give out on me any second now.

CHAPTER 27
Tessa

It's been a week, and I still feel like my heart has been punched out and replaced with an empty hole.

I haven't been able to leave this room or bed. I called out of all my dance classes, show rehearsals, and even the Friday show itself, which surprised and disappointed Dan. But he knew I wouldn't do so without reason.

I need to leave this penthouse, though. I need to get back to my life.

Alec hasn't come to me. Not once this week. After he told me he's the one who put the hit out on James and locked me in his home, I expected him to try and...I don't know what...but something.

I've only left my room when I knew he had left for work, and even then, Tito was sitting in the living room, making sure I didn't try to escape. I don't even have the energy to escape, truthfully. I've only had enough energy to shower and walk to the kitchen for food and water when I've needed it.

Everything I've known is a lie, and I don't know how to process it all.

I thought James was the best man I knew. But now I learn he was a drug dealer, and that's the reason he was shot in the street like a dog. Because someone thought of him as one. Alec and his family thought of him as one.

I know I didn't see him much the last few years of his life with how busy he was, but I never thought...I never thought he'd stoop to that level to make money.

I remember one time I hadn't seen him for a few days, and when I finally did, it had looked like he had bruises on his face. But before I could get a good look, he locked himself in his room claiming he had an accident at the construction site and didn't want to talk about it, and I had to leave for dance class so I didn't press him further.

I spent six years trying to understand that day and trying to get the images out of my head of James lying on the cement covered in blood as I attempted to stop the bleeding. The few people milling about just looked on like nothing was happening. Like it was an everyday occurrence to see a man gunned down in front of them.

Oh, God, it was all because of me. James did all of that for me. He never would have had anything to do with drugs if it weren't because he felt it was his last resort.

Fresh tears start to fall down my face for what feels like

the millionth time this week.

I just want to leave. I need air. I need space. But I'm living under a microscope with Tito always just down the hall.

It makes me angry. Angry that Alec cares enough to have me monitored like I'm some possession he can control, but not enough to try and talk to me. I don't even know why I want him to try to, but I do, and I hate myself for it.

I miss him.

I hate him and I miss him. I'm so fucking crazy. Alec has me all twisted up, and my head, heart, and body are all waging a war against one another.

I'm in love with the man responsible for my brother's death.

I'm in so deep with him that even though I know it's sick to want him after finding out the truth, I do. I can't help it. It's not even a choice for me.

Alec and I...we're more than anything life can try and use to separate us, and I hate myself even more for thinking that. Which is why I haven't left this room. I'm too afraid of what I'll do or say to him if I go to him. But he's obviously not missing me the way I am him if he can stay away like he has.

A burning sensation spreads across my chest. I thought he was as deep in this as I was.

I thought maybe...

I thought maybe he was as in love with me as I am him.

When he shot Enzo, I saw a side of Alec that I never had before. He was only letting me see what he thought I could handle before that point. But now I know the depth of his true nature, and as much as my head is telling me to just get in my car and go somewhere, anywhere far away, my heart is telling me that I'll never be able to outrun what I truly want.

I have so many emotions running through me that I need to get them out the only way I know how – dancing. I hadn't wanted to all week, but I know the only way I'll be able to sort through things is by doing the one thing that brings me absolute clarity.

CHAPTER 28
Alec

I scan The Aces VIP back room and shoot back the rest of my whiskey. Bringing my Cuban cigar to my lips, I take a few puffs, letting the smoke and liquor dull my senses.

For over a week now, I've felt nothing but numbness, with waves of anger and emptiness that hit me when I'm reminded of her.

My mind is filled with the memories of how Tessa's soft skin felt beneath my hands, the way her body moved when she danced just for me, and the sound of her soft moans and sighs that turned to wailing cries as I filled her with my aching cock that only wants her.

The memory of her sexy smile that tightens my chest,

her flowery scent that drives me wild, her sexy voice that makes me hard as steel in seconds, and the way she'd soften and submit to me when I needed her to, all have driven me to the brink of insanity every second of every day since I told her I'm the reason her brother is dead.

When we got back from my mother's, she locked herself in my spare bedroom and has only come out when I'm not there. I have Tito in my place watching her, making sure she doesn't try to escape, but I have to find a way to make her not want to run anywhere but towards me.

It's taken everything in me to give her any space at all, but I know she needs it to come to terms with the truth on her own.

The only way I've been able to stay away is to work all day until I can't keep my eyes open anymore, and then I drag myself up to bed to pass out for a few hours until the sun wakes me up again. I've taken on the work I usually delegate to three other people to keep me busy. Just knowing she's tucked away, safe and unable to run, is the only consolation I have.

I need her.

Tessa is my fucking queen.

She's deep in me. She shined her light into the darkest corners of my soul and gave me hope that I could have something so pure and beautiful all to myself. She lets me give her all of me. She takes my darkness and keeps it as her own, claiming the parts of me that no one's ever wanted before.

She's my perfect little rose, blooming only for me.

I need her to forgive me, and I'm not above keeping her locked away until she does. It would be simpler if she just came to the conclusion that she needs me as well herself, but even if she hates me the rest of her life, at least she'd hate me from the room next door.

Sipping on a fresh glass of whiskey, I look around the room at some of the wealthiest men in the country playing poker. Tonight's game is hosted by some billionaire CEO whose name I can't even remember. I only care about the millions I'm getting from these games.

More money is exchanged in a single night here than the whole casino sees in a week. And that's saying a lot considering The Aces is the most successful casino in town.

With these games, there's no questions as to where the money comes from, there's no recording the winnings for taxes, and there's no limits.

This is what the Triads are trying to establish for themselves in my city. But that's never going to fucking happen.

Vinny is sitting next to me at the bar, and when he opens his mouth, I already know it's going to be about Tessa. He spent two hours in the car with her, and now he thinks he has a right to weigh in on her well-being. "You need to either let her go or beg for her forgiveness."

"I don't beg. Ever," I tell him, despite contemplating begging her every day since I've gone without her.

He barks out a harsh laugh. "I know. Does that mean we're hitting Darkhorse later?"

Darkhorse is the strip club our family owns, and before Tessa, I would go there whenever I needed a warm and willing woman for a few hours, knowing they'd leave when I was done with them and not try and turn it into something more.

But now? The thought of being inside of anyone but Tessa isn't appealing.

"No. You can go, though."

"I think I will," he says. "I've been thinking about having Chelsea's tits in my face all day."

"Jesus, Vinny." I shake my head. "You know she has her tits in everyone's face."

"I know. Don't ruin it for me. And since when does that ever bother or stop you? If I remember correctly, her tits were in your face at one point."

"You have that memory wrong."

"I don't. But I'll let you think that since you're in a mood."

"Vinny," I warn, my eyes darting to his. "Not here."

"You can't keep her locked away in your penthouse. You'll only make her hate you more and she'll find a way out of there. Then she'll have a line of men waiting to sweep her off her feet and lick her wounds. Literally and figuratively."

My blood boils and I turn to face him fully. "Shut the fuck up, Vin," I grind out low, not wanting to draw any attention to us.

Standing, I snuff out the stub of my cigar and button my suit jacket. "I'm done here. You stay longer to make sure this shit goes smoothly. I'm going to go check in with all the pit bosses." Maybe there will be a card counter I can get my hands on. They're itching to inflict a little pain onto someone else.

As I walk past the men in the room, I know they know I'm there, but they don't dare look me in the eyes, too afraid of what they'll see.

Leaving the backroom through the hidden entrance, I

take the short hallway that leads to another hidden door panel that takes me out to a hallway around the corner from the main casino floor.

My uncle was big on discretion and creating rooms within rooms. Everyone who plays in these exclusive games has to be escorted in and out by a member of my security team as no one but myself and my men have access to the hidden doors.

There are cameras everywhere in my casino except inside these backrooms, and each one is equipped with signal jammers so no electronic or recording devices, as well as phones, will work. I'm just as cautious as my uncle Sal, if not more so.

Pulling out my phone now that I'm clear, I see five messages from Leo, and so instead of burning my anger off on some asshole trying to cheat me, I head to the basement to call him.

"The Triads have agreed to our meeting spot for Friday," he says right away.

"What changed their minds?"

"I don't know, but I can't spend the time questioning it. I'll have the men set up and in place on Thursday."

"I'll leave Friday morning and get to you by noon."

"How are things with–"

"Don't fucking go there, Leo," I say harshly.

Stefano and Vinny already knew, but after our dinner at my mother's, everyone else got the memo that our family was responsible for her brother's death, and more importantly, I was. After seeing me with her and seeing how fucking perfect she is for themselves, they've all offered their help in any way I need it to make it right.

"Just be ready for Friday," is all he says, and I hang up.

CHAPTER 29
Tessa

I went back to rehearsal on Wednesday, and started teaching classes again yesterday. It felt good to use my muscles again. For those few precious hours, I was able to use my pain and turn it into something beautiful.

Every night when I've laid in bed, I was left feeling alone and empty, thinking of nothing but having my body tangled up with Alec's. Then I would wake up after a fitful few hours of sleep and I would hate myself for feeling so weak.

I've never been so attached to someone before. Alec was the first man I let inside of me – the first man I *wanted* to let inside of me. He filled me so completely, physically and emotionally, that without him, I feel empty. Like a piece of me is missing.

But right now, tonight, I'm going to try and heal myself and take back a little of the control I've lost. I can't keep going the way I have been.

I have to find a way to survive.

I have to find a way to replace the empty with something else. And tonight, that's me dancing.

I look at myself in the mirror and dab my finger in the pot of silver glitter to add to my eyelids.

I want Alec to be at his table tonight. I want to see him. I want him to see me. For all this time that I've been avoiding him, the stage offers me the perfect distance to see him and know he'll stay there.

"Line up ladies!" Dan yells to us as we all put the finishing touches of our makeup on and make sure our heels are tied well.

When the stage lights hit my skin and I hear the start of our opening song, I plaster a smile on my face, determined to be in the moment. But when my position on stage brings me closer to where Alec's table is, I wait for the lights to dim on us girls on the outskirts and brighten on the three in the middle so I can see into the audience, and my stomach drops.

I can't believe he's not here. For almost two weeks, I've been held hostage in his home with a babysitter, and he hasn't even tried to come to me.

I want him to try and convince me to stay, not force me. I want him to give me a reason to listen to the voice inside of me that says I can't live without him. But his silence is speaking volumes.

Gritting my teeth, I lock my fake smile into place and finish out the routine.

When the show is over, I breathe a sigh of relief that I was even able to get through it, especially my solo. That song...that dance...it's Alec's. It took everything I had to push past the constant urge to break down and fall to a heap in the middle of the stage.

I sit at my station and stare at the hollow eyes looking back at me in the mirror, petting the soft petals of the black roses that were left for me. He's not here, but he still had flowers left for me. I don't understand him.

Lost in my head, I don't notice that Jess is beside me until she places her hand on my shoulder and I flinch, caught off guard. "You should come out with us tonight," she says.

"Yeah, you should," Kayla says beside her with a smile. "You never come out with us, so I think you're due. Plus, I think you could use the fun."

I don't ever go out with them because they've never asked me to...

"And the distraction," Jess adds. "Drinks, dancing, men...what else do you need to have fun?" She laughs.

My mind immediately goes to Alec, thinking about how he would react if he knew I was going to go out with these girls to have men all over me, vying to buy me a drink. But he's not here to try and stop me, and I don't really feel like going back up to that big, empty castle in the sky again so soon.

So, while I've never contemplated going clubbing, the idea holds some value now, and has me saying without thought, "I don't have anything to wear."

They both give me wide smiles. "We've got you covered, don't worry."

Jess runs off and comes back holding a little black dress

that I know will be skin tight, low-cut, and short. "I always carry a second option," she says with a wink. "And are you a 7 shoe?" She holds up a pair of strappy black heels.

"I am, thanks." Taking the dress and heels from her, I get to work on taking my show makeup off and reapplying it with a more subtle look. We all wear our hair in big curls for the show, so all I have to do is quickly go back over it with a curling wand.

Swiping my lips with a deep red lipstick, I blot them on a tissue and stare at myself in the mirror, willing myself to be okay and push down the doubts of what I'm about to do, knowing I'm doing it for the outcome. Alec will have to talk to me. When he finds out I've escaped his new guard dog, he'll use every resource he has to find me. And when he does, he'll be mad and yell, but he'll still have to face me. I'll finally get to see his eyes after going so long without them.

I know it's petty and weak of me, but I'm desperate.

"Ready?" Jess asks eagerly. "You look hot, girl!"

"Thanks. You guys look good, too."

"I need a drink and a hot man tonight!" Kayla announces, making Jess roll her eyes.

"You say that every time we go out."

"Well, it's true every time, bitch." She smirks, tossing her hair over her shoulder.

Standing, I hide my bag under my station and put my phone and small wallet in the clutch purse Jess is also loaning me, and we start to make our way over to the door that will lead us out into the main casino area and not the back hall where Tito is waiting for me.

I know he'll know something is up if I'm not out there within forty-five minutes of the show ending, so I have about a fifteen-minute window left before that happens.

Walking through the casino, my eyes sweep around to make sure no one recognizes me before I have a chance to even escape and put my plan into motion.

Slot machines ring and people cheer, chips clink together as bets are placed, cards slap together as they're shuffled and dealt, dice hit and tumble on felt, roulette wheels spin, and cigarette and cigar smoke puffs from the mouths of those who are either anxious because they're losing, or feeling confident in their skills to win.

The club in The Aces, Royals, has a long line for entrance, but Jess and Kayla walk straight to the front.

"We don't wait in line," Jess tells me. "The bouncer knows us. He loves our show." She winks.

"Oh." I didn't even realize we might be recognized.

"Hey, Santiago," Jess coos, placing her hand on the bouncer's arm.

"Hi, gorgeous." His gruff voice sounds like he swallowed a handful of stones after he smoked a pack of cigarettes. "Who's your friend?" He raises his chin to me.

"This is Tessa. She's in the show, too. Joined us about two months or so ago."

His eyes scan my body from head to toe, and they feel like clammy hands groping me. "I guess I'll have to catch another one soon, then," he says, and I force myself not to make a face that shows my disgust.

Unhooking the velvet rope, Santiago lets us through, and I feel his eyes on my ass as I walk.

The deep bass of music starts to pump through me with each step closer, and when we push past a heavy velvet curtain, the music hits me hard, and my eyes widen at the scene before me.

We're standing at the top of a staircase, looking down at a dancefloor packed with people – their bodies writhing and swaying with drunken abandon. I almost envy them. They're all just trying to escape for a night and get lost in someone who won't even remember their name in a few hours.

The DJ's booth is up on a platform and multicolored lights flash all around from every direction, making it impossible to get a good look at any one spot before your eyes are drawn someplace else.

Jess and Kayla descend the stairs like royals entering a ball while I trail behind them with a little less grandeur, concentrating more on not twisting an ankle in these heels.

Squeezing our way through the tightly packed bodies on the dancefloor, we make our way over to the bar, with the groups of men surrounding it parting for us with ease, all asking if they can buy us our first round.

Jess and Kayla smile and keep saying, "Maybe next time."

"Watch your drinks, Tessa," Jess says to me. "You never know what these guys might put in them."

I nod, and she orders for us, handing me a drink that I quickly take a sip of, needing it to calm my nerves. I feel vastly out of my element here.

"Come on, let's dance!" Kayla yells excitedly, dragging me out into the middle of the sea of people.

Sucking down my drink, I let my body sway to the beat, feeling more comfortable by the second.

By now, Tito has to have realized I'm not in the theater anymore, and probably sounded the alarms. Good.

"Here you go!" Jess yells, handing me another drink. "I

think you're one more away from forgetting that man."

"I think so!" I yell back, hoping she's right. "Wait! How did you know?"

Her eyes widen. "Oh, well, it's obvious!" she yells, laughing. "I know the look of man troubles a mile away! Plus, we all saw what happened at that party we worked!" she adds, and I flinch. Oh, right. Of course. "Just dance, Tessa! Have a little fun!"

Taking a long sip from my new drink, I laugh at Kayla a few feet from me as she circles a very good-looking man like he's her prey. Men have tried to dance with me, but I've skirted out of their grasp every time with sly twists of my hips and torso, content to just dance on my own.

A few songs later, I really start to feel the alcohol take effect, and my head spins with the flashing lights and pounding bass of the music.

Jess takes my arm. "Hey, you don't look so good. Let's go to the bathroom."

"Yeah," I croak out, trying to get the room to stop spinning.

Stumbling through the crowd, Jess wraps her arm around me while Kayla holds my upper arm to steady me as my legs have started to feel a little weird. I blink rapidly, trying to get my eyes to see clearer, but the room remains blurry.

"How far is the bathroom?" I ask, the words feeling heavy on my tongue. I've never been this drunk before.

"We're close. Don't worry," Jess assures me.

Looking up, I see an exit sign right before we walk through a doorway, but my brain is too fuzzy to understand what's happening.

"Come on, Tessa, a little farther," Kayla adds.

My legs start to give out on me as we walk down what seems to be too bright of a hallway to be leading me to the bathroom.

Where are we going?

Warm air hits my face suddenly. Are we outside?

My eyes start to droop, and I feel another set of hands grab my arms. Larger, rougher hands, that don't belong to Jess or Kayla.

I peel my eyes open to see shadows looming all around me, and my heart rate kicks up.

"Where's our money?" I hear Jess or Kayla ask as I'm shoved and pushed around, my brain not able to decipher which one asked.

Money? From who?

My legs hit the cold metal of a car before right before my head hits the lip of what I think is a trunk, and then it all goes dark. Silent.

My head is pounding. It feels like someone took a sledgehammer to it, and there's something wrapped around my head to prevent me from seeing anything but black.

I try and move my arms and legs, but they're restrained.

Panic starts to set in and my heart feels like it's going to beat right out of my chest.

I can't move and I can't see.

Forcing myself to calm down, I can finally hear voices speaking in another language when the blood stops pounding in my ears. The voices get louder, and closer. I think they're speaking Chinese.

The blindfold is ripped off of me, taking a few strands of hair with it, and I hold back a whimper of pain. Everything hurts.

"She's awake," a man says with an Asian accent.

Staying silent, I look around and notice that I'm being held in what I think is a warehouse or an abandoned building.

The floor is cement and covered in oil and dirt stains. Dirty windows are punched out and half-covered up in black fabric that blows in the warm breeze while others are completely boarded up. There's also a faint smell of chemicals in the air that makes me think this used to be a factory of some kind.

Four men stand before me, looking down at me like they want to eat me alive.

"I see why he's taken such an interest in you," one says, looking me up and down with eyes so dark, they feel like death caressing my skin.

Another one, bigger and scarier with a scar running down his jaw and cold eyes that send a chill of fear through me, grips the front of my dress and rips it down, tearing the thin fabric with ease.

"Such pretty skin," he says, his voice as eerie as his appearance. Raising his hand, I see a dagger in it, and he runs the edge of the tip across my collarbone and down the center of my chest. My shoulders move, trying to get out of his reach, but my efforts are futile. I'm tied to this chair and can't move.

"We don't touch her," another says. "She needs to be alive for the deal to take place."

A deal? What deal?

"Time for proof of life," he says, holding up his phone, and the one with the scar steps behind me. He yanks my head back by my hair, and I bite back the pain and stare straight ahead, refusing to give these men anything. "Smile for your dear Alec."

CHAPTER 30
Alec

Leo and I are on our way to our meeting with the Triads, and instead of shutting down my emotions like I need to do, all I can think about is Tessa.

I need her light. I need her to take the sins that stain my hands and heart and replace it with her purity before I become nothing *but* those sins. Before there's nothing left in me that's redeemable or worthy of her.

I told myself to give her a little more time, but after tonight, I fully intend on going to her and telling her her time alone is over. She's fucking mine.

"Alec, we're almost there, get your head on straight."

"It is," I snap.

"I can see you haven't even been listening to me for the past five minutes."

"Because you've been repeating yourself for the hundredth time."

I feel Leo's eyes on me, but I ignore him. "After this, you can do whatever you want. But we have a lot on the line here."

"I know. It's my city they keep coming for."

"Exactly. So focus."

A few minutes later, our car pulls up to the agreed upon location. Leo and I take our guns out to double check that they're loaded and pat our concealed knives in the hidden padded lined pockets in our pants. We're going into this knowing we may have to fight our way out.

We're meeting at one of our shipping warehouses at the Red Hook Terminal, and we've had it set up with men in place since yesterday. They're running surveillance from a few of our shipping containers that have been transformed into safe houses if ever needed.

Both Leo and I hesitated slightly when Lin Chen agreed to meet us on our territory, which is why we've had men in place in case they thought they could surprise us or set us up somehow if we thought we had the upper hand and got cocky because it's our territory.

"Let's go," Leo commands, stepping out of the car. We walk side-by-side into the warehouse with four of our men flanking us to the sides and behind. We agreed ahead of time that each of us would only have two family members and four guards.

The large bay door is open, and I take note of where the five men we have hiding in the shadows around the large space are, that again, have been here since yesterday. We don't take chances when our enemies could be watching us at any time.

Leo and I sit in the chairs at the table that face the open door, staying silent as we wait. Ten minutes later, a car pulls up, and in walks Lin Chen and his brother Sun, with four men of their own.

I don't like the looks on their faces. Almost like they don't have a care in world.

They think they're going to win this negotiation? They clearly don't know who they're dealing with.

This is either going to end in a deal where they stay to their territory in Chinatown, or end with them at the bottom of the Hudson.

Either way, I win.

I always win.

Approaching us, the Chen brothers look around the large space, definitely not seeing our men in hiding, and then settle on Leo and me with their little grins I want to fucking punch off their faces.

"Good evening," Lin says, pulling the chair out and sitting across from Leo – a battle of bosses.

Leo just nods, and I stare down Sun as he takes the seat across from me.

"You know why we're here," Leo starts. "You've been running sex dens and gambling rings in my brother's city. Every time he shuts you down, you just pop right back up. What makes you think you're allowed to do that without his permission?" We learned this week that the places they've been holding their underground games were also where they operated their prostitution business and whore houses.

"I didn't realize we needed your permission," Lin says with a smirk, his eyes darting to mine. Fucking liar. "But even if we did, we would've been told no." He shrugs.

"Yes, you would have," Leo informs him. We agreed that he would do the talking so long as Lin, their head of the family, was doing the talking for them. "Alec runs the underground. He runs the entirety of Atlantic City. He has every casino and club in his pocket. You have nowhere to hide anymore. You have no claim in New Jersey. We do. And you're being told, nicely I might add, to go back to your territory and stay there."

"What if I were to say we have leverage that might make you reconsider?"

Ah, so that's why they agreed to meet us here. They think they have the upper hand. But that's utter bullshit. They have nothing we'd ever want.

"Such as?"

"You can keep your foothold of the city. We just want our own little corner for our businesses. I think that's reasonable."

"What leverage do you think you have?" Leo asks with a little more edge. We both know his request isn't reasonable. It's disrespectful.

Sun reaches for the inside pocket of his suit jacket and our guards take a step forward, but he only pulls out his phone.

"We were at The Broker's party a few weeks ago," he says as he unlocks his phone, and my jaw ticks as my chest tightens. "I saw you with a woman," he directs at me. "And while I normally would have thought nothing of you taking an interest in a sexy little dancer like her, you seemed to pay her an extra amount of attention that looked like you knew her. Like you *cared* about her."

"Who are you talking about?" I ask, tilting my head to the side, keeping my features stone cold. The blood in my veins turns to ice as my mind goes through a thousand different scenarios he could possibly lay out for me. But nothing prepares me for what I see when he slides the phone towards me.

Tessa.

She's tied to a chair with her head yanked back by the dirty hands of a man whose face is cut off in the image. She's wearing some tight little black dress that's ripped at the neckline to expose her lacey black bra and her eye makeup is smudged like she was blindfolded. But her eyes themselves are hard and cold. Distant. Strong.

My woman is strong. She would never cower in the face of danger.

They're the eyes she gave me when I shot Enzo. She was strong then, too.

An eerie sense of calm and clarity comes over me. "I don't know why you thought she'd mean anything to me, but I don't know who that is," I say with practiced control.

I've never needed to restrain myself so fucking badly as I do now. Tessa's life depends on it. I have to pretend like she's nothing. Then I'll put a bullet between his eyes and cut the hands off of everyone who dared touch her. I'll kill his entire fucking family and burn his small little empire to the ground.

No one fucks with me or what's mine.

"Are you sure?" he taunts. "Because if she means nothing to you, then I can give the word to my men that they can have a little fun with her. Out of respect, I told them she was off-limits, but I guess that doesn't matter now."

With one last look at Tessa on the small screen, I slide his phone back to him and keep my eyes guarded and on his. He can't beat me.

Leo's hand drums on the table, his signal for me to hold my tongue. "We don't involve innocent women in our business," he informs Lin and Sun.

"Well, we do. And we have yours. Now, are you ready to discuss the terms of a new agreement so you can have her back?"

I'm not negotiating with this piece of shit and Leo knows that. It takes everything in me to keep my face neutral and not show the fury I'm feeling on the inside.

Drumming his fingers on the table for a few beats, Leo looks between the men sitting in front of us, and then flashes them a predatory grin that's all teeth.

I know what he's about to do, and while every cell in my body is telling me to strangle these fuckers, I know I can't go against Leo. I trust my brother.

He's been drumming his fingers on the table in what anyone would think is a nervous habit, or something he does while thinking, but Leo is too controlled for that, and he doesn't do anything without reason.

"Oh, there's a new agreement. But there'll be no discussion." Their confused looks disappear when Leo makes a fist and knocks on the table once.

Shots ring out from the shadows, and the two bodyguards fall to the cement in dull thuds while Lin and Sun slump back in their chairs. Blood flows down from the bullet holes in their heads, but I'm tempted to take my gun out and put a few more rounds in them.

The soldiers we had hiding in the shadows emerge with their rifles at their sides, and my chair scrapes the cement as I push away from the table. Taking the phone from Sun's hand, I open the message again with Tessa's picture, and my hand grips the phone so hard I feel it on the verge of cracking under the pressure.

"Alec. Focus," Leo commands, gripping my shoulder. "She needs you."

Looking at him, I see both the brother who'd do anything for me and the boss who doesn't let anyone manipulate us.

"We'll have Stefano trace where the number is located and we'll go get her. Give it a little bit, then text the guy who sent it and tell him the deal has been made and to have her ready for transport."

Stefano may be one of Leo's captains, but he's also the family's best hacker and tracker who I know will find Tessa in no time. After all, he found out it was me who was responsible for her brother's death after six years and with us not leaving a single trace.

Giving him a curt nod, I wait while Leo calls Stefano and I pull out my phone, dialing Tito. I pace the area in front of me while the dead bodies are dragged over to the metal drums in the corner and dumped inside. Lye is poured inside with them, and the smell burns my nose from here, which I use to keep control over the anger threatening to break me.

"Boss," Tito answers.

"WHAT THE FUCK HAPPENED?!" I yell, my voice echoing around the empty space, his voice my tipping point. "You had one fucking job. You already know what happened to the last man who failed."

"She slipped out the other side of the theater after the show, and by the time I found out where she went on the security footage, it was too late. They took her."

"How?" I growl, shoving my hand in my hair.

"Two girls from the show took her dancing at Royals, and about a half hour later, the external cameras caught them walking her half-unconscious out the back door. They handed her over to two men who shoved her in the trunk of their car and handed the girls an envelope of cash. They must have been paid to drug her."

They're fucking done.

I don't hurt women, but I'll do any and everything to destroy them so they live a miserable existence and think about what they did every second of what's left of their lives.

"I'll deal with you later. Just go meet Vinny in the basement." Hanging up, I want to fucking hurt someone. I want to kill. I want to maim. I want to feel and see the life drain from the men who took my woman.

"She's in an abandoned building outside of AC," Leo tells me. "Let's go."

Heading towards the car, I turn to the men sealing the barrels. "When you finish here, follow behind us where you'll have more cleanup to do."

"Got it." They nod.

The drums will be sunk to the bottom of the Hudson off the port's docks, never to be seen or found. It's why we wanted to meet at this location.

Once in the car, Alfie peels off and heads straight for Manhattan. The top of Leo's building has a helicopter pad where our chopper will be waiting. It's over two hours by car, even when breaking every law, but only about forty-five if we fly.

"What's up, Alec?" Vinny says when I call.

"Get to the basement. We're on our way back. The Triads took Tessa and she's being held in an abandoned building on the outskirts of town."

"What the fuck? Where was Tito? He hasn't called me with anything."

"I'll take care of him later," I assure him. "But he's meeting you in the basement now. We're almost at Leo's and then we'll be there within the hour."

"I'll have Dante gather the men and everything will be ready for her extraction when you get here."

You could call Dante our head of security, but he's better known as The Executioner to those in our world. If you see him, it'll be the last time. He's walking death, and he's trained some of our best soldiers in his liking. I know he'll have them ready for this job.

"Thanks." Hanging up, I pinch the bridge of my nose and close my eyes, trying to get the image of Tessa tied to a chair out of my head.

She was never supposed to be touched by my world. I was supposed to keep her safe.

This is my fault.

When we're close to Leo's building, I text the number back from Sun's phone, having waited so we could have more time to prepare ourselves to get her out, praying they don't fucking touch her.

Taking the private elevator in Leo's building from the garage that brings us straight up to the roof, the whooshing air blowing from the chopper's blades has me bending forward as I run towards its open door. The pilot we have on call is ex-military, and when Leo, Alfie, and I are all strapped in, he takes off into the night, knowing how to fly with ease under any and every situation.

Staring out at the black ocean, my mind goes over every way I know how to torture a man. That was a part of our training growing up. My father was a ruthless man who knew the depths any man was willing to go to in order to keep his secrets and the ones he loves safe, and he taught us how to exploit those depths and use them to our advantage.

There's always someone trying to knock you off the top of the pyramid, coming from every direction, and we have to be prepared.

Leo, Luca, and I all have the worst of our father inside of us, brewing just below the surface of our controlled exteriors. We were taught that, too.

Our father always said that a man only had two true weaknesses in life – lack of control, and the love of a woman. My brothers and I made pacts when we were teenagers to never let a woman become our weakness. We could have as many as we wanted so long as it didn't go past one night. But that lifestyle gets old. When you can have any woman you want, and the chase is gone, the satisfaction fades over time. Especially when you hit thirty.

Then I saw Tessa, and all of that changed.

She became my chase.

She was something I couldn't have but also couldn't *not* have. Every time I saw her, the pull got stronger. Then I got to be with her, and every time I was, that pull solidified into something I can't even explain.

She's the best gift I've ever been given, and I'll be damned if I let anyone take her from me.

CHAPTER 31
Tessa

I'm so tired.

My arms are starting to tingle and lose feeling from being tied behind my back, and my legs are tight from being bound to each of the chair legs.

I'm trying to ignore the fact that my legs are spread and my short dress does little to cover me. I know the men keep looking between my thighs thinking they'll catch a peek, but too bad for them, I have on a pair of black lace panties that covers me.

No one's touched me since they took my picture for Alec, and I'm thankful for that. I don't know if I could endure the unwanted touch of another.

They're using me as leverage to get something they want from Alec, but I know they won't get it. He's coming for me. I can feel it.

For all that's happened these past two weeks, I know he'd never let anyone hurt me. That fact was made known when he killed Enzo.

Alec always makes sure I'm safe. Even when his methods are over-the-top and impede on my basic freedoms, he does it so I'm safe.

Tears prick the backs of my eyes but I blink them away, refusing to think about how crazy he must be going right now knowing that I'm here. I know he still cares.

I stood my ground and didn't go to him. I could have so easily broken down and gone to him when I knew he was home, telling him I missed him. I know he wouldn't have turned me away. But every time I crawled out of bed to do that and ease the pain I was in, I'd remember why I was in it in the first place, and lie back down.

But right now, I don't even care about any of that. I don't care that he ordered the hit on James. I don't care that he changed my life by taking away the only family I had left. I just want him here. I want to see his dark eyes and let myself get lost in their depths. They bring me comfort and relief.

I'm afraid I'll always want him. No matter the evil's he commits, or the pain he may cause me, I'll always want him.

Despite being my weakness, he also makes me stronger.

When I'm with him, I don't feel like I'm just living to get through each day. He gives me a purpose – to be his.

Closing my eyes, I send a silent apology up to my family. I can't leave him. I need him.

"Good news," a voice says, startling me out of my

thoughts. "You get to go back to him." The way he says it, though, makes it sound like it's not strictly good news.

Another man comes out of the shadows and sizes me up like his next meal. "This is who he's so taken with?" Circling me, he runs a finger around my shoulders, and I flinch away from him. "I can see the appeal. You're quite beautiful. Especially in this dress." His finger dips between my breasts and I clench my jaw. There's only so long that I can stay quiet.

"I know boss said we can't touch you, but you're too sweet to not take a little bite of."

"Touch me and you die," I spit, and he smiles.

"I don't think so, honey."

"He'll never let you live. Alec will kill you."

He comes closer, and I take note of the scorpion tattoo on his neck, with its tail disappearing below the neckline of his t-shirt. His eyes are black. They pierce mine, and I feel like the prey – the scorpion ready to attack and sting me, rendering me immobile before devouring me.

"We took you once easily enough. Your friends were all too willing to hand you over to us for a little cash. Everyone has a price," he says low, his finger now trailing up my thigh.

Jess and Kayla sold me out to these men. No wonder they asked me to go out with them. Jess kept feeding me drinks, probably lacing the last one with something, which is why I can't remember how I even got here. I remember needing to go to the bathroom, and then there's just flashes of light before it all went dark.

"Do you have a price, Tessa?"

"I'm not a whore," I grind out, my jaw clenched.

"Of course you are. Every woman is when they're with a

man like him. A man like me." He's nothing like Alec. Comparing the two would be like comparing a juicy steak to a bologna sandwich. "You're drawn to the darkness. The danger. You eagerly spread your legs, wanting a little taste, and hope he'll keep you around long enough to get as much as you can out of him."

Seething, my vision blurs with angry tears.

Who does he think he is? Judging me for wanting Alec. I don't want him for what he can give me. I'm sure he could buy me whatever I wanted, but it's him I want. It's him I crave. It's him I want right now to come and kill this asshole because I can't. I'm tied up and can't move. And if I wasn't...I think I could kill him myself. I never thought myself capable until this moment, and I never wanted death to greet someone as much as I do this man.

I could do it for Alec. I could take away one life so he doesn't have to.

These men took me because of Alec and some need for negotiations in their business, but I don't blame him. I was the one who snuck out the other exit so Tito wouldn't know. I just wanted a little freedom and to rebel against him so he'd talk to me.

I'm so stupid.

"You'll get back to him soon enough. I just think you'll be a little less...pretty when you are."

Stepping back from me, he nods at the big man with the scar who yanked my hair back earlier, and he steps forward. In his hand is the same dagger as before with a hilt that has a dragon's head coming off of it as if an extension of his hand.

He's silent when he approaches me. He runs the edge of the blade down my sternum and then flicks the tip between my breasts, cutting into my skin. Jumping at the prick of pain, I don't make a sound, refusing to give this man that satisfaction. He clearly enjoys inflicting pain on others.

Looking him in the eyes, I see nothing but evil.

"The Carfanos think they rule everything," the man with the scorpion neck tattoo says a few feet behind the dragon knife-wielding one, "and it's time to show them we need to be taken seriously. We're not going to keep to the territory they say we're allowed to have."

"I have nothing to do with their business."

"But of course you do. If you're with one, then you're their business."

The dragon blade slips inside the rip that's already present in the front of my dress, and he starts to slide it down, the fabric giving way with ease under the sharp blade.

My chest heaves and my nostrils flare with every breath I take as my heart accelerates to a stammering pace.

I don't know how I'm going to get out of this. I don't know how I'm going to stop him from doing whatever it is he wants to do to me.

When the blade cuts through the final inch of the dress, it falls to my sides. The only thing keeping me from being naked are my black lace bra and panties, and I've never felt more exposed.

The blade skims down my stomach, circling my bellybutton, then over to my hip, and when I think he's going to slice the side of my panties off, he instead lifts the blade from my skin and moves to my knee.

My legs jerk under the cold metal, and when he slides it up my inner thigh, he twists the tip near the apex of my thighs to cut into me like he did between my breasts. I flinch and clench my jaw, and he repeats the same move on my other leg.

Flicking my eyes down, I see blood trailing down my torso from the cut on my chest and blood running down my inner thighs, dripping onto the floor beneath me, soaking into the cement.

I pull at my zip ties, but they just bite into my wrists and ankles, and my anger flares. I'm not scared of this man. I'm angry. I want to take the knife from him and slice into him to see how he likes it.

"Such pretty skin. So unmarked," scorpion tattoo guy says as he steps beside his scarred friend with the dagger. "Well, not so much now."

Circling me, he brings the blade down the column of my neck, and when he slides it across to the hollow at the base, he flicks the tip to cut me open. The sting is greater than the other cuts, and I know he went deeper. I can feel the blood running down my chest.

Alec is going to kill him. I know he will. No matter if he gets to me before my entire body is covered in cuts and slices, he'll kill him. And I know he'll drag it out to torture him for doing the same to me, too.

"Let's see how Alec will like seeing you covered in your own blood," scorpion man taunts.

Holding the knife to my stomach, dragon dagger is about to cut into me when a door somewhere behind me bursts open and bullets ring out. The man with the knife jerks up, slicing my arm open in the process, and this time I can't hold in the cry of pain that escapes me.

Three of the men that were surrounding me are now lying dead on the floor with bullet holes in their chests. The one with the dagger only got clipped in the shoulder, and he staggers back, looking around.

He's here. I know he is. I can feel him.

"Tessa!" Alec's voice cuts through every sound around me, and I immediately feel the tension leave my body.

He's here. He came for me. I knew he would, but I wasn't sure he'd come in time.

"Leave him alive," Alec commands to Tito who's putting a pair of zip ties around dragon dagger's wrists, hauling him away.

"Tessa," Alec says, his voice strained, coming around to squat in front of me.

Oh, God, his voice. I've missed his voice. Closing my eyes, tears start to slide down my cheeks, and his hands come up to cup my face, wiping them away.

"*Mia bella rosa*," he breathes.

Cutting my zip ties from my ankles, he reaches around me to get my wrists, and once I'm free, I throw them around him.

Breathing him in, I start to cry harder. I've missed him so much. "Alec." My voice breaks on his name and he holds me tighter. "You came."

"Of course I did, *bella*. I'll always come for you. I'll always protect you. And when I can't, I'll always save you, or die trying."

His words flood my eyes with fresh tears, and he rubs circles on my back soothingly.

Pulling back, he cups my face again, and his eyes hold mine. Two dark pools of endless depth, that for a moment, I thought I'd never get to swim in again.

"I'm sorry," I whisper. "I shouldn't have…" I start, but

shake my head.

"We'll talk later. Let me get you out of here first so I can have Doc look at you." Looking me over, he sees the trails of blood on me and his eyes harden. "What did he do to you?"

"He used his knife on me. That's it. Please take me out of here, Alec," I beg.

Taking his pocket square out of his jacket, he presses it to the gash on my arm and then takes me in his arms, cradling me to his chest. I turn my face into him, needing his scent to keep me from breaking down further.

I hear other people all around us, but I don't pay them any attention. All I care about is Alec.

His arms feel like heaven surrounding me. Two safety lines that I never want to lose touch of again.

Placing me in the back of an SUV, Alec slides in next to me and then brings me back to him, cradling me on his lap.

It's a silent ride to wherever we're going, with just Alec and I holding each other like our lives depend on it. Because they really do.

CHAPTER 32
Alec

Holding Tessa in my arms feels like my world has finally righted itself. She's my axis. Without her, I'm all turned around, and I don't know which way is up.

But now I do.

I see everything as it is clearly again.

Nothing else matters but her right now. I'll deal with the Triads and Tito later. I just want to hold Tessa and make sure Doc looks at her as soon as we get back to The Aces.

Once in the garage, I climb out of the Range Rover and then scoop her up and carry her to the elevators.

"I think I can walk, Alec," she whispers, though her fingers grip my suit lapels in her fists like she doesn't want me to put her down, and I don't plan to.

"No," I say simply, and she curls into me a little more, satisfied with my answer.

The medical suite is only one floor below mine, and the moment the doors slide open, Joe is there to greet us. The whole floor was converted when I took over the business in Atlantic City, wanting to make sure medical service was always close by in case any of us needed it. The bedrooms are now hospital rooms, equipped with everything you'd find in an actual hospital, in addition to a surgical room and another with MRI and x-ray machines.

"What happened?" Doc asks.

"I don't know yet. I found her with blood trailing down her but I took her out of there before I could get a better look."

Laying Tessa down on a hospital bed in the room at the end of the hall, I take what remains of her dress off and then Doc gets to work examining her.

Cleaning off her wounds, the cuts on her neck, chest, and thighs are all shallow enough to not need stitches, but it's the gash on her arm, the one I heard her scream because of, is deep enough for them and may leave a scar.

Tessa keeps her beautiful hazel eyes on me as Joe works. With her hand in mine, I rub circles across her knuckles, needing to feel her touch in any way I can.

"He didn't touch you besides with his knife?" Joe asks her, and she shakes her head no, keeping her eyes on me.

"She'll be fine," he assures me, leaving us alone after he places bandages over her wounds.

Waiting a few seconds before speaking, she beats me to it.

"I knew you'd come. I'm just glad you did before he…before he…" she doesn't finish, but I know what she means to say.

"He'd didn't, though. I'll never let anyone hurt you again, Tessa. I promise you with everything I am that I'll protect you with everything that I have."

"I know," she whispers. "I shouldn't have snuck away like that. I was just angry and missing you and wanting to lash out. But Jess and Kayla…"

Squeezing her hand, my vision blurs. "Don't mention them. I'll take care of them."

"No," she says. "I want to."

Surprised by her answer, I take a second, and then bring her hand to my lips and plant a kiss there. "If you'd like, you may."

"I also want to use a blade on the one who did this to me before you kill him."

The corners of my mouth turn up at her declaration. "Yes, *mia bella rosa*. Whatever you want, you can have. I'd never deny you the satisfaction of revenge. But you may change your mind after you get some rest."

"Will you lay with me? I don't want you to leave me alone."

"I'm not leaving," I assure her, leaning in to plant a soft kiss to her cheek. Tessa's eyes close at my touch and her little sigh makes my chest hurt.

Taking my jacket off, I place it on the chair and then cover Tessa in the blanket that's at the end of the bed before sliding in next to her. She curls into me and rests her head on my chest, her arm snaking around my waist automatically.

She hasn't stopped touching me since I came to her, and

that gives me hope that she can forgive me.

She brings out all of these feelings I didn't know I could ever have for anyone, and I don't plan on letting her go. Not now. Not ever.

"I'm sorry, *bella*," I whisper against her temple. "I'll never forgive myself for causing you pain."

She doesn't answer me, and when I hear her breathing even out, I know she's asleep, so I breathe her in and let myself drift off with her, content at having her in my arms again.

I sense movement to my right and my eyes pop open on alert, seeing Leo and Vinny standing a few feet away.

"What the fuck are you doing in here?" I ask, keeping my voice low as to not wake Tessa.

She stirs next to me though, so I slip from the bed soundlessly, and she curls into the spot I was just occupying as I follow Leo and Vinny out the door. Once I close it and walk a few paces away, I ask again, "What the fuck are you doing here?"

"Is she okay?" Vinny asks first, worry etched on his face.

"She'll be fine. She needed stitches on her arm, but her other cuts will heal on their own."

"He's in the basement when you're ready."

"Tessa gets him first," I tell them, and their eyes widen.

"Alec…" Leo warns, and I give him a wry smile.

"It's at her request, brother. She wants to use the knife on him the way he did on her."

Their eyes widen momentarily, their surprise evident.

Women don't tend to want revenge the way we do.

"I told her to decide again when she wakes up, though," I add, and they both nod their agreement.

"And Tito?" Leo prompts, rubbing his jaw.

Breathing out a lungful of air, I rub the back of my neck. I don't know what I want to do with him yet. I should put a bullet between his eyes, but based off of Tessa's reaction with Enzo... "I'll talk to Tessa when she wakes up."

Both Leo and Vinny remain silent, assessing me. I've never been one to consult anyone when making decisions, let alone a woman. But she's *my woman*, and I want her by my side, not in the dark. Leaving her in the dark only makes her more of a danger to herself and pushes her away.

"Alec?" I hear Tessa call from the room, and the sound of her voice is enough to make my chest hurt. I told her I wouldn't leave her and now she woke up alone.

"I have to get back," I tell them. "Thank you for tonight," I add.

"She's family now," Leo says. "I see that, Alec." He holds my gaze for a beat, making sure I understand his acceptance.

Nodding, I go back inside the room with Tessa, and her worried eyes meet mine in the dim light coming from the cracked bathroom door.

"You weren't here. I had a dream..."

"Shh, *bella*. Let me take care of you."

Carrying her to the adjoining bathroom, I set her down on the bench in the shower and take my clothes off. When the water heats, I remove her bra and panties and lather a luffa with soap. I feel her eyes on me as I gently wash her body, careful to avoid the bandages over her cuts.

As I glide the luffa down her left leg and back up the right, she runs her fingers through my hair and cups my cheek. I look up to see her hazel eyes showing me everything, but neither of us says anything yet. She lets me take care of her first.

When I've finished washing us both, I dry us off and wrap her in a fresh robe from the closet and carry her back to bed.

Sliding in with her, I pull her against me and she splays her hand over my chest, curling her fingers against my heart.

"Alec, I..." she starts to say after a minute, but then pauses.

Propping herself up on her elbow, her face scrunches in pain, but she ignores it to look down at me. She traces my jaw with her soft hands, her touch a comfort I've never known.

"I forgive you," she whispers, her words hitting me square in the chest, and I relax for the first time in weeks, with something akin to hope taking root. "It took me facing not having you to realize I can't live without you. Even knowing the truth about James...I still need you. I can't give you up."

Cupping the side of her neck, I rub my thumb back and forth across her jaw. "You're my everything, Tessa. If I could bring him back for you, I would. There's nothing I wouldn't do for you. Everything I have is yours."

"I don't need anything but you."

"I don't deserve you. Taking you was the most selfish thing I've ever done, and I've done a lot of selfish things in my life. But I need you, Tessa. I need you, *mia bella rosa.*"

Pulling her fully on top of me so I can feel her weight

and know she's here with me again, I bring her lips to mine. Starting out slow, I savor her taste until I can't hold back, and I deepen the kiss. Holding her against me, I slide my hand into her hair and Tessa moans into me, her hands gripping the sides of my face.

I know she can feel me growing beneath her, and she starts to rock against me.

She's so fucking perfect. Even after what happened to her just a few hours ago, here she is, rolling her hips against mine, wanting me.

"*Mia bella rosa*, you should rest." I try and give her an out, but there's only so much I can handle when it comes to her. I always want her.

"I don't want to rest. I want you," she whispers against my lips, biting down. Groaning, I roll her over, careful not to put all of my weight on her. I know she's still hurting from being tied up.

"I'll take care of you, *bella*."

Kissing, licking, and sucking my way down her neck, I stop at the hollow of her throat where that fucker put his blade into her beautiful skin. Kissing the bandage, I feel Tessa shudder under me, and I continue on down the center of her chest, parting the robe to kiss the one there.

Sucking on her nipples, I have every intention of erasing that motherfucker's touch from her memory and replacing it with mine. Always mine.

Her sexy little mewls, moans, and sighs fuel me and light a fire inside of me that burns through my veins.

She squirms under me as I crawl down her body. Pulling the robe open fully, I swirl my tongue around her belly button, and her hand slides into my hair, gripping the ends, making me groan against her skin. Tessa never holds back from me, and I fucking love that.

Kissing her just above her sex, her legs fall to the sides and her hips raise up into me.

So responsive. So ready.

Looking up at her, I find her eyes already on me, and I kiss each of her inner thighs over the bandages where that fucker dug the tip of his blade into her, too.

She's so strong, my woman. She knew I'd come for her, and she didn't let him break her. Only I get to break her – in every way that makes her mine.

I press her thighs open flat and bare her sweet pussy to me like the fucking meal it is.

Locking eyes with her, I dip my head and feast on the sweet cream already waiting for me. Swirling her entrance, I lap up her juices and spread them up to her clit, sucking hard on her tight bundle of nerves. Her hips buck up into my mouth and I press her back down onto the bed.

Flattening my tongue, I press it against her clit to relieve the pressure and then lick my way back down to her entrance. Tessa's moans fill my ears as my blood pumps hard through me, settling in my cock that's now hard as fucking steel. But this isn't about me. This is for her. She needs to forget everything that happened tonight.

"Alec," she chokes out, my name a plea on her tongue. "I need," she pants, and I drive my tongue inside of her, knowing exactly what she needs.

Her deep, raspy groan has me gripping her thighs harder. She's driving me crazy right along with her.

Sucking her clit again, I feel her tremble beneath me, and just when I know she's close, I shove two fingers inside of her and curl them forward, stroking her front wall.

Her resounding scream makes me feel like a fucking king as her pussy squeezes my fingers like she wants to keep me in her forever.

My cock is begging me to give him what he wants, but this was for my woman, not me.

This is my punishment for letting her get taken.

CHAPTER 33
Tessa

Before I even open my eyes, I let myself breathe in the spicy, manly scent that makes my heart dance knowing Alec is right next to me.

He hasn't left me.

My body hums alive just being near him. He has this power over me that I can't explain, and I don't really want to. He's a part of me, plain and simple.

Finally blinking my eyes open, I see sunlight streaming in through the sides and crack of the curtain – a path shooting straight to us and illuminating Alec's face.

God, he's so beautiful.

Beautifully dark, dangerous, and deadly. Even while

asleep, his face doesn't relax from the hard planes and tight set of his jaw. But I wouldn't want him any other way. He's my dark savior I never knew was waiting for me.

Outlining his jaw with the tip of my index finger, I trace his lips. Those lips can both bring me to heaven and drag me to hell, and either way, I never want to live without them.

Lost in thought, I'm not prepared for Alec's quick move to capture my finger between his teeth.

"Ah," I gasp.

"You've been staring at me, *bella*," he says, his sexy raspy morning voice making my stomach knot. He's never with me when I wake up, and hearing it for the first time has both my heart and core clenching.

"How do you know?"

"I can always feel your eyes on me."

"I was just admiring the view."

"Good choice."

I flash him a smile, and then grow serious. "I didn't really have a choice, Alec. You were never a choice. You were always my destiny."

His eyes turn molten, and his hand around my waist tightens. "You're mine, Tessa. From the first time I saw you on stage, owning it like the queen you are, I knew."

"You're mine too," I tell him, pressing closer to him. "But I don't want to be someone you think you can give an order to and I'll just blindly follow. I've never been that person. I want you to see me as more than a duty. As more than an object to keep safe."

"You've never been an object to me, Tessa. You're my fucking world. You're my reason for breathing. A man like me only has two weaknesses — lack of control and the woman he loves. I have both with you, and I don't know how to deal with that. It'll always be a battle for me. But I will never apologize for protecting you."

My heart stops. Actually stops.

Did he just say...?

Did he just tell me...?

Rolling us over, Alec presses me into the bed, his weight a welcomed relief.

"I'm sorry, *bella*. I never wanted to cause you pain. I tried to protect you from everyone else, when it was me who would hurt you most of all. I didn't know. I couldn't have known. But that doesn't excuse it."

He presses his lips to the cut on my chest and the base of my throat, and I shiver, my nails digging into his shoulders.

"He's dead. The man who killed your brother. He's dead. I took care of him for you the day after I found out."

"Alec," I breathe, a tear escaping the corner of my eye. He killed one of his own men for me.

"I don't want you to hurt anymore, Tessa. I don't want you to look at me and see a killer. I don't want you to only see the monster who took your family from you."

Cupping his cheek, I run my hand through his hair and cradle his head. "I do see a killer, Alec," I tell him, and a pained look crosses his eyes. "But I also see a man who would do anything for me," I continue. "I see a man who protects his family. I see a man who's capable of so much more than he believes. I see a man with power who feels the weight of the world. But most of all, I see a man I wouldn't change for anything. I want all of you. Killer and all."

Alec closes his eyes briefly, and when he opens them

again, the two pools of darkness I love to swim in are swirling, sucking me down into their depths.

"*Ti amo, mia bella rosa.*"

Closing my eyes, I let the most beautiful words I've ever heard sink in. Running my hands up the back of his head, I let his mass of silky black hair slide through my fingers.

"I love you, too," I whisper against his lips, and he silences me with his.

This kiss is different than every other one we've shared. It's still possessive and heated, but it has something else added to it that makes my heart feel like it's way too big for my chest.

We pour everything into this kiss, and I feel the electricity snap and sizzle through me like bolts of white lightening in a black sky.

I can feel his love for me. I can feel his devotion. I can feel his sorrow for hurting me. I can feel his every emotion passing through this kiss and into my heart.

Alec runs his hand down the side of my waist and snakes it between us. Kissing his way down my neck, he bites down with a groan at finding me already wet for him.

Kissing and biting his way up to my lips, he takes my bottom lip between his teeth and then smooths it out with his tongue while his fingers rub slow circles around my clit. I melt under him.

No one's ever said they loved me before, and vice versa. But they're more than just words with us. I feel them. I breathe them. I live them.

Deepening the kiss, I wrap my arms around his neck and pull him as close as I can.

"I need you, Alec," I pant, then moan when he sucks my

earlobe between his teeth. "Inside of me. *Now*," I demand, tilting my hips up.

"I'll always give my queen what she wants," he says in my ear, his rough voice holding every promise in the world to follow through on that.

"Then you should get inside of me. And don't hold back. I need you. All of you."

Grunting his approval, Alec aligns himself at my entrance and kisses me hard as he thrusts all the way into me in a single swift motion. He swallows my cry, his tongue sweeping through my mouth to savor its taste.

I asked him not to hold back, and he doesn't.

I feel every inch of him with every thrust, my body welcoming him home after being gone for what feels like forever.

Pulling my lips away from his, Alec buries his face in the crook of my neck – kissing, sucking, biting. As my moans and cries intensify, I'm pushed higher and higher until I reach the edge of a precipice.

Alec drags his teeth over my sensitive nipples and my back arches into him on instinct. His mouth latches onto one of my tight peaks and sucks deep, and I feel the pull straight to my core.

"Alec," I choke out, raking my nails across the breadth of his back.

"Not yet," he rasps.

Biting around my nipple, he drags his lips across my chest to my other one, and gives it the same torturous treatment that drives me to within an inch of losing my sanity.

I can't hold on much longer. I can't take much else.

Looking down at me, Alec's dark eyes capture mine, and every time he's fully inside of me, hitting that spot so deep in me only he can reach, his eyes flare. The dark brown now black as it ripples out like a pebble dropped in a still lake.

"Alec," I beg, holding on by a thread.

"No," he commands, and tears prick my eyes as I hold back, with little sparks running down my legs and up my spine.

I feel him everywhere.

His mouth marks every square inch of skin he has access to, and just when I feel myself reaching my breaking point, he tells me to let go, and I don't hear anything else but the raw scream that's torn from my throat.

White stars dot my vision as I'm thrown from the heavens and plunged straight into the flames of hell — consumed wholly.

My eyes roll back as I burn, with Alec being the only thing keeping me from turning to a pile of ash.

Groggy, I peel my eyes open and see I'm no longer in the makeshift hospital room. I'm in Alec's bed, but he's not here, so I curl into the empty spot he usually occupies, inhaling his residual scent.

I have no idea what time it is, or how long I've been asleep, but I'm starving. My appetite was barely existent for the past two weeks, but it's back full-force now, and I really do feel like I haven't eaten in weeks.

Climbing out of bed, I take a hot shower, mindful of my bandages, and then go into Alec's closet, surprised to see that all of my clothes from my apartment have been moved in here.

When did he do this? How long have I been asleep?

Putting on a pair of leggings and an off-the-shoulder thin sweater, I decide to go in search of Alec to get some answers.

With each step, I feel the soreness between my thighs from Alec's roughness, as well as the ache in my shoulders from having my hands tied behind my back for hours last night. Looking down at my wrists, I see red marks where the zip ties cut into my skin, and I rub them as I walk, hoping they'll magically disappear by the time I find Alec.

He's not in the kitchen, so I keep going through the dining area and around the corner into the next hallway that leads to his office. I don't hear anything, so I knock on the door.

"Come in," he says, and I turn the knob, stepping into his office. He's sitting behind a large mahogany desk with a laptop open and a few papers laid out around him, the setup remarkably close to his office down in the casino.

"Do you need me, *bella*?"

"I woke up and you weren't there. And when I went to steal something of yours to wear, I noticed I didn't need to since your closet housed my entire wardrobe from my apartment. Care to explain?" I cross my arms over my chest and lean my hip against the doorjamb.

"I moved you in," he says simply.

"When? You never asked me."

"I had a couple of men do it after you fell asleep. And no, I didn't ask. I wasn't giving you the opportunity to say no or argue with me about it."

"You let strangers into my apartment and touch my

things?"

"They're not strangers. They work for me. And now they work for you."

"What? Alec, that's not the point. You do realize that means you ordered men to touch my bras and underwear, right?"

"Tessa," he warns, rubbing his forehead. "I do realize that now. But I was a little too preoccupied at the time to consider it an issue."

"You still never asked me if I wanted to live with you."

Standing, Alec walks around his desk and stands tall in front of me. "Are you telling me you don't want to live with me? You don't want to come home to me? You don't want to sleep with me every night and wake up with my mouth all over you?"

"I never said that," I say, breathless. "I just want you to ask me."

"I see." Lifting my chin with a single finger, he stares deep into my eyes. "Will you live with me so I can keep you safe while fucking you every day and night until you pass out and I'm all that's on your mind?"

"Yes," I answer without hesitation or a single doubt that that's what I want. I grip his shirt and bring him down to me, my lips telling him just how much I want that, and him.

Picking me up, he spins me around and walks me the few steps to his desk where he plants me on top. Alec undoes his belt and pushes his suit pants down just far enough to free himself, and then tears my leggings down my body, groaning when he finds me naked beneath.

"Fucking Christ," is all he says before pushing me back against the hard wood and entering me to the hilt.

A strangled cry escapes my closing throat, and I desperately search for something to hold onto as Alec takes me hard and quick. He grips my hips at a bruising strength, and my one hand finds the edge of his desk to grasp.

Digging my heels into his ass, I keep up with his relentless and ruthless fucking. In a matter of seconds, my inner muscles are quivering and then clamping down around him.

Alec is right there with me. He grunts, and then stills, groaning long and low as he fills me with his hot seed. I know I took his release from him from how hard I squeezed him, and I take satisfaction in that I can have power over him too.

Pulling me up into a sitting position, he kisses me hard. "I get to do that whenever I want now."

"So can I," I say back, raising my chin haughtily.

"Oh, trust me, *bella*, whenever you want me, you can have me."

"What if you're in a meeting? Or on the phone?" I counter.

"Just interrupt me and say you need me and I'll take care of you. Always."

"Okay, then." A small smile tugs at my lips and I pull him down to kiss him fiercely.

CHAPTER 34
Alec

I take Tessa down to the basement, and she squeezes my hand when we reach the initial door that leads to all of the others down here. I thought after a night of sleep she'd change her mind on wanting to exact a little revenge on her captor, but she insisted on coming down here. I at least got her to call out of work today. She didn't fight me on it like she did that first day she was with me.

Going through the security process, I hold the door open for her, and her eyes widen as she takes it all in.

Walking her through the first general meeting room area that resembles a living room in most respects, we go through the next set of doors that takes us to the complete opposite.

Standing in a cement and cinderblock hallway that's lined with heavy metal doors on either side, Tessa straightens her back and looks down each way.

"That way," I tell her, lifting my chin to the right where one of my men stands beside one of the metal doors.

Stopping in front of the door, Tessa turns to me, her eyes guarded and unsure.

"You can change your mind. It's your choice." The other men in that warehouse who took her have all been killed and taken up to the Port of Newark for disposal. But this fucker...he's been saved for a special kind of death.

"I don't know if I can," she says. "But I want *you* to. And I want to watch you."

Her request has me reeling, and I kiss her hard, backing her up against the door.

"Leave," I growl at the guard, going back to kissing my woman as he silently slips away.

"You want to watch me?" The image of her standing and watching me as I cut into the skin of our enemy like he did to her, and her enjoying it, has my cock hardening instantly.

"Yes," she breathes against my lips.

Fuck. She was made for me.

Biting her lower lip, I growl against her and then pull away. I open the heavy metal door and let her step through first, with me right behind.

Sitting with his legs tied to the chair and his arms around his back, is Zhang Wu, the main enforcer for the Triads.

He lifts his head and looks at the both of us with the eyes of a man who knows his fate, but refuses to give in to it without a fight.

Tessa walks over to the small table in the corner and picks up the dagger with the dragon hilt Zhang used on her. She turns it over in her hands and then holds it out for me to take.

Brushing my fingers against hers when I take it, our eyes meet, and I see every emotion she doesn't say. Anger, pain, fear, determination.

For her, I can become the monster I was trained to be. He doesn't come out as much as when I was first starting out and had to prove myself, but it's a role I can easily slip back into like a second skin.

"You thought you could cut up my woman and I wouldn't retaliate?" He just looks at me, his nostrils flaring with barely controlled anger. "You don't have anyone or anything to go back to, Zhang. The Chin days are over. Their little empire is being dismantled as I speak, with the pieces being fought over by whoever wants it."

His body jumps, pulling at his restraints, trying to lunge at me.

Holding the dagger up to the dim lightbulb that hangs from the ceiling, I let it glint off the blade so he sees the freshly sharpened edge.

"No one touches my woman without dying. And that death can either be a bullet to the skull, or a slow and tortuous one. You happen to fall into the latter category. You put this blade to her perfect skin to get to me."

Turning the dagger in my hand, I plunge it into his thigh, then rip it out. He only grunts, his mouth pressed firmly together to keep silent.

Plunging the dagger into his other leg, his eyes burn with fire, but he merely grunts again.

I feel Tessa behind me, her eyes trained on me. Feeling her here with me is an experience that fills me with pride.

Her acceptance of me, all of me, is something I never knew a woman would, or could, be capable of. She truly was made for me. Even the things that should pull us apart, bring us closer. And this fucker used her to get to me. He tried to take her away from me.

My anger flares, and I get in his face.

"I know you thought you could make it so I didn't want her anymore. But you overlooked one simple fact." I grip his throat and push his head back so he's looking me in the eyes. "Her beauty is only a small factor in why I love her. And even if you were able to cut her up before I got there, I'd still fucking love her and fuck her harder than I ever have while your blood drained from your body from everywhere I cut into your skin with this dagger."

I'll love Tessa no matter what. I'll avenge her no matter what. And I'll always want her no matter what.

Squeezing his throat, I feel his veins bulge and his pulse pound beneath my grip.

"Alec." Tessa's small voice penetrates through my hazy brain that's sole focus is on watching the life leave the man in my grip. "Alec," she says again, and I turn my head to see her standing right there. "Just kill him. I need you."

Those three magic words snap me into action. I release his neck in a rush, but only to plunge the dagger into the side of it so the dragon's head is flush against his skin and the tip of the blade exits the other side of his neck.

Tessa grabs my arm and pulls me toward her. She throws her arms around my neck and buries her face in the crook, my arms locking around her small, strong frame automatically, holding her tight.

"Did you mean that?" she murmurs against me, and I pull back far enough for her to see my eyes. She'll see the truth there. I always show her the truth when I guard myself from everyone else.

"Yes, *mia bella rosa*." Tears gather in her eyes and I swipe at them before they have the chance to stain her cheeks. "Don't cry."

"I just thought it was me who was feeling this way. This…this is more. You and me. And I feel crazy for feeling the way I do. You've shown me your darkness, and it's slowly consumed me, becoming a part of me in the best, most fucked-up way. I need it, though. It feels right. Wrong, but right. You said you'd love me even if he got to me before you did, and that you'd…" she pauses, swallowing her emotions. Another tear escapes her and I lean forward, licking it from her cheek bone.

"*Mia bella rosa*, I'm going to fuck you right here against the wall so you know how fucking serious I was. I'll always want you, and need you, no matter what. Always."

"Yes," she moans, and I kiss her hard, her nails biting into the nape of my neck.

Garbled sounds from Zhang make me tear away from Tessa, and when I turn to him, I see he's still holding on. I grab the hilt of the dagger and pull it out of his neck, tossing it to the floor. It had acted as a plug to keep him alive, but blood spurts out from the wound at a rapid flow now, and he quickly loses consciousness.

Tessa's wild hazel eyes blaze up at me as I back her up to the cement wall. Cupping the back of her neck, I tilt her head back and kiss her deep, my tongue plunging into her mouth —

tasting, taking, owning, claiming.

She tastes like a mix of heaven and hell — white and black roses. A heady combination that has my addiction growing with every hit.

Tearing her shirt off over her head, I yank the cups of her bra down and twist her pert nipples between my fingers, her sharp cry into my mouth one I swallow and take for myself. Every sound she ever makes I'm keeping as the soundtrack I'll hear play on repeat in my head whenever she's not around.

Biting her bottom lip, I toss my suit jacket onto the empty chair to my left while Tessa unbuttons her skin tight jeans. I could watch her peel them down her sexy legs all night, but I don't have time for that. Unfastening my pants, I push them past my hips and then push her hands away so I can yank her jeans down in a single tug.

She braces herself on my shoulders as she steps out of them, and then grips the small opening of my dress shirt at the top of my chest and rips it open with a strength that makes me need her even more.

I rip her lace thong off with little effort and then grip her ass, lifting and throwing her against the rough cement wall. She moans, her fingers digging into my shoulders as I position myself at her entrance and thrust up into her at the same time I pull her down onto me.

We both groan. *Finally.*

I take her hard and fast, biting my way down her neck. Tessa's cries fill the small room, and when I feel her pussy start to flutter around me, I grip her ass and drive into her harder. I know her back is scraping against the cement, but with each thrust deep inside of her, she moans with the sting of pain, and my chest tightens, driving me to give her more.

"Come for me, *bella*," I demand, my gravelly voice filling her ear as I bite down on her lobe. She screams, her pussy squeezing me so tight that I only need to bury my cock inside of her one last time before I'm letting go right along with her, filling her with my hot release, wanting her to feel all of me.

Tessa collapses against me, but I hold her up easily. Her erratic breathing in my ear and thumping heartbeat against my chest fills me with pride in that I know how to make my woman fall apart and then put her back together.

When we both catch our breaths, we re-dress, all the while Tessa actively avoids looking at the dead man in the room. Gripping her chin, I bring her face up to look at mine. "Don't be embarrassed, *bella*. What we just did was fucking hot, and I don't want you second guessing your desires. I told you I'm here when you need me. Anytime. Anywhere. Any situation."

Breathing a sigh of relief, she closes her eyes and I kiss her, not letting her question herself further.

I don't care that we just fucked with a man bleeding out behind us. In fact, I found it heightened everything. Killing Zhang to balance out the evil in the world fueled me to fuck the wild out Tessa's eyes.

CHAPTER 35
Tessa

Forgiveness can't change the past, but it can change the future.

I never understood the full weight of that statement until I lived it. Forgiving Alec gave me a sense of clarity and freedom that I've never known before.

I can still mourn and love my brother, flaws and all, and love Alec at the same time. He didn't know.

I didn't know the sacrifices James made or the illegal paths he took to make sure I could still dance while having a roof over my head and food to eat. He didn't deserve to die for his actions, but punishing Alec for a choice he made six years ago without knowing the consequences won't bring

James back. And punishing Alec would also punish myself. Denying myself him would bring me more pain and sorrow than knowing and being with the man behind my brother's murder. I've come to realize and accept that, and the only thing I can do is move forward and live the life I want. A life with Alec Carfano.

My newfound resolution has had me dancing differently all week. Alec thought I should take time off if I needed it, but I told him I needed to dance more. It's how I sort through and express my feelings when they build up and I feel like I might explode if I don't get them out.

I even asked Dan if I could change my solo this week to accommodate my heart's evolution. He was hesitant at first, but when he saw me rehearsing a few days ago, he changed his mind. He told me to just give the sound guy my new song and to pick a costume from the rack of extras if I wanted. I knew exactly which one I wanted, too.

I had to have a little talk with Alec about my duet with Jeremy, and while he's not happy that I refuse to stop dancing it, he does feel a little better knowing that Jeremy's gay. He just thinks every man on the planet is out to take me away from him. I told him that it's him I picture myself dancing with anyhow, and to just use his anger at seeing another man touch me to teach me a lesson later on when we're alone. He knows I love his bedroom punishments.

Gone is my usual red costume, and in its place is an all-black one. I put on black sheer tights and then a long-sleeved black unitard that has a deep V in the front to my belly button, and one in the back to the bottom of my spine, with a sheer material between to hold it together. Black rhinestones cover the entirety of the sleeves, as well as the edges of the V necklines. It's sexy and alluring, and meant to make my arms and legs appear longer so the audience will follow my lines as I dance.

Tying my black pointe shoes, I stand and stretch out my ankles, rising and falling on my toes a few times to make sure the silk ties are secure enough.

This is going to be me – real, raw, and unfiltered.

My eye makeup is dark and sultry. I used my black eyeliner pot and brush to draw on swirled lines coming from the corners of my eyes that frame them to look like the beginnings of a mask one would wear to a masquerade party. Adding black glitter on top of it before it fully dries, I turn my head in the mirror to watch the light catch off of it in shimmers.

I hadn't mentioned to Alec that I changed routines. I want him to be surprised. I want him to feel everything that I do in the moment.

The song I chose and the routine I created...it's all for him. I want to *show* him how I feel. Telling him with words and expressing my feelings through our mind-blowing sex is only part of our story. I need him to watch me show everyone else how I feel – let my body talk.

Walking over to the stage left entrance, Dan looks me up and down and smiles, nodding his approval. "Go and kill it, honey."

I chose "Deeper" by Valerie Broussard as my new song for tonight. It's a reflection for how I feel and gives me the perfect chords and beat to dance to on top of the lyrics.

When the lights fade, I walk out to center stage and lift up onto my toes. With my head cast to the side and down, I raise my arms above my head and let my hands fall to behind my head as my opening pose.

When the violin notes start, a spotlight shines down on me and my head snaps forward, my arms moving as waves out to my sides. I lift my leg up and out to the side, spinning slowly in place until the bass beat drops and I look ahead, walking towards to the front of the stage slowly on pointe, dragging out the steps as if in slow motion to accentuate each beat.

When the chorus hits, I drop to the floor, spreading my knees and arching my back so my hands touch my ankles. I spin out of the position, and from one knee, lift onto my left foot's toes and stretch my right leg all the way up into a vertical split, keeping my torso flush against my thigh before straightening and making four pirouettes in equal time to the repeating of the word deeper at the end of the chorus, then slide down into a split.

Time seems to morph at this point, and I can no longer hear the audience in any capacity, only the song. Only these lyrics.

My body moves of its own accord like it did at that party, and I feel like I'm having an out of body experience. I can feel Alec's eyes on me. I can feel his love. I can feel his desire.

I'm his everything just as he's mine, and just as I can feel what he's feeling up here on stage, I know he can feel what I am from his seat. We're tied together. Every fiber of our bodies are woven together to form an impenetrable bond that can't ever be broken. Life will throw whatever it can at us, and we'll never break apart. We can't. We can only turn into the other and share whatever we're feeling – pain, loss, joy, love, hatred.

When the violin hits, I swear I'm floating across the stage, my toes and feet barely touching it. Through the slowing of the beat, I walk on pointe like I'm on a runway, and then as the violin speeds up again, I stutter step and run into a split jump.

I've never felt more out of control while also remaining completely in control.

The song is right – there's no saint without the sinner, and there's no relief without the fever.

We need both the good and the bad in life to appreciate what we have. You can't have good times without knowing what the bad feels like.

Even the brightest of days are when the most shadows are cast.

On the last bars of the song, as the word deeper is sung out four more times, I pirouette in time to each one, feeling myself being cut open deeper each time, with Alec filling the caverns left behind until he's reached the deepest, darkest parts of me that only he can heal and claim as his own.

As the song echoes out when it's over and the lights fade, I collapse to the floor, feeling like I just wrung my heart out for everyone to see. I can't even lift myself up. I gave my everything.

I know I have to move, but I don't have the energy. The next thing I know, two strong, familiar arms are lifting me up and carrying me off stage.

"*Mia bella rosa.*" The sweetest words are whispered in my ear and I curl into him. "*Così bella, amore mio.*"

Alec walks me over to my dressing area, sitting me down in my chair. "Thank you," I breathe, looking into his beautifully dark, yet soulful eyes. "It was for you," I tell him, and he brushes his fingers against my cheek.

"I know, *bella*." Leaning in, the moment his lips touch mine, I'm flooded with his love for me.

I know Alec's not a man who grew up with people around him voicing their love for one another. They showed it in their loyalty, respect, and actions, and he shows me in the same way. It just makes when he does say the words, all that more powerful. Any man can say they love you. It takes a real man to *show* you, and make you *feel* his love and devotion every single day.

CHAPTER 36
Alec

Shrugging on my suit jacket, Tessa comes up behind me and slides her hands around me as she circles around to my front.

"Can I help you pick out a tie? I wouldn't want you to clash with my dress."

My mouth tilts up in the ghost of a smile when I look into her hazel eyes, but then I look down at her dress and *holy fuck*. Every curve of her lithe, tight little body is on display. "I'm going to have to kill every man who looks at you. Are you trying to make me crazy, *bella?*"

"Maybe." She smiles coyly. "I like when you get crazy." Pressing against me, she leans up on her toes to whisper in my ear, "You always fuck me harder when you do."

Growling, I grab the side of her neck and bring her mouth to mine. Her innocence is all mine. And even though I've taken it from her, and tainted her beyond belief, I can still taste its sweet remnants no matter how many times I kiss her.

"I wasn't going to wear a tie."

"You do look plenty sexy like this," she tells me, her fingers trailing along my neck and under the collar of my shirt.

I run my hands down her hips and around to cup her firm ass. "And you look too sexy."

"Are you complaining, Mr. Carfano?" She cocks her head to the side. "I picked this dress with you in mind. I thought after a few drinks that I'd maybe let your hands wander."

A small groan leaves me and I grip her ass tighter, making her teeth sink into her bottom lip.

"Does that not interest you? I could always change into something a lot less accessible."

"No," I bark, and she smiles, my chest tightening.

"That's what I thought. We better go so we're not late."

"Katarina won't even notice."

"It's her birthday party. She'll notice. Let's go."

When we get to the main casino floor, Tito meets us there at the elevator, walking behind us as we make our way around to the entrance of Royals. Tessa told me not to kill him since she thinks it was her fault that she was taken. I know Tito couldn't have foreseen her ditching him, and we both know she's not going to do it again, so I saw her reasoning not to hurt him. For now.

Tessa's hand squeezes mine when we approach the front of the line and I stop, facing her so she'll look at me. "No one will touch you in there. Jess and Kayla have been banned and security has been upped with how many Carfanos will be present. But above all, *I* won't let anything happen to you."

I took care of Jess and Kayla for Tessa. She reconsidered her need for punishing them herself, and let me handle it, so long as I didn't totally destroy them. I had them fired from the show and banned for life from The Aces and all casinos in town so they can't work in this city again.

I gave direct orders to every security team around not to let them inside their establishments, and they have the both of them flagged on their facial recognition systems in case they try and slip through. Those two have nowhere to go in my city anymore.

"I know that, Alec," she says, squeezing my hand. She has no idea how much her trust means.

I'll never forgive myself for the pain she's already endured because of me, and I'm one lucky bastard that she has the heart capable of forgiving a man like me. But I'll be damned if she's ever hurt again while with me.

Passing the new bouncer with a nod, I walk into Royals with my woman by my side. I had Santiago fired real fucking quickly after that night.

Instead of heading down the stairs into the crowd of people on the dancefloor, we go through a black curtain to the left of the staircase that leads to the VIP balcony section, and I nod at the two men guarding the entrance.

The area spans halfway around the club in a crescent moon shape and overlooks the entirety of the dancefloor below.

Music pumps out of speakers all around, and I can feel the bass jump through my veins. I used to frequent the club's VIP section almost every weekend before I took over after my uncle Sal. Vinny and I would invite as many women as we could fit up here and make sure we showed them a good time.

Then I had to get serious, and I didn't have time to waste partying and drinking my way through the weekend.

I had to grow up.

Vinny still comes here on occasion whenever our cousins from Miami or New York visit, but even he takes his job seriously now that it's just us.

Reaching those already here, I reluctantly let go of Tessa's hand so she can wish Katarina a happy birthday and hug Aria, Gia, and Mia, too. Vinny thought Mia was too young to come tonight, but she's 18 now, and it's not like any of us are going to let her drink or ever have her out of our sights.

"Hey, sis. Happy birthday." I hug my little sister and kiss her cheek.

"Thanks, Alec." She smiles wide, her happiness written all over her face. "And thank you for doing this for me."

"Anything for you," I tell her seriously. "You know that."

"I know." She smiles again, her eyes glassy. "But don't make me get emotional on my birthday. I want to have fun tonight."

"Not too much fun."

She rolls her eyes. "Don't start, Alec. Just go enjoy Tessa. I like her. She's really great. You're lucky she tolerates you."

"I know." I nod, looking past Katarina to see Tessa smiling and laughing with my cousins. She's so fucking beautiful.

Patting my arm, Katarina walks over to the bar and orders a drink while I go over to my brothers.

"She's going to give us nothing but trouble, you realize that, right?" I say to Leo and Luca about Katarina.

"I know," Leo groans, rubbing his temples. "She's testing my patience more and more. She just doesn't understand the risks of what she's asking. She wants to travel, move out of mom's, and *date*." He snarls on that last one.

"She doesn't understand that she's vulnerable out there," Luca says. "There are people who won't hesitate to use her to get to us. Look at what happened with Tessa."

I know he's right, but at the mention of what happened only a week ago, my anger flares.

"Sorry, Alec," Luca says. "I know it just happened, but it's the truth."

"I know," I force through my clenched jaw.

"We'll let her have fun tonight and worry about everything else tomorrow." Luca shrugs, sipping his drink.

I leave them to go grab a drink for myself and Tessa, and then sneak up behind her to hand her a glass of whiskey.

"Are you trying to get me drunk, Alec? Because if you are, this is a good start." She smirks, taking a sip. "The quickest way, too."

"I'm just looking forward to the moment you let me test how far you'll let me go with you up here."

With a smile that has the power to make me do anything she wants, she finishes the drink in two gulps and hands me the empty tumbler.

"I'll take another."

Staring down at her, I capture her lips with mine, licking the whiskey from her lips. "Coming right up."

The night goes on, and I spend most of it sitting with Leo, discussing the fallout of the Triads in the week following our takeout of their leaders while Luca is off with Nico, Vinny, Stefano, Marco, and Gabriel down below, choosing the women they want to spend the night with.

Leo is the only one content to sit with me as Tessa dances with Katarina and the other girls up here in VIP. There's no fucking way in hell we're letting them go downstairs where men will put their hands all over them.

"The Russians are taking over a lot of the Triads territory while they scramble to try and rebuild what they had without a leader. But they're no match for the Bychkovs. Those fuckers will annihilate whatever Triads get in their way now that they can't protect themselves. I mean—" he abruptly cuts off, his face turning to stone.

"Leo, what's—" His eyes go dark, murderous, and I follow his line of sight to the woman who just walked in with Nico.

She smiles at something Nico says and he puts his hand on her lower back. That's when Leo growls low next to me, a snarling sound that resembles what a lion would make before attacking its enemy.

The woman is quite beautiful, and when she looks our way, her eyes pass over mine and land on Leo's. She freezes mid-step, her eyes widening in surprise. Nico stops short with her and looks down to see what made her pause. His eyes follow hers, and then he drops his hand from her and steps away, seeing the look on Leo's face.

Leo stands, but with the first step he takes toward her, it's like she snaps out of the stupor she was in and turns on her heel, practically running back out the way she came.

Everyone stops their conversations and dancing to watch as Leo takes off after her with Alfie quickly on his heel.

"What was that about?" Tessa asks, coming to sit next to me in the spot Leo just abandoned.

"I don't know," I tell her. But I think I do know. By the look on his face, I'd say he was just reunited with the woman who ruined him years ago. "I think he knew her a long time ago."

"She was beautiful. I can see why he ran after her."

"Not as beautiful as you, *bella*. No one comes close."

Smiling, she leans into me and kisses me soft at first, then slides her hands through my hair and pulls me down to kiss her fully.

"I think it's time you take me over to get another drink." Her teeth graze my lip. "Then you can casually pull me into the shadows over there in the corner and we can see how fast you can make me come. No one will hear me scream over the music." A soft moan escapes her sexy lips as if she's picturing us doing just that, and my cock lengthens.

My eyes burn down into hers, her fire matching mine, and I pull her up with me, fully intending on seeing how many times I can make her come until she's screaming out my name.

Tessa is my queen, and I'm about to show her exactly who her king is.

ACKNOWLEDGMENTS

Thank you to for the continued support from my family and friends while I pursue my dream of bringing more love into this world through my words.

Thank you to my Organized Crime professor in college who fueled my mafia obsession by sharing his real-life experiences in interviewing the major heads of all the Asian organized crime syndicates – stateside and throughout Asia! I can tell you I never missed a class, and I learned things you'll never find in a textbook or online.

ABOUT THE AUTHOR

Rebecca is a dreamer through and through with permanent wanderlust. She has an endless list of places to go and see, hoping to one day experience the world and all it has to offer.

She's a Jersey girl who dreams of living in a place with freezing cold winters and lots of snow! When she's not writing, you can find her planning her next road trip and drinking copious amounts of coffee (preferably iced!).

newsletter, blog, shop, and links to all social media:
www.rebeccagannon.com

Follow me on Instagram to stay up-to-date on new releases, sales, teasers, giveaways, and so much more!
@rebeccagannon_author

Printed in Great Britain
by Amazon

42634762R00199